Call Me
EVIE

Call Me
EVIE

J.P. POMARE

G. P. PUTNAM'S SONS
NEW YORK

G. P. Putnam's Sons
Publishers Since 1838
An imprint of Penguin Random House LLC
penguinrandomhouse.com

Quotation from Daniel Kahneman on page ix reproduced with the permission of NPR's *TED Radio Hour.*

LIBRARY OF CONGRESS CATALOGING-IN-PUBLICATION DATA
Names: Pomare, J.P., author.
Title: Call me Evie / J.P. Pomare.
Description: New York : G. P. Putnam's Sons, 2019.
Identifiers: LCCN 2018041590 | ISBN 9780525538141 (hardcover) |
    ISBN 9780525538158 (epub)
Subjects: | GSAFD: Suspense fiction.
Classification: LCC PR9619.4.P656 C35 2018 | DDC 823/.92—dc23
LC record available at https://lccn.loc.gov/2018041590
p.   cm.

Printed in the United States of America
10 9 8 7 6 5 4 3 2 1

For P. Pomare
Both of you

Call Me
EVIE

I would forget it fain,
But oh, it presses to my memory,
Like damnèd guilty deeds to sinners' minds.
　　　　　　—Shakespeare, *Romeo and Juliet*, act 3, scene 2

Doubting what you see is a very odd experience. And doubting
what you remember is also a pretty odd experience, because
some memories come with a very compelling sense of truth about
them, and that happens to be the case even for memories that
are not true.
　　　　　　　　　　　—Daniel Kahneman

PART ONE

Shadow and Heat

In the past month, how much time have you spent thinking you will not live a long life?

0. none;   1. a little;   2. some;   3. much;   4. most

AFTER

One

The green first-aid kit is open, with rolls of bandages, eye drops, butterfly stitches spilling out over the vanity like entrails. In my hand are the tiny pointed scissors. Before my eyes, they open and close and open and close. I can hear him coming up the hall. The door creaks.

"Jesus," he says. He palms his forehead.

I stop breathing.

"Put those down, Kate."

I toss them beside the sink and sit back on the stool with my arms folded.

His eyes roam over the floor tiles, the clumps of dark hair. "It's a real mess." He stands for a moment, before reaching in under the sink and pulling out the hair clippers. He plugs them in at the wall, and they purr to life in his hand. "Be still."

Blood throbs in my chest. The clippers sing closer. When the steel thrums against my forehead, I scramble up from the stool. My feet slip on the hair, and I steady myself against the door.

"Kate," he says. The clippers die in his hand.

3

I turn and run. The bathroom door whips closed behind me. I sprint up the hall and through the kitchen, sidestepping the island. It's only when he shouts that I realize how close he is. "Stop right now!" *Never run*, but it's too late.

I lunge for the front door, opening it inward. I twist through the gap and try to pull it closed but his fingers grip the edge, whitening.

I haven't thought this through. I haven't thought at all. Goose bumps rise all over my body. The towel slips from around my torso and pools on the concrete. Pulling with all my strength, I turn my head back and look about me. I could scream. *Would anyone hear?* The door is opening. *If I ran would I make the road? What then?*

"Let go of this door," he says, a sort of stillness on the surface of his voice. "You are only making it worse."

Squeezing every cell in my body, I wrench, imagining his fingers crushed against the frame, clipping off at the tips.

"Please," I say. My voice sounds so pathetic and high, I hardly recognize it. "Just let me go."

The handle slips from between my fingers. My body thumps against the concrete.

"Shit, watch your head," he says, rushing forward, cradling my skull in his hands. "What the fuck were you thinking? Look at you." His face hovers over mine. The concrete saps the heat from my skin. "Come on. Inside now."

"No," I say. "I want to go home."

He looks up toward the road, then back at me. The big wire-framed glasses have slipped down his nose and his cheeks glow red. His teeth are yellow; his voice is low and mean. "If you want to act like a child, I'll treat you like one." He snatches my head back by the remaining hair. The sound is cotton ripping in my skull. An electric shock shoots down my spine, poking between every vertebra to my hips and down the bones of each leg. I scrabble for purchase as he drags me with one hand knotted in my hair, the other under my shoulder. The concrete turns the skin over on one knee. Even though I know I shouldn't, I let out a scream.

I hear the sound first. A gunshot suddenness and my cheek is hot and numb. I look up and he's staring at his hand.

"I . . . ," he begins. His face is still red but the anger is draining. He exhales. "Just stop."

Size is important; the smaller I become, the less he can hurt me. "I'm sorry." My voice is a wind chime. "I was scared."

A tear of blood rolls down my shin, carving a path among the goose bumps. He crouches. Hauling me up, he folds me over his shoulder. Like that he carries my weak and trembling body back inside to the bathroom.

"That was a stupid thing to do, all right? Where were you planning on running off to like that in the middle of the day? They could be anywhere. They could be watching us right now."

I'm back on the stool and now when the clippers start, he positions his lean, muscled body between the door and me. I can feel the naked patch in my hair like a burn. The clippers are whirring again; he brings them up my neck. *Vrrthonk.* The steel teeth gnaw, catching a thatch of hair and jerking my head. Hair brushes my neck. It falls over my scarred thighs to the floor. He thumps the clippers against his palm, blows on them.

"It's too thick," he says.

I stare at the towel veiling the mirror. If I could reach it, pull it away, I would see that it's not real. I would know it's not happening. He runs the clippers through again, this time peeling the hair away from my scalp. A ribbon of it falls apart and strands stick to the dampness of my cheek. He flicks his wrist to whip the cord away. The molars at the back of my mouth are numb. I try to relax my jaw but I can't.

"Be still."

Arms first, then legs, then stomach, but my chest will not become still. It rattles, and within it my heart is the quivering pulse of a bird held in the hand. *Can a heart give up? Slow down, seize its valves, and close like a fist?*

"It's almost finished, darling. Please."

Vrrrthonk. The clippers tangle, clutch my hair like a fist, and pull. The skin of my thighs goes white beneath the grip of my fingers. This bathroom is smaller than the one at home. It's tacky and dated. This entire house is claustrophobic. *Where the fuck are we?* I could scream it and yet the headache looms, sharpening its teeth. And one thought rises through it all: *He hit me.*

Stepping back with one hand on his hip, he examines me.

"It will be fine." My voice is desperate.

"No, it's patchy, it's a mess. You look like a starved dog."

I squeeze my eyes closed and see a teenage girl. She's sitting on the edge of a bed. Then she slips to the floor, where she comes to rest. Her legs are tucked beneath her. Over her nose is a saddle of freckles. She rises with the boneless grace of a dandelion, tilts her head, smiles. It's the video of me. I'm reminded of why I ended up here.

I try to stand but his hand is heavy on my shoulder. It squeezes. I sit back down, tip my head forward, and close my eyes.

He takes most of what's left of my hair in his fist and picks up the scissors. "Almost finished. Just don't move for one more minute." As my hair falls around me, I imagine the scissors puncturing his trachea, lodging between a pair of vertebrae in his neck.

These thoughts come and go as quickly as a sneeze. I remind myself of a time when I loved this man and feel sick with it.

"Oh," he says, letting the word uncoil like smoke from his mouth. "What have we done?"

In the shower, I'm still trembling with adrenaline as I watch the water chase the blood and nicks of hair down the drain. Up in the corners long-legged spiders dance webs on the avocado-green panels. The water pressure is weak and sprays with a panicked hum. Soon the water is cool, and when I shut it off I can hear the pipes shudder in the walls. I dry myself and pull the towel away from the mirror, standing before it. An invisible fist thumps my chest as, for the first time, I see myself.

You can never know the shape of your skull, not until you have peeled the hair away. Even then the skin, the shadows and light, marks and spots, can obscure the bone that lies beneath. Seeing it isn't enough because, as with anything, what you see is not necessarily all there is. I almost don't trust my eyes. It's possible the cord stretching to my brain is knotted, or my brain may have a short-circuited connection or snapped synapse. I see only my skull. Closing my eyes, I squeeze a single tear out. I try to forget but the skin remembers, the fingertips remember. When I touch my shorn head I gasp. The thin layer of skin wrapping the bone cage of my brain is so soft and smooth, like the pink foot of a newborn. I can feel the shape, the planes and the curvature. But of course it's what lies within that is most important of all.

I think: *What I know about the human skull, I learned because of him.*

BEFORE

Two

This is my first memory. I am in the bath at the old house, the house down in Portsea. Mum was sick and we had a nanny who would drift about the house, laying out my clothes for the day, ferrying me to childcare, spreading raspberry jam over my toast and deftly cutting away the crusts. Her name was Eloise. She was the first woman I wanted to be like.

I recall snippets of her time in the house and her abrupt dismissal. I recall Dad passing her in the kitchen, his hand grazing her spine. I remember all the time I spent nestled against her chest as she read to me on the couch while Mum was sick. And, of course, I remember that bath.

Dad would eventually organize to have the hot-water cylinder replaced, but back then the bath would only reach ankle-depth before the hot water ran out. Extreme emotions—rage, bliss, grief, ecstasy, agony—are amber; they preserve memories whole. I remember every detail of that time. I remember the gold locket that dangled from Eloise's neck as she bent to shut off the tap. I remember the cloying scent of the lemon bubbles.

"In you get," Eloise said, her voice sweet and light.

"It's still cold and empty."

She frowned and flattened the front of her blouse. "You don't need to stay in for long, Kate."

"I don't want to get in. It's too cold."

"Come on," she said. "Arms up." She pulled off my top, but when she went to pull off my shorts I held on to them and dropped to my knees.

"No."

"Kate, please. It'll only be for five minutes."

I let her undress me. She picked·me up, deposited me in the water, then I screamed.

"Kate," she said with an owlish lean of the head. "That's enough."

I splashed water over the edge of the bath onto the floor as she left the room, then to stop my shivering I wrapped my arms around myself. When she returned, Eloise slipped and had to grab at the sink to keep from falling. She clicked her tongue. "You've got water everywhere."

"It's cold."

"Do you want to get out?"

"No," I said. "Just make it warmer."

"There's no more hot water, Kate. We can't make it warmer."

"Dad makes it warmer."

"Well, I don't see how," she said. She was on her knees now, dragging a towel over the floor tiles.

"Dad heats the water up in a pot."

From her position on the floor she looked up at me. I splashed water at her. "Make it warmer!" I said. "Make it warmer!" My voice had become a shrieking demand.

She winced. "Okay, okay," she said.

She left the room again.

It seemed a very long time before Eloise returned, carrying a large steel pot. Steam drifted in her wake as she strode across the room and set it down on the wooden seat beside the bath.

"Okay, Kate, move your legs away so I can pour a little in." I drew my legs up to my chest and Eloise poured. A gust of steam rose as the hot water rushed beneath me. It was too hot but it quickly cooled. Eloise set the pot back on the seat. "Better now?"

"I'm still cold."

She tested the water with her hand. "You'll be fine. That's warm enough." She tucked a loose strand of hair behind my ear. "Can you just sit for a few minutes? I have to get your dinner on."

Leaving the door open, she walked away up the hall.

The water was still too cold.

"Eloise!" I called.

No response.

"Eloise!"

Still nothing.

Gripping the edge of the bath, I stood and reached for the handles of the pot. It was heavy, almost too heavy for me to lift. Stepping backward, I dragged it over the lip of the bath. The water rocked within. The edge came to rest against my stomach. It seared. I fell back and a scream ripped from my throat as the pot tipped over my legs. I screamed and screamed as, beneath the surface of the water, blisters bubbled on my thighs.

Then Eloise was there, her hand covering her mouth, her eyes wide. She pulled me from the bath but the pain didn't stop. The screaming didn't stop. I thought it never would. A howl escaped that may have lasted seconds or minutes or hours. Hands holding me under flowing water. I couldn't distinguish hot from cold. A long throat-scorching vowel of pain. This is my first memory.

PART TWO

Out of Its Misery

In the past month, how often have you been upset or scared by something that happened unexpectedly?

0. never;   1. rarely;   2. sometimes;   3. often;   4. all the time

AFTER

Three

He is in the kitchen, thumping about. I've decided to call him Jim. The grinding of the juicer fills the house as the first piece of beetroot churns through. The carrots go in next, then small stringy mushrooms, a pair of Brazil nuts. The spout coughs out a foaming blood-rich concoction. When the juicer thunks to a stop, the classical music coming from the small stereo in the lounge can be heard again. He has made toasted sandwiches, crusts removed and cut into triangles. His glasses are on the island. I try them on but the world through them doesn't change. The lenses are just glass.

"Go on, darling," he says. "Eat."

I'm surprised by how my body responds, how quickly I wolf down the sandwiches. It's as though I haven't eaten in weeks.

"How do you feel?" he asks.

"I'm okay."

"You're doing really well."

"My hair," I say, looking up at him.

He sucks his lips, standing so close that I can see the tiny constellations of blood vessels in his cheeks, the pores of his nose.

"It'll grow."

He stirs a scoop of white powder through the juice and brings it over to me. I block my nose and take a long sip. The taste is earthy and bitter. I cough.

"Good girl. Keep it down."

He goes up the hall and returns with the camera, sliding open the door to the back deck, overlooking the yard and the sweeping bay far below.

We step outside and the air, so cool and unfamiliar on my scalp, sends a ghost down my spine.

"Right there," he says. "In your underwear."

I step out of my tracksuit pants, then grasp the sleeves of my hoodie and pull it off. Standing in my underwear on the deck before the weathered timber wall, I face him. I clutch myself to keep warm.

"Just be still for a minute, then we can take a walk." He holds the camera up and snaps photos of me from front on; I flinch each time I hear the shutter. Then I turn and he takes photos from the side. Looking down, I can see the stencil of my ribs, the sharp ridges of my hipbones. It's as though I have stopped aging, no longer a seventeen-year-old girl but working back to being a child.

"Okay," he says. "Let's go."

As we trek up to the headland, I draw my fingertips along the skin of my head; I palm the planes of my skull.

At the top I step near the edge and I can feel the nervous energy coming from him, radiating in waves. The boom from the sea is so loud that I widen my stance, as if the wind driving up the cliff face could reach out like a hand and pull me over. Below, the water twists white in the channels between the rocks. He breathes almost silently and he's light on his feet, yet I can feel he's close.

"Well, you've seen it now," he says from behind me. If I didn't know any better I would say there was fear in his voice. "Let's head back. It's not good for you to be out in the cold."

Stepping a foot closer to the fence, I peer down over the edge. There are people, tiny from above, standing along the crescent of sand.

"Hey," he says, not disguising the strain in his voice. "Come on. Now."

I turn and start back toward the road. He looks grim, his eyes weary behind the clear glasses. His face is stiff as I pass. *Does he regret shaving my head now?* I stuff my hands into the pockets of my hoodie. We cross the farmland. There's a rusted iron shed in one of the paddocks, the type of thing someone might take a photo of. I make a rectangle of my thumbs and forefingers, close one eye.

"Funny how some things are different here." I wonder if he means the shed, or maybe the bird with the blue bill watching us from its eave. Thinking about home is a twist in the heart. I bite my cheeks and force my face to remain neutral.

We climb the wooden steps over the last fence and continue along up to the road. Nearby, the black skeleton of a car leans down the bank. The grass, which is richer and greener than at home, reaches up to the door handle. This country is a million shades of green. Ferns plume out over a neighboring fence like small emerald explosions, branches hang down toward the road under the weight of fat leaves, and there are those strange brown fingers from which the ferns unfold—*punga*, he called them. Some properties are fenced in almost entirely by them.

Somewhere far off an engine rumbles. I press my hands into my thighs to help with the incline. In a way, my body has become unfamiliar to me; the drag of breath that comes with some small effort, the hardness of my skin where it's drawn tightly over my femurs. I look up, shocked.

"I know," he says. "Need to get meat on those bones."

Back at the house, I leave him in the kitchen. Stepping out onto the deck once more and leaning against the balustrade, I look out over the steep yard, toward the curl of the bay and the hills, moss green in the twilight. Two streetlights near the beach flicker on. I'm shivering with cold but I make a study of the land, particularly the road out, from where a pair of headlights can be seen tracing the route into town. I had tried to memorize the drive—the turns, the landmarks—but we drove for so long and the pills had made me so sleepy that it had all faded by the time we reached the house. I recall a tower; a steel-trussed structure of red and white thrusting toward the sky and held in place by wires.

I see then, down toward the corner of the block, a steel shed, the roof thick with foliage from an overhanging tree. I climb down the steps and cross the yard to the shed. The door is clean, recently painted with a new steel door handle. I try it but it's locked. I climb back up the steps to the deck as the back door slides open.

"You'll catch your death out here," he says. "I've made you a hot drink."

"What is it?"

"Dandelion and chamomile. Good for the liver apparently."

I drink the tea. Then, when I hear the shower drubbing in the bathroom, I pull on a sweatshirt and my Chuck Taylors. I'm allowed out of the house with him. *What about on my own?*

I open the door, step through and silently pull it closed behind me. The driveway is steep and gravelly. It's an effort to climb up it toward the road. *We could have gone anywhere in the world,* I think, *but he dragged me here.* An old bus shelter juts out at the corner, flimsy wood and a rash of flaking brown paint. I feel eyes and glance over. Inside, in the near darkness, sit two boys and a girl. One of the boys throws his head forward, narrows his eyes at me. I look away.

"You're a lesbie, eh?" he says, ugly and mean.

I turn again and let my gaze creep up from the road. I remember my bare skull and feel a sudden urge to run.

He flicks his tongue between his fingers. The others' laugh. "Fucking lesbie," the girl says. She holds a paper bag to her mouth and sucks in a breath.

I quicken my pace and when I get to the bottom of the hill near the beach, I can't convince my feet to go any farther or to turn back, so I stand rubbing warmth back into my arms. I look out around the bay, following the road with my eyes. Nearby, a white dog sniffs at the grass. By the way it hops along, I see it's missing its front left leg. That narrow head turns to me. Its eyes are black and glossy as oil seep. It turns away and continues on in a rolling gait. The town is in shade now as the sun disappears. If I can get far enough away, if I can make it to the highway . . . *then what?*

Something strikes the asphalt. *A stone?* Then a sharp sting strikes the back of my head. I hunch forward, touching where I was struck. Spots of blood come away on my fingertips. The headache is back, grinding just below the surface. Where the bus shelter sits at the road's edge, the silhouette of a head pokes out, then disappears. I stand there weeping, holding myself together in the cold. *Why here?* I think. A lacquer of hopelessness pours over me, standing alone as the occasional car passes and the last light fades from the sky. There's nowhere to run. We are so far from the airport.

After we landed, before we got into the car, he made me swallow a small diamond-shaped pill. A calm rolled over me at once, and on the drive I drifted in and out of sleep. I regained consciousness to find we had stopped at a service station. I was too drowsy to get out, but I watched the world from the passenger seat. I listened to the strange accent of the other customers, short formal vowels, hard stops between words. I thought we were on the other side of the world. The birdsong, the quality of light, everything is different here.

Soon enough the sedan comes around the bend. He pulls up beside me and when I climb in, he just stares. I brace myself.

"What the hell are you doing?"

"I don't know."

"Shit." He thumps the steering wheel with the heel of his hand. "What do I have to do? Tell me, what the hell do I have to do to make you realize what sort of trouble we're in?"

"I'm sorry."

A knot pulses at his jaw. I wait for pain, for anything. He shifts the car into gear and silently we glide away from the curb.

"I just felt like a quick walk."

He lets all the air out of his lungs at once. "We had a bloody walk today. You know what will happen, don't you? You know what I will have to do."

When we pass the bus shelter, I look in. The kids are gone.

. . .

All houses have their own quirks. This house is nothing like home. This house is nothing like anywhere I have been before. The cupboards don't quite close all the way. Windows shudder when a door is slammed, and when the wind picks up the structure seems to yaw.

The light is on above the deck outside and a pair of moths fly about it in delirious elliptical whirls.

"You can't disappear like that," he calls, marching down the hall. "Just say if you want to go for a walk and I'll take you. It's dark out there."

"I'm sorry," I repeat.

"What if someone saw you or recognized you on the road? What then?"

He comes back, pulling a sweater on over his shirt. He slams something down on the counter. It's a dead bolt. I look up into his eyes.

"It's not that I don't trust you. It's just something that will give me peace of mind in the evenings." As he says it, I notice the loops of sleepless bruising about his eyes. He didn't sleep on the plane. "You don't seem able to grasp what is at stake here. I'm protecting you from yourself." Then he's off down the hall toward my room. "From now on, you don't leave this house and you don't leave this room, not without my permission."

I wonder if it is loneliness, his fear of my escaping, that seethes inside of him, or if it is something else.

The headache still looms as I sit at the kitchen island. I hope it's just an echo of the slap or the stone that hit me, not something I now live with like the phantom pain of a missing toe. I press the bump at the back of my head with my thumbnail. Fresh blood seeps out. The pain is addictive, like worrying an ulcer with my tongue.

I hear Jim testing the lock, sliding it into place, blowing the wood shavings away. The cutlery drawer is across the island. It would be easy to reach in and pull out a steak knife, slide it into my pocket. Just something small to make me feel safe.

When he comes back up the hall, he stands before me, hands on hips. "You go taking off like that and things are going to get a lot worse. Right now, you're free. But that freedom is tenuous. Understand?"

I nod.

"I've been through this before, and I'm not going to let you leave me."

Jim finds me balled up on the couch with my blanket wrapped around me. I didn't sleep well. Maybe it's the spongy mattress, or could it be the lock on the door? There is something about the idea of being trapped that keeps me on edge. More likely it's the dreams. While I lay in bed, eyes wide open waiting for sleep, I heard the floor as he paced back and forth. He didn't sleep well either.

"I'll light the fire," he says, looking down at me. "It'll get warmer soon. It's almost spring."

Spring. He plans on keeping me here until spring.

He heads outside to search for wood.

The television sits in the corner. He lets me watch it during the day, but it's not like home. We don't have all the channels. No guilty pleasures, no *Keeping Up with the Kardashians*, no *Ex on the Beach*; the world through the screen is not the one I know. It seems absurd that there are only a few channels. Apparently he no longer believes in the Internet or smartphones—not for me anyway. He's trapped me in the nineties.

It's only been a couple days but already I miss what I know. Even the small things: Boost Juice; catching trams to the city; the Yarra River, churning with plastic bottles and shreds of rubbish. On sunny afternoons we used to watch the rowers from the banks as they dragged themselves along and the heat bleached the grass. One night, Willow and I pushed a shopping trolley into its depths without a second thought. Isn't it strange how one moment you can be taken by a destructive impulse and the next you're fine?

I rise from the couch, shed the blanket, and go to the kitchen. The old steel tea tin is where the white powder for my smoothies comes from. I pull the lid off and sniff. There's something in it, strange smells that weave into my sinuses. He told me it's a mix of protein and carbohydrates to help me gain weight.

"Leave that," he says, coming through the back door. I jump. He crosses the room and takes the tin from my hand.

"I was only—"

"It's fine, just don't. There's no wood."

"Oh."

"I'll organize some. For now we can collect driftwood and use that. How's your head? Feeling better?"

"It's okay."

He takes me gently by the back of the neck and presses his lips to my forehead. I wince, resisting the urge to wipe the dampness away.

"I'll give you some pills," he says, stepping back, opening a drawer.

"No," I say.

He swivels at the neck like an owl. "Why not?"

"I'm okay."

There is a tray of sealed pills in his hand. He punches two out onto the island. "Come on. Take these."

"What are they?"

"Ibuprofen. They'll help with the headache."

I hold them in my hand and steady my breath. When he hands me a glass of water, I swallow them, then show him my tongue.

"Good girl."

"How long until you take me home?" I hate the pathetic lilt in my voice.

"You know what will happen." He reaches up and gently taps his forefinger against my temple. "Only time will heal this, and what happens out there"—pointing to the backyard, the world beyond—"that's out of your control, but it will only get better when everyone moves on."

"I know."

"Do you remember? Is it coming back to you?" He leans forward, his eyes sharp.

"I just remember the car. I remember being in the car."

But I can remember more. I can remember gripping the steering wheel, the crunch of the car hitting something. Then there is only darkness. There is only me, my body thrumming with adrenaline.

"I remember small things. That's it."

"Like what?"

I shake my head. "Not much." I can feel the tears coming.

"It's okay, we'll get there."

"Can I send a letter now? You promised."

He regards me; I know he doesn't want anything going out or coming in. Only he is allowed to use the Internet—using a special Tor browser and VPN, only visiting certain websites. "Yeah," he says. "Fine."

. . . .

I take up the pen but I can barely hold it. I go to my room and sit on the edge of the bed, plotting each word before I press the nib to the page.

> *He doesn't want anyone to know where we are. The first thing I want to tell you is I'm safe and happy. We must stay hidden for obvious reasons. I'm not allowed to text or use Instagram—he won't even let me on the Internet.*
>
> *I've actually been thinking about you a lot lately. Thinking about what we did. I do miss you. I miss spending afternoons lying in the study, listening to music. Maybe one day we can go back to that time.*

I sit with the letter in my hands, carefully folding it into thirds. I slide it into the envelope and leave it unsealed.

When Jim calls to me I return to the lounge room and hand it to him. He removes the letter, unfolds it, and scans my words while his cracked lips make subtle movements. "It's fine," he says, stuffing it into the pocket of his jeans. "I'll send it on our way." He steps back and gestures to the door.

"On our way where?"

"The doctor."

Four

t takes forty minutes to drive back to civilization. I watch out the window, counting intersections, memorizing the route to the highway. *Left, right, straight through, right.* I repeat it in my mind like a mantra. *Left, right, straight, right.* Focus on landmarks: tall trees, a rusted-out shed.

"Are you okay?" he asks. "Is it all right in the car?"

My breathing is loud. "It's okay."

Eventually we pass a McDonald's and a BP, and I almost feel normal. A sign declares that a small square building, a place that looks just like a house, is the Te Puke police station. I stare as we pass by.

Pulling into the doctor's surgery, I see it also appears to have been a house once. A sign is stabbed into the lawn displaying the doctors' names with all their suffixes and above them all: AROHA MEDICAL CENTER.

Inside, it looks like any clinic, with posters for flu shots, a crate of children's toys in one corner, and magazines so dog-eared they no longer stay closed but splay out over the low coffee table.

A nurse with hair she gave up on years ago and clacking plastic bangles leans over the desk.

"First time?"

"Yep," Jim says, squeezing out a smile. He thumbs his glasses back up his nose.

She hands me a clipboard. I look him in the eye pointedly as I let the pen hover over the name section. He takes the clipboard and pen from me. I watch him fill in the boxes with his leaning scrawl. "Evie Turner" under name, then our new address. He checks his mobile for his new number, before scribbling it down. He takes the clipboard up to the receptionist, then returns and folds one leg over the other, looking down at his phone. The benches and seats are full. There is a child with a cast on his arm sitting beside his mother, who has sunken cheeks and the last millimeter of her thumbnail between her front teeth. An elderly man sits beside her, clearing his throat periodically. He hawks up a wad of phlegm, then deposits it into his hanky.

We sit there as the afternoon stretches out. The mother and son disappear up the corridor with the doctor. Eventually the nurse calls another patient. She calls the name again. She comes over, places her hand on my wrist. "Evie?"

"Sorry," Jim says, "I was daydreaming. Come on, Evie, doctor's ready."

Why has he brought me here? It's as if I'm peering at their faces from the bottom of a well. I can hear them, feel their hands on my arms, under my shoulders. They lift me to my feet but at first I can barely move. I'm as still and rigid as a china doll.

"Are you okay, dear? Do you need a drink of water?"

"She's fine," I hear him say. "She's a little tired is all."

White walls, anatomical posters, a blood pressure machine. "Dr. Simon," says a tall man in an off-white doctor's coat, taking my hand in his. I'm surprised by its softness, the way his fingers curl around mine. I sit on the bed and stare at a pink mouth and throat cut lengthwise, pinned up on the wall. The tongue looks so thick I wonder why we don't all choke on them.

"She's been quite unwell for the past couple of weeks or so; she's had some issues with eating and sleeping." Jim runs through my history, though of course he leaves out the most important, incriminating parts. "There was an incident; she's had a bit of a tough time and you've been feeling a little blue, haven't you, Evie?" Jim says.

I nod.

There was an incident. Dr. Simon nods gravely. He scrawls notes, asks questions, pokes something cold into my ear. They speak in euphemisms. *Incident, unwell, trauma, stress, history.* Jim says just enough to get through the appointment. Eventually the doctor leads us to another room, where a nurse slides a needle into the hinge of my arm and draws out blood.

"Not so bad, huh?" Jim says afterward as we cross the car park.

"It was okay."

"Soon you'll be better than okay. Trust me, and it will all end up fine."

The next morning the air is cold and gritty with salt. We descend toward the private beach at the foot of the headland.

As we walk on the pale sand, we collect driftwood for the fire. I carry a few pieces in my arms back up the track that splits farmland. Wind-polished bones, boars' tusks, shinbones, antlers sit on top of the dog cages. An old woman with eyes as dull as oysters watches us from the yawning doorway of an iron shed. Jim turns to look; even he can't ignore her stare.

When my breathing gets too heavy, we slow down a little. "I've got a couple of questions," he says.

"Questions?"

"They might help you to remember and understand, eventually, you know?"

"Sure."

"If it gets hard to answer, let me know."

"Okay."

"We can walk and talk."

We start walking back up toward the house.

"What do you remember about that night?" he asks.

"Well, I remember in the morning . . . I remember waiting at the table."

"No, not the morning. The night before."

"Umm . . ."

"Do you remember drinking?"

I recall the scorch in my throat. Tipping the bottle back. "Yes."

"Anything else?"

"I remember being on the couch."

"What about seeing him? Seeing him lying facedown?"

I can see him, see the blood spreading. I squeeze my eyes closed. "Stop," I say. "Stop it!"

"Okay." He pauses. "It's not looking good for him, you know."

My chest feels weak. "What do you mean?"

He sighs. "It means I don't like his chances."

His chances . . . his chances of what? I try to block it out again.

"How do you feel when you try to remember?"

"Afraid."

"So you do remember?"

I don't answer. It's not that I want to keep it from him; I just don't know what to say. It's as though the kinetic energy is working to dislodge something in my mind, but how can I possibly distinguish between what is a memory, what is a dream, and what I have invented from everything he has planted in my head with his stories?

We're approaching the fence at the road's edge; sheep watch us from a distant corner of the paddock. He climbs over and holds his hands out to help me. The questions keep coming.

"Do you have bad images, like memories that come when you're not expecting them?"

"Yes."

"Let's talk about that," he says. "What images come to you?"

Tears start, silently running down my cheeks. I try to think about Melbourne. When I speak, I gasp. "I don't know."

"It's okay," he says. "Do you remember who else was there?"

"No."

"I'm not there, in your memories?"

"I don't know. I don't know. Please can we stop?"

"Just a few more questions, all right? Have you thought about how you were feeling? What you went through?"

"Never."

"Not once?"

"No." We pass the bus shelter; staring white eyes float in the spill of darkness, becoming wide and fierce when they meet mine.

"Regardless of what memories come back to you from that night, I want you to know that you weren't yourself, okay?"

But it can't be true. I can't have done anything. . . . I just know that it wasn't me. When he tells me big lies, how can I accept the small things as truth?

I'm in the shower the following morning when I hear an engine groaning. A knock at the door. My breath stops. I turn off the tap and stand in the cold, hands to my chest. I focus. A spider creeps down the wall of the shower to eye level. Jim goes to the door. Something crashes down out there, a rumbling like a landslide. Eventually the engine comes back to life on the driveway and chugs back up to the road and away.

I towel off, dress quickly, and go outside. A pile of firewood.

"Come on," Jim says. "Give me a hand."

We're stacking the wood behind the steps beneath the back deck when his phone rings inside. Our eyes meet for a second. Jim runs up the steps to answer it.

A minute later he leans over the balustrade. "Let's go," he says. "Results are back."

We set off in the car. Jim is wearing the glasses again and a blue baseball cap. The winter sun arcs out over the water on one side and there's a hitchhiker on the other, chin down against the cold and his thumb defiantly thrust in our direction. He holds a cardboard sign that reads AUCKLAND. I never saw hitchhikers in Melbourne. I turn my head to watch the man as we pass.

Jim flicks his eyes at me. "What is it?"

"Nothing," I say, turning back to the road.

At the surgery, Dr. Simon reads through a sheet of lab work from a clipboard, looks up, and says, "The blood test results look pretty good. You could do with a touch more iron in your diet, Evie, but I think we can rule out any underlying deficiency." He places the clipboard on his desk, looks me in the eye. "Let me just say that it's absolutely normal to be having some issues adjusting, particularly given your history." I swallow. *What does he know about my history?* "I'm going to prescribe medication to make you feel better for the time being. You just take a pill every morning and we can check on you in a month's time. If you're feeling drowsy or nauseous, then give me a call and we can look at other options. Aside from that, you're perfectly healthy."

"Is it possible she might get worse? There's potentially a family history."

Why is he talking about my family?

"It's possible, but I'm perhaps not the best person to advise about that. I would also like to refer Evie to see someone else."

Jim frowns. "Who?"

"Anne Lachlan; she's a psychologist with a clinic in Rotoiti. It's only a half-hour drive. I think it would help her."

"Oh, well, that won't be necessary."

"Medication will help with the symptoms, but if Evie speaks to someone we can help to address the underlying causes."

"I appreciate the recommendation, but Evie is already seeing someone."

He's losing patience.

"That's good to hear. Do you mind if I ask who it is?"

He tries to smile but it doesn't reach his eyes. "I'd really rather not say."

"Well," the doctor says, taking a pen and a notepad from his desk. "Let me give you Anne's number just in case."

Jim takes the note and presses it into his pocket. "Thanks for your help, Doc."

We drive to the pharmacy, where Jim leaves me in the car. I look out at the street, at the people passing by. The clock on the dash reads 2:19 p.m. It's a new car: leather seats, touchscreen navigation. It's almost a relief to see technology, a touchstone of the life we left behind. I open the glove box. There is a plastic case containing the car's manual and service record. I open it and feel the shape of a spare key within one of the compartments. The door to the pharmacy opens and Jim is striding toward the car with a bottle of pills in his hand. I snatch the key and jam it into my pocket, then push the case into the glove box and snap it closed.

As we speed along a straight road toward Maketu, Jim winds down his window enough to toss the note from the doctor out. I feel the throbbing convulsive fear growing inside my chest. My brain is full of static and it doesn't matter how quickly I breathe, I can't get enough air.

"Kate," he says. "Are you . . . are you okay?"

I try to answer but the words come out in clots between my rapid breaths. "I—don't—know."

My stomach clenches. The car seems to be slowly corkscrewing. My vision blurs and my face pounds with heat. We're slowing but it's too late. The panic takes over. I yank the door handle and throw my weight against the door. It doesn't open. Jim slams on the brakes, veering off the asphalt. I feel my pulse, my heart slamming in my chest. I breathe faster and faster but the darkness closes in. I squeeze my eyes closed. There are no sounds but my wet, shuddering breath and the thunder of my heart.

A voice tells me to breathe in. *One-two-three-four. Hold. One-two. Out. One-two-three-four. In. One-two. Out. One-two-three-four. Hold. One-two. Out. One-two-three-four.*

When my violent shaking begins to subside, I realize Jim is holding my head, speaking right into my face. "Keep breathing with me, you're going to be okay." He's holding me firmly but I can't contain my body. "Come on, Kate. Look at me." There's a scratch that starts at his jaw and runs down his neck.

In. One-two-three-four. Hold. One-two. Out. One-two-three-four.

It helps. I'm rocking hard against the seat belt, but it's beginning to feel like I'm sucking in enough air.

"The doors won't open when the car is moving. It's a safety feature. One of the reasons I opted for this model."

I think of the hitchhiker and my throat constricts. I could never do it. I'm still rocking but everything has slowed; I can focus again.

His leg jiggles up and down and the pills rattle in his pocket.

"Will they help, the pills?"

"I think so, yes."

As cars pass I avert my eyes, keep counting out my breaths, and look out over the glistening water of the long, sweeping estuary into the village.

"Better now?"

I nod. My thighs ache where my fingers dig in. The car starts again and we slide from the gravel shoulder back onto the road. This time he drives slowly, carefully, glancing over.

"You lied," I say.

"I would never lie to you."

"You lied to the doctor. You said I was seeing someone."

"You are," he says. "You're seeing me."

It was so easy for him to lie. It came out like the truth.

"The doctor said it would help."

"The people he wants you to see can't help you, Kate. They'd only make it worse."

There's a faded map of New Zealand hanging off-kilter near the fireplace in the lounge. The house is still, motionless, safe. What I feel is not comfort but a numbing fear. For a while I stare at the map. The two long islands are drawn in all the colors between yellow and green, like an underripe mango. Maketu is a point in the middle of the bay. It sticks out like a jag that could tear the skin. I trace my finger down the coast, measuring it out against the key. Three hundred kilometers to Auckland, maybe more. I try to find Te Puke, where we went to the doctor's office. It took over half an hour to get there but on the map we barely traveled any distance at all. The emptiness comes on again, the realization that home is so far away.

If I were still in Melbourne, I would be preparing for high school exams. We would already be talking about end-of-year parties, planning ways to stay in touch as we stepped into adulthood. Isn't it amazing how quickly plans can derail, how life can break apart like a flock of startled birds?

Even if I still had school and my friends, Melbourne will never be the same without my old dad. I pull the bottom drawer of my dresser all the way out so I can drop the car key into the cavity between the drawer and the floor. Slowly, silently, watching the doorway, I push the empty drawer back in.

Jim is outside stacking the last of the firewood. We found an old ax to cut kindling. If nothing else, at least we have the means to protect ourselves.

BEFORE

Five

People will say *I did it just for attention.* Here's the truth: almost no one does anything *just for attention.* Admiration, freedom, love, obligation, revenge—these are more likely motivations. Before you can understand why Thom and I did what we did, you must know one thing: I envied the girls who got attention but not the attention itself. Rather, I craved the comfort they took from it, the way some girls waded through it. I wanted to be like that. Instead, I shut down when I felt eyes lingering on me, when people expected me to say something cutting or bitchy, when boys joked in that sly way, anticipating my laughter. I hated the sound of my laugh, how unnatural it was, the shapes my mouth made. And around other girls, I was treading on eggshells; just one comment about the size of my ankles or the thick hair on my forearms could ruin an entire week. That comfort I so longed for, it was something I knew I would never have.

Willow, my closest friend, was magnetic. What you first noticed about her was her hair, dark and chaotic in a deliberately structured way. Mine frizzed out from neglect and a refusal to cut it more than once every few years. Willow was the same height as me, but where I was drawn and thin, she was strong and filled out. Her green eyes were enigmatic, with a feline quality. Eyes designed for eyeliner ads. Mine were brown, doelike, and boring.

Willow was different from me in so many ways. Her father was a musician; she went to a coed public school. I went to Windsor Girls' Grammar, a private girls' school, which I suppose conjures images of violin lessons, plaid skirts, and school trips to France, but the reality was cigarettes, cagey bulimic friends, and talking about blow jobs. The reality was trying to fit in; that's something everyone goes through, I guess.

We had only known each other since I changed swimming coaches and moved to the pools closer to home a year or so earlier. I might never have met Willow if not for the pool. Everyone assumed I would be athletic like my father, but the only extracurricular activity I stuck with was swimming. I told Dad it was so I could interact with people outside of school. Truth be told, it was the boys I was most interested in. One boy in particular. Had it not been for the pool, I might not have met Thom.

At the end of the summer before junior year I was eager to return to my regular routine—maybe not so much school, but definitely swimming. Seven weeks had passed since I'd last seen Thom. We'd been flirting and sitting together each day before swimming, but then the holidays came at the worst possible moment. He was the first boy to show me that sort of attention. He was the first boy I wanted attention from.

Dad and I had been away for most of the summer, leaving our five-bedroom home empty, except for occasional visits from the cleaner. Dad opted for a rusty camper in Torquay rather than the house on the beach in Portsea. For Dad, the Portsea house was a place where Mum's ghost still lingered like a fog; he couldn't bring himself to sell it but he couldn't visit it either. For me it represented the bath and all that happened in it.

Things had changed since Eloise the nanny, and those days I spent in the hospital recovering from the third-degree burns on my thighs while Mum was sick. After Mum died, Dad decided to hang up his rugby boots to raise me himself. He reinvented himself as a financial analyst and by the time I reached high school Dad's new career occupied him until late most afternoons. This meant I had a lot of alone time, but since he didn't let me take my phone to school, I had to wait for him to get home before I could use it.

I was bubbling with excitement to see Thom and Willow at swimming. The afternoon before our first training session back, I rushed downstairs from my room the moment the front door closed. In the foyer, my dad unbuttoned his cuffs and looked up, his eyes finding me.

"Hello, Kate," he said, lowering his head and turning his cheek toward me. I kissed it. "How was school?"

"Good, thanks," I said. "Can I have my phone now?"

"And here I thought you were running down to see your dear old dad."

"Please? I want to message Willow."

"Oh, you want to message *Willow*." He winked. "If it's Willow, I'd better hurry then."

"Dad." I tipped my head forward so my hair fell over my face.

"All right, all right. I'll bring it down soon." He headed for the stairs.

Thom Moreau. While I waited for my phone I wrote it, holding the pen close to the nib to keep my handwriting tight and neat.

Putting the name on a page made it tangible, gave my thoughts a place in the real world. Again and again I wrote it, with serif twirls, in block letters, scribbled in ovoid flurries like Dad's signature. My journal was filled with small encounters, jokes, and observations. I thought of ways to describe him, things he did that no one else did. *He turns one ear to you when he listens. He blinks quickly when he's thinking. He bumped his shoulder into mine on the way to the changing room.* My heart was there on those pages; anyone could have seen it if they found the journal. I was attracted to him before I knew what attraction was.

He didn't seem to try when it came to swimming, unlike other boys; he just *did* it. I imagined him, imagined the future him, imagined the future versions of *us*: private kisses, school dances, attracting the envious eyes of all of my friends. I was almost fifteen and could still believe in these things. The burning ideals that keep us warm when we're young, before colder, harder times temper them.

I slipped the journal under my pillow and went to wait outside Dad's room. Drawers opened; the floorboards sighed under his weight.

"Dad, can I have it now?"

He emerged and slapped the phone into my hand. "Just make sure I don't see it at the dinner table."

I lay down on my bed and messaged Willow:

Ready to start swimming again?

If I must. I know you're chomping at the bit to show off that summer tan. Maybe turn up in a bikini and watch Coach Mark's head explode. The boys would enjoy the show.

I could actually feel myself blushing. It has been a bit boring without swimming.

> Speak for yourself. Don't tell me Thom Moreau is the
> most exciting thing about your life these days?

The blush got worse. Who said anything about Thom?

> Sorry, did you move on while you were in Torquay?
> Some lifeguard you haven't told me about maybe?

> With my dad nearby? Not likely.

> Too bad. You could do better than him. Not sure if
> you've noticed, but he's kind of annoying.

> You're just being a bitch.

It was easier to be confident in the cyber-world. Digital Kate never felt flustered or shy.

> Look I think you need to get over him. I know some-
> thing about him you don't and it will change EVERY-
> THING.

> What is it?

I didn't hear back, so after dinner I sent another message.

> Willow what is it? Tell me please.

No I don't want to disappoint you. Just don't get
obsessed.

I could hear Dad coming up the hall, his footsteps irregular,
which meant his knee was particularly bad. He reached up and
scratched the small scar across the bridge of his nose. He had told
me he was born with it, like a birthmark, and I believed him until a boy at primary school showed me the video on YouTube of
when it was broken in a rugby match. Boys had a way of ruining
the things my dad would have had me believe.

A knock at my door. "It's nine o'clock, Kate. Any homework?"

"I've done it."

"Okay, five more minutes."

Seriously, what is it? Did he do something?

It's not what he has done, it's something else. I
shouldn't say.

Dad came back as I was typing my response. I held my phone
out for him.

I couldn't help but think about Willow's message as I lay there
in bed. I tried to push it out of my head, dismiss it as Willow
being her melodramatic self, but for some reason those words
stuck.

In the stands beside the outdoor pool, Willow, Sally, and I hud-
dled in our towels to stay warm in the chilly air. My leg bounced
in anticipation. Willow stood and adjusted her towel like it was a

maxi dress. She sensed her own charm, something that was irresistible. It was easy for boys to overlook her flaws.

I kept my towel wrapped tight around me. The faint pink continents that mapped my legs had faded but would never disappear. I smeared oil on the scars every day and in summer, when my skin darkened, you could barely see them at all. The towel was just long enough to conceal them when I sat. We all develop our own little movements and habits to keep the ugly parts hidden, the bony, ill-proportioned parts.

Willow nudged me. I looked up to see Thom walking briskly into the changing room. He was wearing a hoodie and his school socks were pushed down to his ankles.

"So I've been chatting with a boy from Brisbane," Willow said. "He's going to come down and visit me. Guess how old he is?"

Thom came out of the changing rooms, his brown hair down over his ears, eyes as dark as black coffee.

"Sixteen?" Sally asked. Was Thom heading in our direction?

"Eighteen," Willow said. "He's got a Ford."

Thom sat down between me and Sally. I could feel my pulse in my chest as the girls' chatter fell silent. Warmth diffused where our bodies almost touched. I hunched forward to cover my thighs.

"Hey, girls," he said.

"Hi." I smiled. My cheeks were aflame.

"I see we're all excited to be back at swimming," he said with a sarcastic fist pump. "How was everyone's break?"

"It was okay," I muttered.

Before Sally could speak, Willow had changed the subject. "Thom, would you go out with an older girl?"

"What?"

"How old would you go?"

Thom sniffed, straightening his back. "Sixty-five," he said, deadpan, to a chorus of giggles. "The nanas love these dimples, my boyish charm." I noticed then that Thom's leg was almost touching Sally's on the other side of him. When I looked up I met Willow's eyes.

"No, but seriously, Thom, what do you find hot in a girl?"

"Why?"

"Well, I heard a rumor about you. I want to know if it's true."

"A rumor?" he scoffed.

"Just answer," Willow said, rolling her eyes.

"Brown eyes, brown hair. Tall, but not taller than me. A nice smile."

"What else?"

"I don't know. Someone who doesn't take herself too seriously. Someone who can take a joke and likes the things I like."

"Someone like Kate then?"

My cheeks were searing. He had described me—well, kind of.

"Wow . . ." He sucked air through his teeth as if embarrassed. "I don't know. Nice way to put me on the spot."

"Don't be a bitch, Willow," Sally said in a rare moment of courage.

"Am I? Kate, do you think I'm being a bitch?"

Before I could think of anything to say, Coach Mark strode past. "Come on," he said. We stood and made our way down to the blocks, shedding our towels like coats.

We lined up and began laps with all the others. Three lanes of girls and boys. I found it calming, the rhythm of breathing, turning my head, stroking, kicking, rolling at the end.

Willow came by in my lane, going the other way, her tall body stretched as she drew another stroke through the water. It was quiet in the pool. Not silent, but without distinguishable sounds, only the muffled wash and thump of kicking. Thom passed, his head rising in a caul of water. His hair slicked back. You could see the power of his shoulders, his full chest as he pulled through the water, with a quiet determination on his face and his nose dragging chains of silver bubbles.

That night Willow texted me.

> So are you going to ask me what I know?

> Only if you're actually going to tell me.

I was on my bed and whenever my phone vibrated I snatched it and held it close to my face.

> Ask me what Sally and Thom have in common . . .

I knew then what was coming. I never should have asked.

> What?

The door opened.

> They like each other. A lot.

I stared at the screen.

"Kate," Dad said, solemn. "What's wrong?" I looked up. His brows climbed up his forehead.

"Nothing."

"Well," he said, stepping into the room. "It's just gone nine." He was in his tank top and veins stood out in his shoulders. He had been doing his evening press-ups.

"One more text."

I quickly punched out a message.

How do you know?

Dad stood with his hand out. "Come on."

The phone vibrated.

Sally told me. They've been texting. She said they're
going out now.

I swallowed, then turned the phone off. I placed it in Dad's hand while heat started behind my eyes. I just wanted him to leave.

"Brushed your teeth?" he asked.

"Yes."

"All right, well, good night then." He leaned down and kissed the top of my head before walking out of my room.

Willow wasn't at swimming the next day, and when I walked in I saw Thom and Sally sitting beside each other. I couldn't stay there, so I sat in the foyer and Coach Mark called Dad for me. A couple of the older boys arrived for swimming and saw me hunched over. *Got your period, huh?* They erupted into sniggers. I swallowed, tried to smile because if I spoke my voice would break and if I shook my head the tears would fall.

Dad watched me in the rearview mirror as he drove us home. I covered my eyes with my forearm so he couldn't see me crying. The empty feeling inside lasted weeks, then things were back to normal but I cut down on the swimming and I would have quit altogether if I could have. Knowing Thom had chosen someone else made me want him so much more.

Dad might have seen something tragically familiar in my sadness. It's a painful thought now: at those times when I feared that I would never be with Thom, the foundations of all that was to come were laid.

AFTER

Six

There is a stranger inside everyone, an animal that doesn't think but responds only to its instincts and impulses. Some people will let the stranger take over once, possibly twice in their entire life. It's only afterward, when your body has cooled down and your mind has returned, that you realize you had no control, that you realize something else took you over. I've seen it in Jim; I've seen it come and go.

It's been five days since he shaved my head but my skull is still apparent beneath the skin. It draws the eye to the concave shape of my cheek, the hinge of my jaw, and the veins tracing into the stubble of my hair. Even my nose seems narrower and longer. I want to wear a woolen hat or perhaps one of his caps with some loose-fitting clothing, but when I try it all on I look boyish and ill, with a bald head and dark pouches under my eyes.

Cracks run down and across the mirror like the wings of a butterfly. He said I had pitched the clippers at it. Why? I guess I couldn't look at myself any longer. The clippers felt so reassuring in my hand, the weight of them, I must have drawn back my hand and thrown them with all my strength.

Classical music sings through the house from the lounge. A knock sounds at the door and I hear Jim opening it.

I go through to the kitchen and peer around the corner, up the driveway. Jim is standing in his jeans and a woolen sweater, one hand on his hip, the other holding a steaming cup of tea.

"So you must be the cousin?" a stout man with a walrus mustache is asking. He offers his hand to Jim. "Terry Wallace," he says. He has a crooked smile and a broad flat nose like a sheep's.

Jim shakes the proffered hand. "Good to meet you, Terry." He too has shaved his head—in an act of solidarity, I suppose. Or perhaps he did it so people were less likely to recognize him too. But now he looks dangerous. He could be a cage fighter. His hair is so dark pressing through beneath his skin that it gives his scalp a bluish tinge.

"We've just been here for the weekend but your cousin Drew called me to say you'd be staying," the man says. "Didn't mean to give you a fright or anything."

"Oh no, it's fine. It's nice to see a friendly face."

"It can be a bit like that hereabouts," Terry says, grim now. "But you won't find a much better spot to fish."

"You're a fisherman?"

"Does the pope shit in the woods?" He lets out a hack of a laugh. "Yeah, I love my fishing, and my hunting too." Then he stands on his toes to look back over to his side of the fence. "I'll pack that up, dear. Come say hi to our new neighbor."

"I'd love to do a bit of hunting while I'm here," Jim says.

A short lady with long graying hair wanders around the fence. She shakes Jim's hand, then looks over his shoulder toward me. "Is that your son?"

Jim turns and his eyes widen behind his glasses. "Oh, er, that's my niece."

"Oh my, how rude of me. Sorry, dear, I couldn't see you properly in the shadow."

I look at Jim and he gives a small nod. I step forward.

"I'm Angela," the woman says.

"Evie." The new name doesn't roll off my tongue easily yet.

"It's good to see the house occupied again," Terry says. "The last bloke your cousin rented it out to"—he leans in conspiratorially—"was a bit on the loopy side, if you catch my drift." He hacks another laugh. Jim just gives a weary smile.

"Are you on school holidays?" Angela asks me.

"I'm finished," I say. "This was my last year."

"Oh," she says, blinking rapidly. "How old are you, Evie?"

I'm thin and bald; I can hardly blame her for thinking I'm thirteen or fourteen. "Seventeen."

Before Angela can respond, Jim asks Terry a question about fishing and their attention is diverted from me.

Finally Terry says, "Well, we'd best be off." He turns to leave, then pauses and glances back. "Keep an eye on the place for us, would you?" He gropes his pockets for his mobile phone. "I'll leave my number. We don't get here much and we've had a couple of break-ins in the past."

I go back inside and soon I hear their SUV start up and pull out onto the road. I begin to write.

I told him I miss Melbourne. He said it was too early to return. He said they would "maul" me, and I believe him. I don't know why but somehow I know it's true. I think about what I did to your family. Do you ever wonder what would have happened if my secret didn't get out?

> *Something else I have been thinking about is lying in the*
> *sun while your family was out, talking about what we would do*
> *if we ran away together and left everyone behind.*
>
> *There is Scrabble here. We watched a movie last night*
> *about a train, three brothers, traveling through India. You*
> *would have loved it.*

Later I hand Jim the letter.

"What is this?"

"Could you please send it?"

"What exactly do you think the letters are going to achieve?"

"I don't know. They . . . they make me feel better. They make me feel less alone."

He gives a short nod and goes to his desk, shoves the letter into an envelope and seals it. *Maul.* I imagine hands on me, my arms, my legs, and I begin to shake.

In the midday stillness we walk down the hill. I wear sunglasses and a hat. The trees at the roadside hang a damp rug of shade over the grass and the frost breaks beneath our feet. The winding road has homes on one side and paddocks on the other, until houses sprout in paddocks and eventually paddocks become lawns, all overgrown and some with rusted cars, or goats and horses chained up, picking at the grass.

I hear a grating sound. Turning, I see an old man, white hair and long gray beard. He is bent, in a faded flannel shirt cinched into blue jeans. He doesn't stop sweeping his driveway as his myopic eyes find me. I turn away and we continue down the hill.

We come around beside the beach and the square car park

with a gravel of broken bottles. I look out into the water and see with each receding wave a head of black rock lurches from the sea, lined with mussels like a thousand razor teeth.

As we continue along, we pass knots of people sprawled out on the wedge of grass near the beach or leaning against cars watching us. I feel their eyes crawling over my body. *Look all you want, so long as it's my strangeness you're looking at.* It's something I'll get used to. I thought I would never miss what I had, all my old soft edges and childish long hair. I thought I knew what it was like to be self-conscious. I knew nothing.

A breathy voice utters the words, "Stick up the ass," and then there's laughter but I don't look. I should have worn track pants; I should have dressed like a sick boy.

Did you know a human skull can withstand up to 2,100 pounds per square inch of pressure? A heavyweight boxer might exert a force of 700 psi. A claw hammer, on the other hand, could exert enough pressure to dash open a human skull. The same could be said for a fall from a great height, even onto a relatively soft surface like wet sand. The front of a car going 100 kmh would also do it.

Finally we reach the shop, which sits beside the last roundabout before you leave town. Nearby, the forecourt of the abandoned petrol station is spiraled with black tire marks.

The shop is a cube of wood and brick, plastered with graffiti. It's a dark place with barred windows and a steel grate to roll closed every night. It's the kind of place that has one of everything. I survey the tiny tags marked with exorbitant prices. I'm still not used to the exchange rate. The shopkeeper leans forward in her seat with a vacant grin. *Just look at the magazines, don't look up,* I think as Jim moves about briskly, filling his basket with canned tomatoes, beans, bread. She's staring. I feel it and can't help but look over again. The woman raises her eyebrows and smiles. I pick up a copy of *Us* and flick through the pages, imagining just for a second that I see myself in them. Jim seizes it from my hand and puts it back in the rack.

"I was just looking."

"No," he says with finality. His eyes shift to the shopkeeper, then back to me. Quietly he says, "Just leave it." He approaches the counter with his basket.

"Kia ora," the shopkeeper says.

"Hi," he responds, pulling his wallet from his back pocket.

Burned skin climbs out of the collar of her hoodie, marbled and with a stretched quality. A scarred girl, I see, just like me.

"Where are youse from?"

"Australia."

"Aussies, eh? I can tell from the accent. I got cousins in Brissie, got a mate in Melbourne too." She punches prices into the cash register and bags the groceries.

"We're from Melbourne," I say as Jim digs into his wallet.

He hands over a note, then says, "Oh, I've a letter to post." He pulls out the envelope from his jacket. "To Australia." *Did he get the address right?* When he places it on the counter I read the name and the address. "Shit, I forgot the stamps."

"It's okay, we sell them."

She draws a sheet of paper from beneath the register, her eyes scanning down, and taps a number into the till. Jim holds a handful of coins, fingering through them for the right amount.

The woman smiles, puts her palms on the counter, and props her big torso over it to look out through the door. She would be about twenty. "Well, it's nice to meet you guys. Where are you heading after Maketu?"

Jim's gaze slides toward the door. "We moved here. Just take this," he says, pocketing the coins and holding out another note.

"You're not up the hill, are you? In the old wooden place with the flat roof? The lodge." The light coming through the entrance darkens as a cloud passes before the sun.

Jim draws a long breath. "We're in a bit of a hurry." He turns his head; his eyes say, *What's her deal?*

"What do you mean, 'the lodge'?" I ask.

"Oh," she says, "just a nickname for the old place. Had a cousin lived there a while back." The woman licks a pair of stamps and presses them onto the envelope. She takes the note from Jim and hands the change back.

"Kate," he says. He has broken his own rule. He should have said Evie. "Come on." Taking me by the wrist, he pulls me toward the door.

"See you around."

Outside, as we cross the road, he casts a furtive glance over his shoulder. "Shit." He runs his palm up his forehead and over his trimmed head. "It slipped out. Did you see the scars?"

"What?"

His sarcastic expression makes him look ugly for a second. "You didn't see the scars up her neck, under her jaw?"

"Yeah," I say. "I saw them."

We are walking along the footpath beside the beach.

"Oh, wait here a second, I forgot something." He rushes back to the shop, disappearing inside.

I stare out toward the deepest part of the estuary that divides the main beach from a tongue of sand that runs down toward the next point. There's an old broken structure of bricks and a group of boys are standing on it, shirtless, arms folded, and shaking with cold. One launches himself off, curling his body so that when he hits the water, a spray of seawater explodes up over the others. One by one the others follow him in. I shiver just thinking about the chill.

Jim returns and we set off walking again. "We've got to be more careful," he says. "You told her we were from Melbourne. It wouldn't be too difficult to put two and two together. What would you say if someone asked about us—I mean, who we are and what we're doing together over here?"

"Um, I'm not sure."

"What you say is this: I am your uncle. I am looking after you. If anyone probes you, tell them you would rather not talk about it. Some people are human lie detectors, they can spot a lie just by how you answer, so it's easier to avoid the questions altogether."

"Why did you bring me here?"

"Don't start this, please."

"But why here?"

"It's hidden away. I can barely get coverage for my phone. They won't find us here."

I swallow. It feels like I have an apricot pit lodged in my throat. Heat rises in my cheeks. He is still talking.

"You can't keep me forever," I say, low and harsh.

His eyes narrow. He drops the groceries there on the footpath, snatches my wrist, and pulls me close.

"Don't you fucking push me," he says. He's twisting the skin of my wrist. I pull away but he just tightens his grip. He looks about him, then releases me. "We're both damaged, you and me. We're stuck in this together. Just think about what they're going to do if they find us."

We are silent for the rest of the walk. His face is gaunt and gray with anxiety.

. . .

The following morning he sends me up to the letterbox. He's waiting on mail from the bank, a new card for his New Zealand account. He wants to hire a trailer and buy some new things for the house.

I see a glossy folded edge poking out of the letterbox. *Us*. The one from the shop. No stamp or envelope. Someone left it. There is also a letter for Jim.

Shoving the magazine under my hoodie, I go back inside, drop his letter on the kitchen island, and walk straight to my room.

"Anything?" he calls from the deck. He's holding the binoculars up to his eyes, scanning the bay.

"There's a letter for you."

"Anything else?"

"Nope." As I say it my heart slams against my sternum.

"No magazines?" There's laughter in his voice. "Don't worry, Kate. It's a treat. I don't mind."

I fall on my bed clutching the magazine to my chest, breathing in that clean new smell. I hear him walking across the deck, down the steps, and a few minutes later the rhythmic knock of the ax rises from the yard. I let my imagination run loose and see the ax striking the back of his head. The thought makes me cringe, and for a moment I feel sick. *Keep it together, Kate*. Perhaps when the impulse to hurt people weaves itself into your brain you are changed forever.

I draw another long breath through my nose. Was it a test? Did he place it in the letterbox to see if I would lie? I must earn his trust. I think of the girl at the shop, the way she looked at me. I finger the knotted flesh of my thigh and bite my lip softly as I open the cover.

Seven

here is nothing poisonous in this country, Jim said. No snakes, and the spiders are harmless. Last night when he lifted the wood box, a mouse dashed across the room and beneath the fridge. Jim heaved the fridge out, but he couldn't find the mouse; he couldn't even find a hole. He placed mousetraps in the dark recesses of the house, in cupboards and crooks where a mouse might hide. He bought a yellow box of rat poison and scattered half of it around the fridge. There is nothing poisonous in New Zealand except us.

Jim is out in the night collecting a desk for him to work on. It's going to sit beneath the map near the corner of the lounge. While I wait to hear the car crunching down the gravel driveway, I do as he asked. I sweep the wooden floor, then fall on my hands and knees to polish it with a cloth.

In the kitchen I see the old landline hanging from the wall. This could be my chance to contact someone from home, to find out if he is telling me the truth. He doesn't want me on the Internet because I could be traced, but he didn't mention the phone. I glance once up the driveway, then take the phone to my ear. I dial the only number I ever learned by heart. It doesn't ring. A voice in a New Zealand accent tells me that the number I dialed is incorrect or disconnected and to try again. I need to dial Australia, there must be a code. I pull the drawers out in the kitchen and search under the sink for a phone book, for anything. I check the hot-water cupboard. I find stacks of old newspapers, yellowed and bent. Then my hand grips something thick: *Bay of Plenty White Pages 1998/1999.* It's old and faded, dusty with age. On the island I open it out and flick through the pages before finding what I am after.

Dial out international prefix: 00

CODES BY COUNTRY:

Afghanistan 93
Albania 355
Algeria 213

Scanning down the list, I find Australia.

This time when I dial the phone number I add the codes and the phone begins to ring. I hold my breath listening, my heart speeding faster and faster with each ring.

"Hello." I'm surprised to hear a woman's voice.

I can't move or speak. I can't think.

"Who is this? I can hear you breathing." I slam the phone on the hook and step back, palming my chest, waiting for the phone to ring again. Surely they couldn't trace the number back to our location. I try to allay my fears with reason. It could have been a telemarketer or a wrong number. No one would go to the trouble of tracking down a call, and even if they did, what could they do with this number? Would she guess that it's me? I put the phone book back where I found it. Suddenly the room feels cold.

I go out to the yard to chop kindling for the fire. I hold the ax by the throat, just as Jim showed me. It reminds me of the shape of the land here: valleys are cut as though struck by a blade, opening up the earth for native fern and bush to erupt. The bush is so wild and so swift that old bicycles and broken fences in yards are quickly swallowed up.

I knock thin tinder from the wedges of wood and stack them in the wicker basket. I try not to think about the phone call. Jim will be angry. Jim might hurt me but there is nothing I can do about it now. I go slowly at first, taking careful aim before each strike. Gradually I work faster, with more precision, each blow passing cleanly through the wood. Occasionally I hit a knot and the ax stops, sending a shock through my wrist.

There's a memory like smoke in my fingers. It's so close yet I can't quite grasp it. I'm in the car alone, my head swimming, the wheels rolling silently beneath me. Is this a memory or a dream? *What did I do?*

Jim says the memories will break through, like grass *pressing between cracks in the pavement.* One strand at a time, making up patches of those lost hours. He says I need to remember the truth of how it *actually* happened. When I have remembered it clearly, only then can we formulate a plan and begin to move on. I remember gripping the wheel, the pull of the car. I can *imagine* it the way he says but not *remember* it. *I* didn't hurt anyone.

Inside, I set the kindling in the fire ready to light. As the potatoes boil and the pot lid rattles, I sit and wait, watching specks of rain appearing on the window. A fog is drifting down over the hills.

The magazine sits open on my lap. I flick through the pages, looking at photos of celebrities and reading about the affairs of the rich and the famous. In the middle, the magazine folds abnormally at the seam; some pages have been cut away.

The landline rings. I turn and stare at it hanging on the wall of the kitchen. It rings and rings and my stomach is up in my throat. It could be *them*. Someone could have traced the number and maybe they're coming for us right now. As suddenly as it began, the ringing stops. Slowly I release my breath. There is silence. Then the ringing begins again. I walk over and place my hand on it, feeling the vibrations of the sound. I pick it up and just wait and listen.

"Kate?"

I don't speak.

"Kate! Stop playing games."

"Jim?"

"God, what took you so long?" Jim's voice is tight with frustration.

"I thought you didn't want me to answer the phone."

He breathes out down the line. "I've pulled in at a service station. The rain's getting heavy down here and I don't have a cover."

"Oh," I say, eyeing the potatoes boiling on the stove. "Will you be long?"

"I need to keep the rain off the desk. Servo's closed. I'll just have to wait until the rain's eased. Is dinner on?"

"Yes."

"Good girl. If the rain looks like it's settling in, I might have to haul the desk off and come back with a tarp. But I don't really want to leave it here; someone might grab it. Can you light the fire?"

I ball the newspaper and stuff it into the open grate; outside the fog has settled around the house. *Good, quick-burning tinder,*

Jim had said. I'm beginning to see how proficient he is as an out-doorsman. I had helped prepare the fire but had never lit it. There's an art to those simple things we take for granted, those things that we grappled with for millennia.

Building a tepee with each individual piece of kindling just how he showed me, I lean over and ball the newspaper at the heart of it. When I strike a match, the newspaper burns too quickly and the kindling doesn't catch. I try again and again. Finally the fire spreads and the flames grow and slide up the wood's edge. I blow at the base of the fire, driving oxygen into the burgeoning flames. I stack more kindling in and then a larger wedge of wood. The fire gnaws at it.

The rain has cleared. I wait for him. Even if I knew where I was and had a plan to escape, what could I do without money or a passport? Out in the cold and dark I wouldn't get far at all. Would anyone help? Certainly not those locals with fierce eyes.

When he opens the door, the wind tears it from his grasp, slamming it against the wall. "Quick, give us a hand."

The desk I can only describe as *grand*. Scrolled feet, hand-tooled trimming. Jim shuffles it to the back of the hired trailer. We lug it to the front door.

"All right, let's get it inside."

We lift it through the door onto an old towel. He gets in behind it and pushes while I pull from the front.

He encircles the top with his arms. When he has enough purchase, he heaves it up. His arms bulge in his sleeves. He drops it down in the corner.

I can't tell if his face is damp with sweat or rain or both, but without his glasses framing those green eyes and with the stubble on his head, he looks like a prisoner himself. He is all power, a compressed spring.

He sits on the arm of the couch, frowning down at his hands. "What is it?"

"I've got to duck back out."

I step closer. "Why? Did you forget something?"

"I almost hit something," he says, glancing up at me. "What?"

His eyes lose their sharpness. He's looking through me. "A kid was out there on a bike. He rode in front of the car and I think he slipped at the bend. I couldn't stop in the wet with the weight of the trailer."

"Did you . . . did you hit him?"

He sighed. "No, I didn't hit him. He flew past me and over the bank at the road's edge."

"Did you stop?"

"No. I"—he sniffs and pulls his lips to one side—"I couldn't stop. I mean, I slammed on the brakes but I couldn't just stop in the wet."

A familiar chill washes down my back. I have a flash of my dream again, in the car, but the vision passes. "Where?"

"Couple of hundred meters down the hill."

I stare at him.

"I'll head back down now. It's probably nothing. But I better check to make sure the kid's okay. I should have stopped and got out, but the rain . . ." His hands are shaking. He looks gruff, worn, with stubble covering his cheeks. He tries to smile. "The car is fine."

He rises from the armrest of the couch and heads for the door. I follow him.

"Stay here."

"I just want to see."

"It won't be good for you; it might trigger something."

He closes the door behind him.

I wipe the desk down with the towel, then use a rag to polish the top. I get the plates out and set the table. I'm too young to be a wife, but that's how he treats me.

It can't hurt to have a look, just a look, that's all. I pull a steak knife from the cutlery drawer and walk outside. The gravel of the driveway is cold and sharp on my feet. The roar of the sea sweeps over all the rustling sounds and the rising wind in my ears, but I keep moving. He is lucky that he didn't hit the boy. It's easy to imagine what the weight of a car could do to bones and organs.

When I get to the top of the driveway I can see him up ahead; he is a smudge of darkness. In a nearby paddock, sheep are grazing. Then, as my eyes adjust to the dark, I see that a group of people have gathered near the bend in the road.

The steak knife is tight in my fist. I can feel my pulse in my fingertips and quivering away in my chest. The wind drives up the road again, bringing the chill and sharp beads of rain. Someone aims a flashlight beam at the road, then the beam rises. I press myself into the bushes near the roadside. Silhouetted by the light, Jim holds up a hand to shield his eyes. I can hear his voice but not his words. He steps closer, extends his hand. The flashlight stays on him. The figure doesn't accept his handshake. I see now that it's a woman and the rest of the group are children—it's a family. *Please don't make him angry.*

She says something that is stolen by the wind before it reaches me. I need to get nearer. I move forward. Leaves crunch. He is speaking again, murmuring an apology. I hear *evil you have brought.* At least I think I hear it, but the wind is still whirling around me and my blood hums. The chill has numbed my skin, my feet, hands, and ears. I can no longer hear the sea.

A child has fashioned a sling out of his T-shirt. Is that blood running from his head? The child swings his foot at Jim, but the old woman yanks him back by the collar so his kick barely grazes Jim's shin.

Despite the chill, sweat rises under my arms, down my back. Jim speaks again. Just a murmur from here. He offers his hand once more but they all just look at it. The woman holds the child and gestures wildly at the others to retreat.

Jim draws himself up. I know that stance. The primal hunch of the shoulders, hands clenched into fists. For a few heartbeats, no one moves. Then they all turn away and the family walks back down the hill in the damp evening air. I'm sprinting back toward the house before Jim has a chance to turn and see me.

Off in the distance, through the patter of the raindrops, I hear something. It sounds like someone shrieking; it might be the wind. I turn back to look. He is walking with his head lowered.

Inside, I drop the knife in the kitchen sink and fall onto the mat near the fire, my knees pulled up to my chest, my arms wrapped around them. Then I get up and wheel his filing cabinet in beside the desk. It has nothing inside but empty folders. I put his penknife in his penholder, the silver handle winking at me in the firelight. I'm opening the oven to dish up dinner when he enters, closes the door behind him, and slams home the dead bolt.

"The boy came off the bike and hurt his arm," he says. His expression is grim.

"Oh."

"Nothing really—he understood it was an accident," he says. He sits down on a stool and leans forward, his fingers splayed on his thighs.

"Was he badly hurt?" I say.

"Does it matter?" He eyes me, his patience evaporating. "I

don't know. He had a knock, he'll survive. Shouldn't be out in the wet riding around."

"Was he a local?"

"What difference does it make if he's a local or visiting from Mars? What difference does it make?" he says. He forces a laugh. "There was an old lady there." His eyes wander from mine to the fire. "Nice enough people, accepted my apology, shook my hand. That's all I could do." I watch his face for a hint of the lie but he clamps his lips closed and walks down the hall. "What's a boy doing out on the street like that, though? These people need to accept responsibility. It's dark and wet. It's plain stupid."

"Yeah," I say, because there is nothing else I can say. I almost feel bad for him.

"I'm going to have a shower," he says over his shoulder.

"What about dinner?"

He lets out a breath, then replies, "I'm not that hungry. You start without me."

I place the steak knife back in the drawer, and for the first time I can remember, I eat dinner alone. He's in his room most of the night and I can almost believe that I'm alone in that house. But when I go to bed, I hear his bedroom door open and the lock outside my door sliding into place, then his bedroom door closing once more.

BEFORE

Eight

old it in, suck in some air. Keep it in your lungs as long as possible." The joint glowed in my fingers. I had smoked a cigarette but that was easier: pull the smoke into your mouth, blow it out. I didn't like it at first, but after doing it once, the thrill of that small adult act brought on a bubbling excitement.

In the way that groups of girls are always looking for strays, I had been passed around from group to group within and outside of school, never settling too long before moving on. Willow was the only constant; I never was close to Sally again. Willow and I were enough for each other at swimming, turning away with our little inside jokes whenever Sally approached. I was surprised by how freely Willow could spit venom. At once she seemed almost aloof with her eyebrows raised, mouth pinched, then something sharp and mean would come out. Sometimes she would make small clever remarks, or sometimes she might just speak over Sally, interrupting her, suppressing Sally's voice with her own.

We never talked about Thom or about what Willow had told me. I couldn't let them see how much it upset me.

It was easy for me to talk *about* Sally to Willow, but I was only bold in private. I could never look Sally in the eye when I heard her sharp intake of breath, saw her face drop. Willow, though, seemed to relish her power. The power to hurt. The power to exploit vulnerabilities. It made me fear her. I hoped I never found myself on the receiving end of one of her barbs. I became distant with Thom; I felt betrayed in a way. Then he left swimming with promises to everyone that he would keep in touch. It felt like something had been severed. It felt like I might never see him again. Why did I care so much when I had been trying to distance myself from him anyway? It should have been a good thing he was leaving; that way I could get over him faster. Willow left swimming too. She had been "over it" for months. And then it was just me.

Fortunately Willow lived close by and most days I went to her place after school—though sometimes when my dad thought I was at Willow's, we were somewhere else completely.

That day it was the garage of a random friend of Willow's. The smoke burrowed into the fibers of my lungs, breaching my chest, itching all the way up my throat. All the eyes were on me. A small cough started it off and I tried to contain it but it kept coming. I coughed so hard my eyes watered but coughing didn't stop the itch. I tried to swallow it away, but as the others smothered their laughter it came on again.

Dad previously had banned me from using my mobile phone for two weeks when he smelled the cigarettes. *Who gave them to you?* He had asked. I blamed Sally. I wanted him to hate her.

We swam in the cloudy garage. Laughing, sitting on the tacky leather couches. The awkwardness was evaporating with the smoke. Willow propped her legs across the lap of a barrel-shaped boy and his body seemed to stiffen with the touch of her bare skin.

Maybe it was my imagination but everyone seemed to be watching her. I rolled my tongue around the inside of my mouth, smiling. It was easier to smile with the pot pouring itself over my brain. I undid my hair tie and ran my fingers through my hair, letting it fall over my shoulders.

Walking home later as the sun sank in the sky, we coated ourselves in Impulse to mask the bitter herby scent. When we got to Willow's house we went straight to her room and fell back on her bed. The light was fading outside. We lay there together, looking up at the ceiling, on the edge of some vast crater of laughter. The fragrant aroma of dinner rose up the stairs and my mouth watered.

"Just act straight when we eat, okay? My parents don't really give a shit. It's best not to get caught in case Mum is in a mood."

We went downstairs and sat at the table. I knew I was acting different but I felt untouchable. Willow moved her fork to scoop up peas, which spilled over the edge of her plate. A grin unfurled on her face. Her mum cleared her throat and her dad just sipped his red wine.

"Kate," he said, "you're looking particularly happy."

I realized I was smiling. "Oh, well, I am." Willow let slip a cough-like laugh.

"Good to hear. And how's school?"

"It's okay."

Reaching for the butter, Willow's mum knocked over a glass of water. It raced across the table and dripped onto my lap.

Her dad flicked his eyes up, gave his head a little shake.

"Good one, Mum," Willow said.

"I'm sorry, dear," she said to me, rising to fetch a tea towel. I felt a foot slide up my shin and looked into Willow's eyes.

When the spill had been mopped up, Willow's mum reached out to pat my hand. "I'm so clumsy."

"It's okay."

"A little water isn't going to melt you, is it, Kate?" Willow's dad said with a wink so subtle I almost missed it.

I noticed the face Willow's mum made. She looked ugly for an instant and I wondered how Willow's parents met. He was lean, handsome in a scruffy way. She was doughy, her jeans stuffed with middle-aged fat, but you could see she had once been pretty.

The television was still playing in the lounge. I remembered something Willow had said recently: *My dad has the hugest crush on you—he's always on his best behavior when you come over.* Sometimes if you bite into a joke you find a stone of truth at the center. I looked him right in the eye. His irises were a galaxy of different shades of green, his eyelashes dark and cheeks peppered with stubble. I swallowed.

After dinner, we watched *CSI.* Willow's dad disappeared to the study, which was more of a studio than a study, and I could hear the melodic plucking of a guitar unwinding into the house. After some time, I went to the bathroom. Passing through the study on the way back, I saw him sitting with his feet crossed on his desk, the guitar lying across his lap. A piano stood in one corner and guitars of different shapes and sizes were in racks beside it. I avoided his gaze, staring instead at the bookshelf.

The guitar paused. "Help yourself," he said. I turned to him. He thumbed a curl of dark hair behind his ear, then resumed plucking the familiar tune from the guitar.

"Thanks." I tried to smile, but it wouldn't take shape. There was something else, a tickling in my stomach.

Back in the lounge, I sat on the couch with Willow and her mum and watched the TV. The weed was wearing off.

Around nine a knock came at the door. I knew it was Dad: two curt taps. He had been away for work and was picking me up on the way back from the airport. Serious face, pants, and shirt. I tugged my hair back into a ponytail and stood to leave.

The detached feeling from the pot was gone, replaced with a washy gray ambivalence. Most men looked at my father in awe, but Willow's dad didn't care about my dad's sporting accolades; he may not even have known about them. Dad was just another man.

The warm breath of the heater in the car brushed my face like fingers. *Are my eyes red?* I didn't want to check. My dad steered with his fists, his arms straight. The big Range Rover wheeled around the bend. *Yuppie tractor.* I almost laughed. He veered through the gate and into the garage. The Mercedes was there, dark and sleek as a wet panther.

I skipped swimming again the following week to get high with Willow. This time her parents weren't home, so we sat on her windowsill looking down into the backyard, blowing the smoke out the window and burning a stick of incense.

"Why don't you just quit too?" she asked, handing me the joint and climbing onto her bed. I hated swimming; there was nothing in it for me now that Willow and Thom weren't going anymore.

"I can't, Dad won't let me."

"Fuck that. Just say you hate it."

"Yeah, I should." But of course it was not that easy.

"What has Sally been doing?"

"Nothing. She hangs out with Cara now." I took the last pull on the joint, then coughed out the window as I emptied my lungs.

"Cara? She's like thirteen."

"She just turned fourteen but yeah, Sally can't make friends her own age," I said, not mentioning the fact that I always sat alone.

"I want to go down to the pool," she said. "Come on—let's go fuck with her."

I felt anxiety thrumming below the surface of the high. There was no way I could be caught down there; I was supposed to be sick.

She rose from her bed. "Come on," she repeated. "I've got an idea."

I crushed the gray stub on the windowsill and let it drop into the garden below.

She slung her backpack over her shoulder and I followed her downstairs, along the hall, and into the garage. Willow took something from a bench, jamming it in her bag.

"What are you doing?"

"Let's go," she said, ignoring my question.

We made our way along the tree-lined streets. Willow strode purposefully, her wild brown hair swinging down her spine.

As we passed the shops and rounded the bend toward the pool, my skin prickled with anticipation. The familiar cars were in the car park and the bikes were in racks near the door.

"Follow me," Willow said.

I hesitated. "What are you going to do?"

A smile played on her lips. "You'll see."

"I can't go in there," I said. "Dad will kill me if he finds out I was lying about being sick."

"We're not going inside."

Willow drew her fingers through her hair so it fell down

around her face. She stopped at the bicycle rack, lingering beside a white step-through bike I recognized. The lock threaded between the spokes of the front wheel and the loops of the helmet where it hung near the pedals. Willow unzipped her backpack, her eyes fixed on the sliding doors of the aquatic center. "Watch this," she said. She pulled out a pair of sharp pliers and squeezed them over the series of cables that ran down from the handlebars. The cables twanged as they broke and curled back.

I clutched her shoulder. "She's going to notice."

She eyed me peevishly. "It's just a prank. Don't be such a Debbie Downer. She knew you liked Thom, right? Don't get mad, get even."

I'd been holding my breath; I let it out. "Okay, be quick."

She glanced once more toward the entrance, then reached down and clipped all the cables at the other end. Pulling them free, she wrapped them around the pliers and dropped them in her backpack.

"Come on," she said.

It was a joke. As we rushed away, we were giddy, cackling. The euphoria felt oddly satisfying. It still hurt to think about Sally and Thom, the things they would talk about and do. I hadn't seen him in the month since he had left swimming, but every time I saw Sally it reminded me that he had chosen her over me.

I didn't really understand the gravity of what we had done at the time, how a small act can have such consequences. Sally's injuries weren't serious. She hadn't ridden far at all, nor was she going too quickly when she discovered she couldn't stop. I didn't know anyone who saw it happen, but apparently she was hurled over the handlebars onto the footpath, breaking a small bone in

AFTER

Nine

Jim controls everything. That's why we are here in this town. He says he is protecting me, he is protecting us both, and I have no choice but to trust that he knows what he is doing. Everything I see, everything I experience has been filtered through Jim. So when we park outside the shop and he hands me a ten-dollar note and says, "Grab some butter, won't you?" I just stare at him, searching his face for any sign of intent.

"Me? By myself?"

He smiles and reaches out to unclip my seat belt. "You're a big girl, Kate. I'm sure I can trust you to buy something from the shop." He takes his glasses off and begins cleaning them on the hem of his shirt. "I need butter for the cheese sauce tonight," he says. It's been seven days and for the first time, he trusts me to interact with someone else without him. Is this another test? Maybe he is working with the shopkeeper.

I climb from the car and cross the car park. In the shop, the scarred woman is at the counter.

"*Kia ora*, Kate," she says. *Kate*. "How are you?"

I look at her. She's grinning from ear to ear. "I'm okay. But my name's actually Evie."

"Evie, huh?" she says with a big knowing grin. Blood rushes to my cheeks. "I must have misheard your uncle. How's the place treating you? Settling in?"

"Good," I say, walking around the shop. Did Jim tell her he is my uncle? The silence prods me to continue speaking, so I quickly add, "We're settling in well. It's very quiet here."

"I bet. Must be weird in Maketu after living in the big smoke. What's the story with your hair? Just like to keep it fresh and short?"

I chew my lips. "Yeah," I say, looking over at the magazine rack.

"Have a read," she says, kicking a stool out beside the counter.

"I can't—my uncle is waiting out in the car."

"Your uncle buys up loads of them. I reckon he's my best customer."

"Really?"

"Yeah. He loves them."

"Yeah," I say, frowning. "I guess he does."

"My name's Tiriana, by the way." She holds out her hand and I shake it. I don't sit, but I quickly flick through *Women's Weekly*. I don't know what I'm looking for. There could be anything in there.

A police car stops outside and I catch my breath. Has Jim seen them?

Drawing my hood lower over my eyes, I hold the magazine close to my face. An officer enters the store. Sweat rises on my chest. He nods at Tiriana, crosses the shop to the pie warmer. *Is he looking at me?* If I run, I won't get far. Tiriana's movements are jerky when she reaches to accept the money for the pie. The officer takes a bite as he strolls out the door to the street. She scowls as the car starts up outside and pulls away from the curb.

"Wonder why they're in town," she says. "Bloody nuisance."

I jam the magazine back in the rack and wait, looking out through the door across the car park. I can see Jim waving me over.

"What's up?" she says. "You look like you've seen a ghost."

"No," I say, trying to keep the panic from my voice. "I just need some butter."

"Down the back in the fridge."

I find the butter and take it back up to the counter.

She pauses, sitting on her stool, shrugging her denim jacket higher up her shoulders. The collar doesn't quite conceal the scars on her neck. "Three ninety for that."

I hand over the note.

Jim is holding his mobile phone to his ear as I step from the shop. He eyes me on my approach to the car. The engine starts. The phone slides into his pocket.

"Jesus, that was a close one."

My heart is still thumping. "Could they be looking for me?"

"I doubt it, but it's possible. Maybe we should take a long drive, in case they're waiting for us at the house."

We cruise down through the village, then up over the hill to the neighboring beach. I grip the door handle, focusing on my breathing. After half an hour we reach the next beach along on the coast. We stop at a park at the end of the beach and watch the sets of waves. Jim is chewing his lips with a pleat in his brow.

"If they are there, waiting for us, we'll just have to abandon the place and our things. We'll have to move on."

Gulls stand on the grass watching over the beach down below. Out near the receding tide, I see more. I walk close to them, and then I throw out my arms and rush. They take flight; the sound is like reams of paper falling.

Jim watches without speaking. This beach is longer than the

one at Maketu, more exposed, and every so often a salty breeze comes off the sea, sending a chill over my naked scalp.

A car pulls up and an old couple with cruise ship tans climb out. The man has a newspaper package of fish and chips.

"G'day," he says as he passes us. The woman just raises her eyebrows.

The man stares at me a beat too long. *Have you seen the video too?*

"I want to go," I say. "Please."

Jim nods and we head to the car.

We drive back along the road, up over the hill lined with curling ferns and the dark twisting limbs of those damp native trees. In places the trees lean toward each other from either side of the road as though they just want to touch.

When we're near the house Jim pulls over to the side of the road and yanks the hand brake up. He switches off the engine.

"Stay here while I check the house."

He gets out and starts up the road, then turns and comes back. He taps his finger on the window. I lower it.

"Hand me the keys."

I reach across and pull them out of the ignition, then pass them through the window. He jams them in his pocket.

"I'm sure the cops aren't waiting for us, but better safe than sorry."

Jim walks up the road. When he has been gone for a few minutes, another man comes back the other way and down the hill in my direction. He's dressed all in black and raises something to his eye, aiming it toward me. I avert my eyes, reaching for the button to raise the window, but it won't go up. He's got an urban paunch and a lawyerish thin face.

"Lovely day, isn't it?" the man says as he approaches. It is not a New Zealand accent. It's familiar. He's from back home. I glance at him and try to smile, but there's something mean in his eyes. Could he be here because I made that phone call? Did they trace it back to us? It can't be a coincidence.

The man is not long gone when I see Jim returning, striding briskly down the hill.

"All clear," he says, and we drive the rest of the way home.

Inside, he sets the butter on the island and puts a pot on the stove. I open the fire and scrunch up newspaper, but there is no wood in the wicker box, so I carry it out through the sliding door. I stop almost immediately. There is something red and shiny by the back door. My throat clenches. I recognize it straightaway; shaped like a tiny bean, no bigger than the top half of my thumb, it is a heart. The creature it belonged to was small.

"Jim," I say, my voice trembling. I drop the wicker box and stumble backward into the house, falling to the wooden floor.

"What is it?"

"There," I say. "By the back door."

He rushes forward, drying his hands on the thighs of his jeans. "What the fuck is it now?"

Tears are coming, my chest heaving.

"Oh, that? Come on, Kate. That's nothing." He plucks the heart between his thumb and forefinger and hurls it out into the backyard.

"It was a heart," I say. "Why would someone leave it there?"

"It would have been a dog or a cat," he says. Stepping closer, he squats down and strokes my cheek with the back of his hand. I imagine the animal's blood smearing on my skin. "Nothing to worry about."

"Could it be a threat? Maybe someone knows we're here." Someone left it where it could easily be stood on, split beneath the sole of a foot. I look out at the yard, watching for movement.

"Nonsense, no one could have found us and arrived so quickly. I've been careful," he says. I think of that phone call I made. "It's wild around here, you have to remember that we're not in the city anymore. Cats will often leave part of their prey for their owners as a gift."

There is no blood, no dash of red to mark the spot where it was left. I imagine it sitting in a mouth, the blood curling in the saliva beneath the tongue. I imagine it warm and beating.

"You're okay," he says. "It's okay. It's gone now. All gone."

Breathe, I tell myself over the pounding of my heart. *Breathe*.

"Go lie down, Kate. Go on. I'll do the fire and make dinner. Let me get you one of your pills." He lifts me from the floor and lays me down on the couch, where I curl into a ball. Classical music fills the room, and outside the rain starts pattering on the tin roof. The sky is darkening. I haven't seen the sun in days.

"Swallow," he says, fingering the pill into my mouth, holding out a glass of water. My heart beats like a hummingbird. Some small things can trigger this anxiety. The bath in Portsea, that creamy porcelain seashell with gold feet; I imagine it now.

The rain thickens outside. A drip sounds in the corner of the room. Our eyes meet. We hear another one. Jim walks toward the sound, then clucks his tongue. "There's a leak. It's only small but we'll need to get it sorted."

That night rain runs over the gutter, sheets of it distorting the world outside my bedroom window. It makes me want to pee, so I knock on my door and soon he comes to let me out. Walking to the bathroom, I hear the metronomic plop of water dripping through the roof into the pot in the lounge.

. . .

The next day, the rain has cleared, although the thick clouds threaten to break open again. Jim is on the roof repairing the leak.

At his desk, I pull out a fresh sheet of paper and begin writing.

> *This morning, I had a vision. I was standing in the hall-way at home, drinking from a bottle, some spirit that burned inside. Then I was driving. If I remember that, then perhaps he has been telling the truth about everything else but I just know I did nothing wrong.*
>
> *I'm starting to look better, healthier. I wish I could be back with you. Maybe one day soon I will, but I need to get happy and feel good again. I'm eating lots and walking and I also chop wood in the afternoons. Can you imagine me with an ax?*

I hear Jim calling from the front door. "I just rang Terry from next door. He's got some silicone out in his shed and a ladder. Won't be too much longer."

"Okay," I call back.

I read through the letter once more. Chopping wood implies we are somewhere cold, I suppose. But wouldn't it be obvious from the postage stamps what country we are in? Perhaps that's how the man who was dressed in black found us? It strikes me that Jim, who has been so careful about hiding us, has been lax about sending letters. I saw him hand over the last one at the shop, but there's no guarantee that it was sent. I add a line.

> *He locks me away at night. I am scared of what's going to happen to me and I don't know what to do.*

I seal the letter in an envelope. There are no postage stamps in his desk. He must have hidden them. In the kitchen I pull out drawers and open cupboards, searching. I stash the letter in the cupboard above the fridge while I keep searching. Moving down the hallway, I open the linen closet and lift up the towels to scan the dusty wooden shelves. The hot-water cylinder is pewter, spotted with age. I slide my hand along the top of it. I imagine spiders scattering from my fingers. My hand hits something. It's rigid with a velvet feel, like something stuffed. I pull it down. A mouse snapped in the steel loop of a mousetrap. I drop it, a quick inhale, hand to my heart.

The front door slams open and Jim rushes in. "Get down," he hisses. "Get on the fucking floor."

I stare at him.

"Now!"

I drop with my chin to the wooden floor. Blood pounds in my chest. The letter is in the cupboard. He can't be angry because of that. The mouse is inches from my face. He crouches, staring out through the lounge and into the yard. "Stay there." His eyes are wide, searching. He has a piece of paper screwed up in his hand. He creeps to the kitchen, makes a gap in the blind with his thumb and forefinger, and looks up toward the road.

"What is it?" I hiss.

"Someone's found us."

T hese are the types of events that serve no purpose other than to stir a semblance of loyalty from the masses." That's how my dad always saw the public meet-and-greet days with his old rugby club. To him, anything that wasn't about playing better and developing the game was pointless. In better moods, he saw such events as a means to an end: keep the fans devoted, retain members, get more money, and pay players and coaches more. Normally I would try to get out of going, but I didn't have any other offers and I knew Dad didn't want to go alone. He appreciated my company.

Dad pulled on his coat with the Melbourne Gators badge on the chest and his green scarf. He had had his hair trimmed and on the morning of the event he dragged a razor over his cheeks. He even slapped on some of the aftershave that he still had from before Mum died.

We walked down, opting to take public transport to avoid the standstill traffic heading into the city. He perched himself on the seat of the rattling train, watching the world out the window while I stared at my phone. A man on the train approached to shake Dad's hand and take a photo. When he smiled, really smiled, he could light up the whole carriage, but when he forced his face into an approximation of a smile for selfies, it looked like it hurt.

When we were alone again, I asked if he was excited. He smiled and nodded. I couldn't tell if it was sarcasm.

"Really?"

"Of course not," he said with a laugh.

His last full year of playing—while Mum was sick—people remembered as the best, most fierce year of his career. He was fearless. Then Mum died, Dad hurt his knee, and in his own way he, too, vanished, retiring from the sport in his late twenties.

Families clogged up the paths of the park surrounding the stadium. There was barely enough room to move without the occasional fans approaching Dad for a photo, or a signature, or simply to shake his hand and express their admiration. They seemed startled to see him, no longer that nugget of muscle they remembered but a man who was simply in decent shape for his age but otherwise entirely average. He could've been anyone. Photographers asked me to stand next to my father and smile into the camera. It wasn't until a few days later that I saw myself in the newspaper, Dad's arm draped over my shoulder and that pained smile on his face.

I pulled out my phone. I was bored already. Without thought, I found myself opening Instagram, finding Thom's page—a habit I'd fallen into. Almost a year had passed since I last saw him in person, since he had stopped turning up to swimming; fortunately I could keep an eye on him via his Instagram. I checked for new photos or to see if he had any live videos, but he only seemed to post photos of other people. I was too afraid to comment on any of his posts but I always "liked" them; in return Thom had liked the few photos I had posted too. It was a sort of torture checking his social media accounts because I knew eventually he would post a cute photo of him and Sally, which would break my heart all over again.

I found something new on his page. It had been uploaded four minutes ago. I could see the stadium in the background and all the purple scarves. It had been taken from up on the hill looking down over the crowd. The crowd I was standing in. I turned back, glancing up. People were streaming toward us. He'd been there four minutes ago.

Dad continued doling out signatures. I called to him. "I'll be back in a minute. Just going for a walk."

He raised a thumb.

I pushed through the churning mass of people and up toward the hill. Glancing down again at my phone, I attempted to locate the exact spot in which the photo had been taken. I moved through the thinning crowd higher up the hill, scanning faces, but there was no sign of him.

I opened Instagram again. The photo had been posted nine minutes ago now. I looked out over the crowd. I was standing near the spot he had been in but now he could be anywhere. Feeling lost in the crowd, I rushed back down the hill, searching each passing face. What would I say even if I found him? I could feel the moths beating about my chest. *He's here.*

Back beside where Dad stood, I pulled my phone out. I was getting desperate now. *Posted 14 minutes ago.* Despite my better judgment—and Willow's advice to stay distant, cool, and avoid being needy—I decided to write a comment beneath the image.

Omg I'm there too!

I hesitated before posting. I was staring at my words when I felt a gentle nudge at my elbow. Turning back, I looked up into his eyes. *Thom.* He had grown a little taller. His brown hair was raked back. Eyes dark and pinched at the corners—eyes made for smiling. Black jeans slashed at the knees. He still had strong swimmer's shoulders beneath his white long-sleeved T-shirt, but now the rest of him had filled out too. Hanging down one shoulder was a camera.

"Hey, stranger," he said.

"Hi," I said, blood flooding my cheeks. I wondered if he knew what I'd done to Sally.

"So," he said. "How have you been?"

"Okay. I mean, good."

"Right." Wry smile, fingers running back through his hair. "This shouldn't be so awkward, right?"

I laughed a little, shook my head. "I'm sorry, it's just been a while."

"Yeah, it has. I knew you would be here," he said. He had grown surer of himself. He flashed his white teeth. "I mean when I saw your dad." He nodded in the direction of Dad. Was it possible he'd sought me out?

"So what have you been doing since you quit swimming?"

"A bit of photography," he began, lifting his camera in his palm. "School. What else?"

"And Sally? Are you ..." I didn't know where that came from; impossibly, my face felt even hotter. I tried to smile but couldn't.

"Sally?" he echoed, brow furrowed. "Do you mean Sally from swimming?"

I couldn't hold his gaze. I recalled how acutely I had felt the ache of jealousy in my gut when I found out about them.

"I thought maybe you two were still going out."

"Going out?" He shook his head with an uncertain smile on his lips.

"But . . . I thought—"

"Me and Sally? I mean, Sally's cool but . . . no. What gave you that idea?"

Willow. "I don't know." I attempted to laugh through the heat of embarrassment, but it sounded more like a deflating balloon than genuine laughter.

"It would be good to catch up properly. I mean without all the"—he threw out his hands, indicating the crowds—"families."

"Yeah," I replied, noticing Dad close by fidgeting in his pockets as he tried to wrap up a conversation with a fan.

"So," Thom continued, suddenly shy, "maybe I could text you or something."

"Yeah," I said. "It would be cool to stay in touch."

"Do you want to give me your number? I mean unless you've still got a boyfriend?"

Still. "No boyfriend."

"No boyfriend?" he asked. He raised his eyebrows. "That's the best news I've heard all year."

I couldn't form a response. Everything was happening too quickly for me to think clearly.

"Here, give me your phone."

I pulled it from my pocket, unlocked it, closed Instagram, and handed it to him.

He punched something in. "Okay, I've put my number in *your* contacts. So it's up to you if you want to catch up sometime."

"But what if I don't text you?"

Those dimples, I thought as he smiled.

"You'll text me," he said. "I give it an hour before I hear from you."

"Is that right?" I said, raising my eyebrows. "I'll see if I can hold out."

That old feeling stirred inside, the fizzing excitement spreading to my fingertips, my toes, tugging at the corners of my mouth. It was really happening.

"I've got to run, actually. Believe it or not, I'm not just here to charm you, I'm meeting friends." As he walked away he held up his phone and mouthed, *One hour*, with a wink.

After Thom had left, Dad found me. "Don't leave me alone again please, Kate." He was looking around as if scared. "These people are relentless." He met my gaze. "What?" he said. "What is it? There's something on my face, isn't there?"

"I'm not smiling at *you*," I said.

"What is it then?"

My phone began vibrating in the pocket of my jeans. An alarm was sounding. Dad looked over. I pulled the phone out. It wasn't an alarm; it was a reminder.

Have you texted Thom yet—Mark as complete?

"You're doing it again," Dad said, with laughter in his voice. "Look at that smile. What is it?"

"It's *nothing*, Dad."

Another alarm sounded on the train home exactly one hour after I had seen Thom.

If you haven't texted Thom already, maybe you should do it now?—Mark as complete?

I found his contact and sent him a message.

Whew. One hour and one minute. That was tough.

A second later he sent one back.

A valiant effort. So tell me, what happened to the
boyfriend?

What had Willow told him? I guess it was easier to go along
with it than to try to explain.

It didn't work out.

Well I'm eternally grateful. You know I used to have the
biggest crush on you.

Used to?

A few minutes passed as the train rattled along, excitement
blooming in every inch of my body.

Okay, maybe I still do.

AFTER

Eleven

A strange energy surges through my body. *Someone has found us.* I swallow against the claustrophobic press of the hardwood floor on my throat. Jim gestures to me to rise, then points toward my room.

"Stay in your bedroom," he says. "Someone is out there, looking for you."

I hurry down the hall. At the bathroom, I stop and climb up to stand on the toilet and peer out the window toward the street. Looking up through the branches of the tree at the front of the house, I can just see the road but I don't see anyone standing on it. I head back into the hall to my room. There I close the curtains and sit on my bed with my arms wrapped about myself.

Who are they? Who are we running from? The police? The media? The men online? It's been eight days since we fled. They've found us and now we'll have to leave again. Or I could travel alone. *Me llamo Evie.* I could go to South America, or Japan or Europe. *Bonjour, je m'appelle Evie.* I could escape him and everyone else.

He comes into my room and sinks onto my bed. He pulls me against him. My shoulders hunch at his touch. "It's okay. They'll go away." His body is warm against mine, and I can hear him swallow. "We are going to need to be more careful. It's not the police, Kate. Well, not yet anyway. It's someone else."

It sucks everything from inside of me; I'm reminded of the life I will never have. "No one was there. I looked up toward the road from the bathroom window." I don't go so far as to challenge him.

His jaw knots and his mouth barely opens when he speaks. "Don't even begin to think that we are in the clear. Don't think they won't come after us again and again. I'll make sure they never take you but you've got to listen and trust me." He presses his face against my damp cheek.

"I'm sorry," I say. He leaves and closes the door. Sometime later, I hear his socked feet come up the hall. The lock on my door slides into place.

I haven't been out of my room for two days except to go to the bathroom. Yesterday, while he thought I was in the bathroom, I rushed up the hall on the balls of my feet to collect the letter I'd stashed in the cupboard above the fridge. It was gone, which means he found it.

We didn't run away; he just keeps me hidden now. Sitting in a square of sun on my bed, watching the sky outside, I sense he is close by. The mattress compresses behind me as he kneels on it, resting his hands on my shoulders. I shrink away.

"They will still be in town. They'll be waiting on their bellies like snakes. But for now, we can wait too." He clears his throat. "I'll make your juice." He rises and soon that excruciating, churning sound of the juicer comes as he feeds vegetables into it. I've become acutely aware of the sounds we make, the treacherous noises that might give us away if someone was listening outside. I hear the teaspoon scraping around the glass. He returns and hands me the concoction, folding his arms, looking down into the backyard. I follow his gaze to a family of rabbits grazing on the lawn. They are fully grown and the color of thunderclouds. Jim turns to face me, watching as I swallow the bitter liquid.

My hair prickles through the skin, beginning to grow out. It has taken eleven days to get to this length; it'll take years to grow back to how it was. For the other hair on my body he still hasn't given me a razor; a fine blond down covers my legs. I want to write in my journal, write what I remember and what I feel, but I know it's only for him to read later. I have tried to write, but every time I open the first page I lose the impetus.

Again I wonder about that letter. What did I write? *He locks me away.* He must have read it. Is it possible that he sent it? It could lead the police in Australia to us. Just like with the phone call, I acted without thinking, and just like with the phone call, I put myself in danger.

He's been out once or twice over the past couple of days—without a word, I hear the front door close, the car backing out of the driveway—and when he returns he carries boxes of groceries to unpack. In one instance, I watched from my bedroom window as he carried a narrow steel case that looked like something a musician would use to carry an electric guitar. It went straight out into the shed.

He's out now as I sit in my room, dressed in layers—tights and track pants, a sweater—to keep warm. I eat the leftover fruit salad he brought me this morning and think about all the food we used to eat: smashed avocado, spicy shakshuka, eggs Benedict, and corn fritters at our local café. I think about playing Scrabble with Thom's family at the beach and my heart squeezes. The last private place I have is in my mind, the last place no one can take from me. This is where I keep those memories of the time before.

I go to the bottom of my wardrobe and pull out my escape bag. It was his idea: *Think of it as an evacuation seat.* If we must leave suddenly, the bag is all I will need. On the bed, I unpack and re-pack it, folding the clothes, counting the money. But as I am putting the bag back I notice something: the carpet in the bottom of the wardrobe is peeling back. I reach in and tug it gently. Something hard and rectangular has fallen in behind it. I feel it in my hand, the thickness and weight. Drawing it out, I smell the sour must of an old book. I take it in my hands, bringing it into the light pouring in through the window. It must have slipped from my bag when we arrived. I began to read this book at the airport before we left. It's old and dog-eared. Jim gave it to me. I flick through a few pages and pause to read one. Something snatches my attention. Toward the bottom of the page, in the middle of a word, the letter o has been underlined. Why would someone underline a single letter? I turn the page and find there are no underlined letters. I scan through, one, two, three, four pages. Then there it is. The letter n underlined. *O-n.* What could it mean? I continue the process, next finding a t and then another. I grab a pen from my bag and write the letters on my palm. *Ontt.* I flip forward and find the next letter: r. A pattern emerges; the under-lined letters are on every fifth page. I go back to the start, five pages back from where I found the first o, and sure enough there

Twelve

on't trust him. My mind is reeling. Something bad is going to happen if I stay here much longer, if I let him keep me locked away, feeding me pills and blocking the world outside. Who made these words? I can feel an attack digging its claws in beneath my collarbone. *Breathe. You can think your way out of this if you stay in control.* I steady my nerves, block out all the conflicting voices in my head telling me to run, to stay, to attack, to hurl myself out the window. Over them all I can't escape the words I found. *Don't trust him.*

I stay in my room all night, choosing not to eat the dinner he brings in, leaving it sitting on my dresser. Later that night I hear party sounds floating up from down the hill. The noise doesn't stop until after I've fallen asleep. But it is the other night sounds that chill me. I hear things . . . breaking glass, the squeal of tires, voices whispering. These sounds come every night and Jim says it's the trees, the branches scratching at my window like witches' fingers, but now I can't take anything he has told me for granted.

When I wake in the morning I'm watchful. I take one sip of

my morning juice, then tip the rest out the window after he has left the room. I hide the vitamins and the pill from the doctor inside my cheek and spit them out. The pills from the doctor are the worst of all; they make me drowsy and pliable. This happens every day. The same routine. He tries to talk to me, ask me questions. After three days he says, "You know, Kate, I want you to be free but we just can't risk you going out there until we know it's all clear. That doesn't mean you have to stay in your room all day, why don't you come out into the lounge?"

I just nod because if I try to speak I might scream.

After almost a week inside the house, he lets me out to help him clear the blocked gutter, the one that causes rainwater to rush down over my window. It's my job to hold the ladder as he climbs.

"Hold it steady," he says.

He trusts me. Does he not know what I'm capable of? This is my chance. I could push the ladder. A hard shove at the side and he would come tumbling down. A fall from that height could snap his neck. The image is so clear, it comes to mind so easily, but still I cringe at the thought. When I escape it will be with as little violence as possible.

"I've got it," I say. He is standing on the second-to-last rung, leaning up against the house. He lifts both hands off the ladder and takes the pruning shears he tucked into his belt.

"Look out," he calls as he closes the shears on the first branch. It falls to the ground with a soft thump. Slowly he works his way along, clipping the branches hanging over the roof, tossing thatches of damp leaves from the gutter.

"Do you think that's clear enough now?" he asks, coming back down.

"Yeah," I say. "Thanks."

We have chicken salad for lunch and I'm so famished I eat it all this time. In the afternoon, he locks me in my room again. A man comes to drop off another load of firewood, this one much bigger than the first. I hear the thunder of it all pouring onto the driveway.

When the man has gone, Jim lets me out to help cart and stack the wood beneath the steps in the cool midday sun. Between trips I eye the road. It's so close that I could make a dash for it, but there is no point running without a plan; I need to be tactical.

I pick up a piece of wood and a spider crawls across my hand. The wood slips from my grip, falling onto my foot. I drop to the grass and clutch where the wood landed as hot tears come.

"Oh, darling," he says, coming around the corner with another load. He dumps the wood and, crouching beside me, pulls my shoe off.

"Fuck, it hurts so bad."

"Shhh," he says, peeling off my sock. He leans forward and presses his lips to the spot where the skin has bruised, then he rubs my foot between his hands. "What happened?"

"There was a spider."

"Really? How big?"

"Giant." I show him with my thumb and forefinger.

A smile plays on his lips. "They don't have spiders that big here, Kate."

"I know what I saw. It was on my hand."

"Was there *really* a spider, Kate?"

I ball my hands into fists. "I fucking hate this place," I say. The pain and adrenaline have turned to a cold, sharp anger.

"Hey," he says. "It's okay. We're safe."

I pull my foot from his hands. "We're *not* safe. You said that they're here. They've found me. You promised they wouldn't."

"If they had found us—I mean, if they knew for certain—they'd already have us, wouldn't they?"

They. That's what he calls them. But he never says who. Is it possible that no one is after us at all? Or perhaps he is only telling me half the truth. I think about what I know: someone was hurt, I was there, I drove a car, we fled together, and now I can't leave.

"Kate, please don't overthink it. Let me do the thinking."

"I just don't want to be sad. I hate this feeling."

"The pills should be helping. What's making you sad?"

He doesn't know that those pills end up out my window, or under my bed, or spat into the toilet. "I don't know. You keep me locked up. You don't trust me."

He huffs out his breath and rises, resumes stacking firewood. "I trust you, but I don't trust your judgment. You can understand why I am worried about what you might do, right?"

"I'm not going to do anything crazy, but if we are staying here, I want to be able to be normal." I need enough freedom to begin planning my escape. I need some time alone, away from this house.

In spite of the chill, a single pearl of sweat runs down his temple. "What are you suggesting?"

"Maybe I can go out by myself sometimes."

"You're free to do whatever you want, Kate. If that's what you truly want, there's nothing stopping you."

"Well, there's a lock on my door."

A little chuckle. "If you think you're locked away now, wait until they get their hands on you. Then you will see what *locked away* really means."

"I'll be careful, I won't talk to anyone. I'll stay out of sight."

He shakes his head. "I can't protect you if I don't know where you are." A moth lands on his face. He pauses, swings at it with his palm. "Why do you need to go out? Why can't you just wait?"

"I want to go for walks again, I'm not asking too much. And you said they might not know where we are."

He jams another wedge of wood in under the steps. "You think that some of the people here in this town don't know? You don't think they're trying to sell us out as we speak? And even if they don't know for sure, they're definitely suspicious. If they don't know the whole truth, the ugly truth about who you are, they will in time." He straightens up. "The longer we keep you hidden, the better." He turns away and climbs the steps into the house. "You'd better get some ice on that foot."

The bruise still pulses with pain when I pull on my shoe. I kept it elevated all afternoon yesterday, a bag of ice pressed to the sore spot, but it still swelled. From my window, I watch Jim cross the lawn to the shed, his laptop under his arm and his head down. He unlocks the shed with a key and pulls the door closed behind him.

The lawn is a few meters down below; too far to jump. But then I notice something: the ladder is still by my window. I could reach it, if I tried. I could climb down it.

As I push the window open wider, I watch the door of the shed. Even if he found me I could say I was busting and couldn't get to the bathroom. The prepared excuse does little to abate the fear. I climb up onto the windowsill and slowly lower myself down, reaching with my bare toes. I feel the top rung of the ladder. Lowering myself farther, I feel the next one. The ladder moves a little beneath me but I hold tight to the window's edge. Slowly, carefully, I climb down the rungs. Then when I reach the grass, without thinking I'm off up the side of the house to the road with my heart slamming.

There's a white sedan farther along our road, so I go the other way, setting off down the hill. As I approach the bus shelter I try to resist the temptation to look in, but when I feel eyes on me I can't help but turn. A small child of five or six with a straight bob of black hair sits on the bench. I stop.

"Hello," I say.

"Hi," the girl says.

Jim might find me gone, I've got to keep moving, but I'm drawn to the girl. I step forward and she leans so her face moves from the darkness into the light. I see then the shining trail of mucus beneath her nose. She's not crying, but it's clear from the tear tracks down her cheeks that she has been.

"What's wrong?"

"Nothing," the girl says.

"What's your name?"

She scratches at her hair. "Awhina."

"Awhina? That's a nice name."

I say it how she said it. *Ah-fee-nuh.*

She shrugs. "What's your name?"

"Kate," I say. The word is out before I can stop it. I feel anger at myself at first, replaced quickly with a light buzz in my chest. It feels good to say my old name.

"I don't think you're supposed to talk to me," the girl says.

"What do you mean?"

She stands up and steps out of the bus shelter into the muted sunlight. I see then how skinny she is, how her sleeves don't quite reach her wrists, how her bare knees poke out from beneath her shorts. A car crawls past but I don't turn to look at it. When I do glance over my shoulder a few seconds later, I see it has parked farther up the hill. A man dressed in black is climbing out.

"Awhina, can you tell me what you mean?"

She looks at my bare feet, then back up to my face, before stepping past me.

"He told me."

"Who?" I say with growing alarm. I step closer to the child. "He told you what?"

"Not to talk to strangers."

"Oh, well, you know my name now, so I'm not *really* a stranger." I push my hood back so she can see my face. "What happened, Awhina? Why were you crying?"

She is staring at the ground. "I made him angry at me."

I swallow hard. "Who?"

"My dad. He got angry at me."

"What did he do?"

"He hurt me. That's why I can't go to school today."

I wince. "Does he often hurt you?"

She scuffs the ground with her shoe. Then, as if it takes all the courage in the world, she looks up at me and gives the smallest of nods.

"Where do you live?"

"Down the hill."

"Where?"

"I'm going home," the girl says, suddenly shy. She begins walking briskly away down the hill. I could go after her to see if I can help, but it's easier just to hope that she will be okay. I savor her name in my mouth. *Ah-fee-nuh.* The car is still parked up on the shoulder of the road, the white sedan with a rental sticker in the corner of the back windscreen.

The black-clad man stands near the mouth of our driveway, a cigarette hanging from his lip. I can't be sure, but it looks like the man who was near our place a few days ago. I pull my hood back up.

He walks toward me, holding something up to his eye, something small and square. The camera lens finds me. I look down the road and realize I am too exposed. I turn and start back toward the house, beginning to run. Clicks machine-gun behind me. I quicken my pace and turn into our driveway. My heart is thundering.

The shed door is still closed. I fly up the ladder, tip over the window ledge, and tumble down hard onto the floor of my room.

"Jim," I call toward the shed.

There's no response.

I close the blinds, then curl myself into a ball on my bed and rock. *Where is he?*

"Fuck," I say. Then I say it again, louder, and again, louder still.

The back door slides open. For a second I'm chilled to the core. I think, *They've come for me and now they're inside.*

"Kate," the voice calls. It's Jim.

I rush to my door as the lock slides and the door opens. I fall into his arms, racked by sobs. I realize he is holding me, that I want him to hold me. *Don't trust him.* But what choice do I have? "It's okay," he says. "What happened?"

"Where were you?"

"I was just in the shed," he says. "Did something happen?"

"No," I say. "Nothing happened, I—" The sobs shudder through my words. "I was scared that you'd gone. I don't know what I thought. I heard someone outside." My chest flutters. The pain and fear wash over me like the angry sea. He holds me tight, containing me. My throat constricts. It's a full attack coming on.

"Hey," he says, more softly than I've heard him speak. "It's going to be okay, I've got you. Breathe with me." He places his hand on my back.

We sit like that for some time. My chest rises and falls as I breathe in and out.

When everything is calm and still, he pries my arms from around his neck and stands.

"Kate, can you make me a promise?"

"What is it?"

"Promise me that if you ever feel like you are going to do something rash, you'll just pause and take a few breaths."

Sagging in the fatigue from the unspent adrenaline leaving my bloodstream, I utter the words, an empty promise: "I will, yes."

"I heard you calling when I was in the shed and came straight-away. That's all you need to do. Just call out to me."

He leaves my room and I hear him walking up the hallway. Then comes the knock of his tools being dragged out from beneath the sink. I go to my bed and sit there waiting to see what he will do. In the door frame he aims the electric drill at the roof and tests the battery.

"Trust me and I will trust you. If I tell you to go to your room, you go there and stay there until I say you can come out, under-stand?"

I nod.

"Say yes."

"Yes. I understand."

I stand and watch him drill. When he's done, I follow him as he carries the dead bolt down to the kitchen and slaps it on the counter. "All right," he says. "I'm going to put this away for now. Please don't make me regret it." He opens the fridge and takes out the ingredients for my juice. The juicer grinds to life. He begins feeding the vegetables through, then the fruit.

"You've been eating everything I make?" he asks, speaking loudly to be heard over the din.

"Yes," I reply.

"Good," he says, killing the juicer, holding the glass out to me. "Let's see how much weight you've put on."

We go to the bathroom and I stand on the scales. He leans over my shoulder to read the number, then scribbles it into his notebook.

"You're getting better, Kate. That's almost four kilos. Not bad for less than two weeks. Soon, when you're feeling up to it, we can talk more about what happened that night back in Melbourne."

It's dark when I wake. I have no idea how long I have slept for, but I know it's still nighttime. The light is on in the hallway; a voice comes from the lounge.

"It needs to happen sooner rather than later." A murmur just clear enough to make out. Slowly I rise from my bed and press my ear against the crack between the door and the door frame. "I've got her with me. But does anything change, I mean the longer it takes?" He's on the phone. "What will they do with her?" His voice is steely. "Then what? I mean what legal options do I have if things go pear shaped?"

I ease my door open and creep up the hall. He sighs. "She's healthy, I'm keeping her healthy. It's her brain that's the problem." One more step and the floorboard creaks.

He turns, his eyes widening when he sees me. "Let me call you tomorrow. I've got to go. . . . Yep, will do. Bye." He hangs up.

"Kate," he says. "What's going on? Can't sleep?"

"Who was that?" I ask. "Who was on the phone?"

"Just settling some affairs, nothing to worry about."

"Why are you up so late?"

"Late?" He glances at his phone screen. "I guess it is getting late." Then the cold weight of his eyes falls on me. He's not wearing his glasses. "I suppose you're not the only one losing sleep these days."

I lean against the dark wood-paneled wall in the hallway. "I want to use the Internet. I want to see what they're saying."

"You can't."

"Why not?"

"It's too soon. You're not stable." Annoyance is visible on his face now. His brow creases. "You don't even remember what happened."

"I know, but I just want to see what they're saying."

He sighs. "You have to see things for yourself. It's not enough that I tell you, is it?"

I don't know how to answer, so I stand there until he waves me closer, turning toward his desk. He opens the laptop, and I watch his fingers punch in the password. There is a P and an E but his fingers travel too quickly for me to pick up anything else. He opens an anonymous browser. I watch him as he chooses a city from a list; if anyone could see this search, they would think we were in São Paulo, Brazil.

"I give up, Kate. I don't know what is working and what's only making it worse."

He clicks on a message board with hundreds of messages. The title is *Kate Bennet*. I take a breath to quell my nerves before sitting down on his office chair. I was convinced he wouldn't show me and now I'm here, with the screen loaded before me. I can't look up.

"You don't have to do this, Kate. I don't think you're up to it."

He doesn't want me to look and so I must. I swallow, a tension coiling in on itself inside. I exhale and look at the screen.

If I encounter this virus, I would love to dispatch her. One bullet. That's all it would take. Hundreds of likes.

> She's pretty hot, but clearly crazy. I'd still fuck her, but then again she'd probably consume me like a praying mantis after.
>
> Lol.
>
> So true.
>
> Let's start crowdfunding a PI to find her. She can't have disappeared.
>
> Does anyone know where she is?
>
> She won't have gotten that far. Maybe Sydney—it's not hard to hide.
>
> Can someone share the tape? It's been taken down . . .
>
> Try this: http://www.vilefile.com/share/kate-bennet -leaked or if you have a Tor browser you can buy the HD version on the dark web.

I'm shaking. My inner organs have plummeted. In their place is a cold vacuum. Jim only shows what he wants me to see.

"Click it."

"What?"

"The link," I say, steadying my voice. "Click on the link. I want to see it."

He closes the lid of the laptop, stands, and wraps me in his arms. "It'll be fake. The video has been taken down." He gazes into my eyes, his jaw firm, his nostrils flaring.

I scream so loud that he covers my mouth.

"Shh," he croons. "Let's go to bed."

"No!" I yell. "Don't you tell me what to do. You're not my father!"

I collapse to the floor and he comes down with me. He holds me like he's sinking and I don't have the energy to push him away.

"You're being nasty," he whispers. "You don't want me to get angry."

We stay like that until I have nothing left, no energy, no tears, just a trembling in my chest, in my limbs, in every cell.

BEFORE

Thirteen

Was it something I said?

That was the first message I read from Thom in two weeks. I had other messages from Willow and school friends too. Thom and I had exchanged texts for the better part of a month, the flirtation gradually growing. At first it was the inclusion of a single x at the end of each message. Then he began to call me babe. We hadn't seen each other again but did it matter? We realized that we lived within walking distance from each other, it was only a matter of time, then Dad confiscated my phone.

I'd been keeping a plastic water bottle under my bed half filled with liquor I had skimmed from the bottles in the hallway cabinet. I got the idea from Willow. We had drunk together and I thought next time I would provide the booze. I'd originally gone to her house to confront her; I wanted to know why she lied to me about Thom and Sally, but I couldn't bring myself to say the words. I didn't even tell her about bumping into Thom and the text messaging that followed. Instead, up in her room she pulled the alcohol out from beneath her bed. We sat against her headboard watching *The Bachelor* on her iPad and passing the bottle back and forth. With a buzz in my chest and the alcohol's lacquer-like effect on my thoughts, we cackled at the desperate contestants. I was confused and annoyed about the lies she told but I knew that I wasn't ready to have that conversation with her. It was, after all, through Willow that I had made so many of my other friends, and without her I wondered if I would still have any of them. Besides, I was just happy that Thom was back in my life.

When Dad found the liquor cabinet open, he realized the seal of a previously unopened bottle had been broken. I'd only just got full-time phone privileges, which meant I could FaceTime Thom late into the night and fall asleep as if he was there, beside me. Then my phone was gone again.

How could I lose Thom so soon after all this time? I nagged for him to give it back, reaching for it in his hand. I wouldn't leave him alone until he snapped. *You want it that bad? Here it is.* He took it in his fist and pitched it across the room so hard it shattered against the marble backsplash in the kitchen. I rushed over and took all those broken pieces to my chest so my fingertips bled from the broken glass.

When he came home from work the next day, he had a white box. Inside was a brand-new phone, the next model up from my old one. "I'll give it to you in two weeks but only if you behave yourself, and it comes with two conditions." He counted them with his fingers. "No passcode on the phone, and you talk to me if you ever want to drink alcohol or anything like that, okay? You're growing up, I get it, but there's a right way and a wrong way to do things."

After two weeks, at the breakfast table he handed me that white box. I opened it up and plugged my SIM card in. That's when the messages I had missed from Willow and Thom came through, but it was Thom I cared most about.

> OMG Dad took my phone. He found out about the
> booze stashed under my bed. I'm so sorry! I missed
> you.

He replied almost instantly. I saw you hadn't posted on Instagram or Facebook so I thought something was up. I knew you wouldn't just blow me off. ;) I was tempted to walk up your street and try to guess your house but thought that would be too stalkery.

I was grateful he hadn't. I didn't know what I would tell Dad if Thom knocked on the door. His next message popped up before I could reply to his previous one.

> Glad you're back online, even if you did set my plans
> back two weeks.

> Plans, huh?

> Well by now I would have asked you for a date. But I
> guess that'll just have to wait.

I considered my next message carefully. I couldn't help but wonder why he had chosen me. I imagined the way his body had changed since our swimming days.

> That's lucky because I probably wouldn't have said yes
> so soon. Out of curiosity what would this date involve?

> I was thinking we could take a walk.

Something was blooming inside. I smiled.

> A walk? Really? I think I might almost be ready for that.
> Almost.

Dad came into the room carrying two plates. "Eat up or you'll be late to school."

We sat together at the table. I felt the phone vibrate in my lap.

> Do you think you will be ready this weekend?

Dad cleared his throat. "Not while we're eating, please, Kate."

"Sorry."

I put the phone back in my lap and felt it vibrate again. I couldn't do anything but scoop my omelet into my mouth and chew faster.

My school friends were candid with their parents about boyfriends and parties. But it wasn't like that with Dad; I felt a kind of shame. Maybe it was because we only had each other. Would it have been different if Mum were still alive? My closest family members were Grandma up in Wagga Wagga and my mum's sister, Lizzie, in England. I hadn't seen Aunty Lizzie since the funeral when I was only five, although we had Skyped sometimes on birthdays. After Mum died, Aunty Lizzie flew over and stayed with us for a month. There were times when Dad and Aunty Lizzie would begin talking and gradually their voices would rise until they were both yelling and I would block my ears and bury my head beneath my pillows. Then she went back to England.

"Look after your new phone at school, Kate. It's not cheap, that thing."

"I will, Dad."

Squares of light fell through the window, rising partway up the fridge. It was a clear day and the jagged angles of the cityscape stood out stark against the September sky.

I took the steps back up to my bedroom two at a time, tense with anticipation. I opened Thom's message.

So?

I messaged back.

Where and when would said walk take place?

My suggestion for said walk would be this Saturday in the city.

It had been six weeks since I'd seen him, so surely a few more days wouldn't matter. But I already knew that Saturday couldn't come soon enough.

When the day came it was blustery. Leaves worked themselves into gutters, blocking drains so puddles crept up onto the road. I had settled on jeans, dark flats, a white top beneath my good black coat. I did my hair, ironing out the flicks and curls at the tips, but spent the most time on my face: foundation, Willow's eyeliner, a pale lipstick, the tube of mascara I had bought with my pocket money. All just to make it look like I hadn't given it much thought at all. Dad cocked one eyebrow when I came down the stairs.

He drove me into town, pulling in near the gallery Thom had named. I had told Dad I was meeting Willow and a few others. *The girls.* I guess he was just happy it was a gallery and not the mall.

The street bustled with the standard Saturday fare: women in yoga pants, men with groomed beards. A homeless man thrusting his cup out toward the passing crowds.

The exhibition looked quiet from outside. A few people floated from one piece to the next. Then I saw Thom. He stood alone near the window, gazing at something on the wall.

I moved in beside him and spoke in a French drawl. "Hmm, the angles and light, it's magnificent." Leaning in, I added, "If you look closer, you will find this piece pays ho*mage* to the impressionists."

He didn't turn from the picture, but his grin crinkled his eyes. "You know, if that wasn't so ludicrous, you could pass as someone who actually knows what they're talking about."

"Who says I don't?" Now he turned to face me.

"Maybe I just hope you don't. Otherwise you wouldn't need me to teach you."

He was dressed in black skinny jeans, a black T-shirt, and brown boots that had lost their shine. Over the T-shirt he wore a dark tweed coat with the collar up. He didn't dress how most teenage boys did. He dressed like the guitarist in an indie band. I hadn't known I'd be into that kind of look.

"You made it."

"I did."

"That accent was a thing of beauty," he said.

"I take French."

"You would get on with my mum then. She was born in France."

We walked around the gallery looking at the work of a famous photographer from Ankara, Turkey.

Stopping before an image of an old man, we stood side by side, my hand so close to Thom's that my fingertips tingled. I could feel his warmth, a sort of energy between my skin and his. I looked down at his hand, then up at the image again. The colors were saturated. The creases in the old man's skin were dark, as though filled with grime, and his individual facial hairs stabbed through his skin like a thousand blades of grass.

Thom tilted his head and I wondered what he was seeing. His parents had bought him a *real* camera and his Instagram account was stocked with hundreds of photos he had taken. Some were abstract—a blue sky bisected by a plane's vapor trail. Others documented his trips through India, Japan, and Europe with his parents.

As if reading my mind, he said, "Great photographers can take something ordinary and find a way to make it beautiful." I expected him to be joking, but he wasn't smiling; he looked earnest. "I want to take photos like that."

I smiled, wishing he would take my hand as we continued around the rest of the exhibition. I stood close to him and when it came time to leave, he touched my lower back, guiding me toward the exit. When he took his hand away again, my skin tingled with warmth.

"What's next?"

"Gelato, of course."

He led me along Flinders Lane to a tiny shop. Inside, we sat by the window and shared a bowl of gelato. The rain had stopped, although the wind was still strong. A newspaper flapped in the gutter like an agitated swan. Thom pointed out couples passing by the window, putting on funny voices as he invented their conversations. When I tilted my head back to laugh, he raised his phone and took a picture.

"Show me," I said, still laughing at the voices he had given the strangers outside.

He held the phone behind his back. "It's good," he said. "Very photogenic subject."

I took another scoop of gelato, then reached past him for his phone. Our faces were almost cheek to cheek. He tried out another voice and I clamped my lips together to keep the melting gelato from dribbling down my chin and onto my white shirt as I laughed. Instead it erupted out of my nose. *Fuck.* Then he was laughing too. I buried my face in my hands, tears of laughter pricking the corners of my eyes.

"That was the cutest thing I've ever seen."

I was aware that I would probably never look more ridiculous than I did now, with passion fruit gelato dripping from my nose, but part of me didn't care. He'd called me cute. His hand landed on the back of my own before I realized it. When I looked up he was watching me, his smile traveling from his lips to his dark eyes. It hurt how badly I wanted him to kiss me.

We headed to Flinders Street station, and on the train home he took my hand in his and I rested my head on his shoulder. He walked me to the corner of my street but I wouldn't let him come any farther. I didn't want Dad seeing us.

"We live so close," he said.

"I know."

"Here, I got you a souvenir." He pulled something from the pocket of his coat—a postcard. On the front was the photo of the old man from the gallery. I hadn't seen him buy it. We'd been together the whole time.

"Thank you," I said, holding it to my chest. "How did you get it?"

He gave me a wink. The idea of his stealing something was exciting. I should have given it more weight, but the hammering of a smitten heart is so much louder than the conscience.

Our first date established the pattern for the next few: Dad dropping me at the movies or the mall, Thom walking me home afterward and presenting me with some small token—a snow.

globe, a pen, a flashlight—when we parted at the corner of my street. "It's easy," he would say of his newfound hobby, producing a key chain still in its plastic. "Like magic."

Walking home from school that next week, I stopped to take some photos of myself in front of the city skyline, faded blue in the spring light, thinking I would choose one to send to Thom. I'd found that when he took photos or short videos of me, it gave me a surge of confidence. I'd hated the idea of selfies until we started going out.

A car pulled up to the curb beside me. I didn't look at first, just resumed walking, plugging my earphones into my ears, my gaze fixed ahead.

The window on the passenger side slid down. "Kate, is that you?"

Willow's dad. Had he seen me taking selfies?

"Hi," I said, my cheeks burning. I tucked a strand of hair behind my ear. "Where's Willow?"

"She's at home. You need a lift?"

"That's okay—it's not so far."

"Come on," he said, pushing the door open. Poking out of the sleeve of his linen shirt, on the inside of his forearm, I saw a small black tattoo of a heart. A real heart. A beating human heart. His arms were tanned and thick with hair. I wondered if he had any more tattoos hidden away.

I climbed in, closed the door, and reached for my seat belt. "Thanks," I said. "I'll direct you."

"Kate . . ." He turned to me with a smile. "I know where you live."

Fourteen

The day I met Thom's mum it was an *anniversary*. That's what he called the fifth day of each of the three months that had passed since our first date, the fifth day of September. I was thrilled he took the small milestones so seriously.

We met at the place we'd dubbed *the spot*—where we had finally shared our first kiss—right under the eucalyptus tree in the park at the end of Thom's street. There had been other kisses since then, but I felt an inner warmth every time we passed by the spot. I would always think about that moment when I stood on my toes and leaned forward, our lips touching, my hands on his biceps.

It wasn't excitement I felt as he led me to meet his mum. My nerves were crackling and my stomach twisted.

"Mum knows you're coming," he said as he led me along by my hand. "I've told her all about you. Let me guess, Bomber Bennet hasn't even heard my name yet, has he?" He was right; I hadn't mentioned him to Dad.

"He can be a bit protective," I said defensively.

"A bit?" he said. "What about the thing with the paparazzo? The guy is a legend."

I didn't know what he meant at first, then the incident came back to me. It had been more than a decade ago. There'd been a guy hovering with a camera as Dad led Mum from the hospital to the car. Dad had snatched the front of the man's shirt and drawn his fist back, but at the last second his fist had transformed into a pointing finger, veins in his throat, his teeth gritted between words. That's the image a lot of people associated with him. Dad ripping the camera from the man's hand, holding the man against a wall with his forearm, and placing the camera on the footpath before driving away. Six months after that photograph made it onto the front page of the *Sun*, Mum would be dead.

"The guy deserved it," I said, controlling my voice and my impulse to defend him. Not that he needed defending. I didn't want this conversation heading in the direction of Mum, I didn't want Thom to talk about her. So I added, "Dad is nothing like that in real life, you know."

As we neared the door of Thom's house—small and neat, white weatherboard with terra-cotta roof tiles—I pulled my hand from his and tightened my ponytail; I cut my hair so rarely that when it was loose it hung almost to my waist. I shoved my hands into the pockets of my jeans.

When Thom opened the door a gust of heat rushed out, followed by the rich aromas of rosemary, garlic, a lamb roasting in the oven. I could picture his mother: floral apron, red lipstick, loving gaze.

Inside, the walls were stark white, except for the art: single-colored paintings of shapes I could recognize but couldn't quite place, as if I were looking at something familiar through an unfocused lens. We stopped to remove our shoes, placing them in a steel rack.

"Come say hi to Mum."

I followed him up the hall, the polished wooden floorboards chilly through my socks.

"Mum," he called.

We emerged into a small kitchen with copper pots hung above the stovetop.

"Well, hello," she said. Her voice had the crispness of a school-teacher, and her demeanor was serious, almost stern. She was rinsing her hands at the sink. "You must be Kate."

"Hi," I said. "It's nice to meet you, Mrs. Moreau."

"Call me Suzie." She smeared her hand down her apron, then offered it.

"She speaks French, Mum," Thom said with pride. I rolled my eyes at him.

"*Peux-tu parler français?*" she asked.

"*Oui. J'apprends lentement.*"

"*Très bien. Persévère,*" she said. "*Thom m'a tout dit de toi.*"

Thom raised his eyebrows. "All right, Mum, I can understand *that*. You're just showing off. You too, Kate."

His mum batted him with a folded tea towel, then turned back to the stove.

"I'm still learning, so I'm not great," I said.

"Nonsense, your pronunciation is perfect," Suzie said.

Thom showed me around. The lounge room was small and con-spicuously TV-free. One corner was lined with built-in bookshelves. He pointed out to the yard, where rain was beginning to fall.

"That's the veg garden and out there in the kennel is Che, our Labrador. Named after the socialist revolutionary or barbaric ex-ecutioner. You know, depending on who you ask."

He led me back down the hallway, pointing out his parents' room and the bathroom, then his mum's studio, where he stopped. "No one is allowed in there."

I supposed that room for Thom was like the upstairs bathroom at the house in Portsea for me—somewhere I could never go.

He led me into his room and closed the door.

His room was big, almost as big as the lounge. The walls were plain white, with no posters or pictures except for a long string of photos, mostly black and white, pegged along.

"So no TV, huh?"

"You noticed?" he said, flopping onto his bed. "Growing up it was kind of weird. I know it's a bit of a trend now, the whole 'no TV' thing, but my parents have been like that since I was little. If I wasn't into photography they'd probably have a thing about me having my laptop in my room."

"What did you do for fun?"

"I don't know. Scrabble. Thankfully the iPhone killed off all board games."

"Scrabble's not dead."

"Of course *you're* into Scrabble. I should have known you were too good to be true."

I looked around the shelves and walls for any memento of his swimming days, but there was nothing. My eyes fell on the string of photos.

He leaned back on his bed and laced his fingers behind his head. His eyes met mine. A subtle wink. I could feel a blush coming on in my cheeks.

"What's your favorite photo?"

"That I've taken?"

"No, just any photo."

"Well, there are a lot from the Vietnam War . . . a whole series of them that are really powerful."

"Powerful how?"

"There's this photo that won the Pulitzer Prize. It's of children running from a napalm attack. And a photo of a man seconds before his execution. Literally standing there with a gun to his head."

"Sounds gruesome."

"It is. But that's reality." He smiled. "It's important to see the world the way it is. You can't do anything about it if you're not aware."

"I guess."

He sat up and gently nudged my arm with his fingertips. "Also, if my mum asks, my favorite photo is anything by Henri Cartier-Bresson."

"Can I see your camera?"

He reached beneath the bed to retrieve a black case. He pulled the camera out and handed it to me. I clicked back through his photos: dozens of pictures of a tree, the twisting limbs reaching up into a marbled gray sky. Then a photo of a bloody dead bird.

"Gross," I said.

"Oh, that—Che managed to finally catch one in the yard." He took the camera from my hands, twisted off the long thick lens, and put on a short stubby one.

"Smile," he said, bringing the camera to his eye. The shutter snapped with a crisp click, then again and again. He looked down at the screen. "You photograph really well. You're beautiful through the lens."

Beautiful. The word reverberated in my head. "Let me see."

"Nope. I'm a man of principle; I never share my raw material."

The camera disappeared behind his back. I reached for it. He drew me closer, on top of him.

"A man, huh?" I teased.

He took my hand and placed it on his chest, leaning up for a kiss. "Is this man enough?"

I slid my palm over his shoulder and down his arm. His hands roamed my body, working down my spine. . . .

Thom's house became our routine after that, his room our haven. I knew at some point I'd have to bring him home to meet Dad, but not yet. Not while things still felt so new.

PART THREE

Something Has Happened

In the past month, how often have you experienced memories that have made you upset, sad, or afraid?

0. never;   1. rarely;   2. sometimes;   3. often;   4. all the time

Fifteen

DISPATCHER: Emergency Services. Do you require police, fire, or ambulance?

CALLER: Ambulance. And I think police too.

DISPATCHER: Okay. Can you state your name?

CALLER: Peter Turner.

DISPATCHER: And the address where you require assistance?

CALLER: Well, I'm near the park on Central Road. I don't know the street. I was just walking along and there's someone slumped on the curb.

DISPATCHER: Central Hawkesburn.

CALLER: Correct. Yes.

DISPATCHER: Hawkesburn Park.

CALLER: Yes, I think so.

DISPATCHER: Are you with the victim now?

CALLER: Yes. He's facedown on the road. There's blood. As in under his head.

DISPATCHER: Have you touched the victim?

CALLER: No. I've just found him. Can you hurry, please?

DISPATCHER: Does the victim appear to be breathing?

CALLER: It's hard to tell. I called and he didn't move. I mean, he's not moving at all.

DISPATCHER: Does the victim's air passage appear to be obstructed in any way?

CALLER: Um. No. I wouldn't say so.

DISPATCHER: An ambulance and the police are on their way. Can you stay put until they get there?

CALLER: Yeah. That's fine.

DISPATCHER: It's important that you do not touch anything.

CALLER: Yes, I'll just stay here.

DISPATCHER: *They will be with you shortly.*

AFTER

Sixteen

The door slams and the house shudders. Jim drops the bag of groceries on the table and jams the charger into his mobile phone. He breathes deeply, holding himself over the kitchen counter. Taking his glasses off, he presses his thumb and forefinger into his eyelids. An electric mood fills the room with the weight of the air before a storm.

I turn back from where I'm sitting on the couch. "Hey," I say.

He doesn't look up.

"What's wrong?"

"Nothing." Eyes flick open, glasses back on.

I step closer. "Did I do something?"

He traps me with his eyes. He's aged. The withering of the past three weeks is there in the lines bracketing his mouth and the skin hanging from his jaw. Then the moment passes and he looks away.

"No, it's not you." He goes to the sink and rinses his hands. "I just chipped the windscreen."

The color in his neck climbs to his cheeks, shines at his crown through his brown hair, then fades. He sighs.

"Did you have an accident?" I ask.

"No, no, nothing like that," he says, frowning. He studies me as though I am an equation on a blackboard, something he knows he can solve if only he really focuses. There's a pulse visible at his temple. "I just wish things could be easier for us, that's all."

I shift my gaze to the hills out the window. Is it only this time of year that the grass is damp and frosted in patches all day and the windows are fogged until noon? Some trees are electric green, some pale with spindly arms. Behind me a pot slams in the kitchen. "For fuck's sake." A cupboard bangs closed. "Why are these dishes out? Kate? You need to put the fucking dishes away."

"What happened while you were out?" I ask, anxious now. "It makes me scared when you're like this. Did you see someone?"

He shakes his head, the anger coming off him like heat. "Why is it important to you?"

I turn to face him. "You never tell me the truth."

He's on me in a flash, grabbing my upper arm.

Angry tears are stinging the corners of my eyes. "I'm seventeen," I remind him. "Not a child."

"Well, you've shown me just how much of an adult you are, haven't you? Why else would we be in this town?" As if noticing my tears for the first time, he makes an irritated sound with his tongue. "Don't cry, all right? Just stop it with the crying."

"You used to treat me like an adult."

"I know," he says through gritted teeth.

"What happened today? Why are you so upset?"

"Just some kids throwing stones. Down near the estuary. They were eight or nine years old, they threw stones, that's it. It just made me angry. When I stopped the car they didn't even run away. I wish I could call the police."

"Can I see?"

He frowns, but he doesn't say no. I walk outside. Over by the car, I peer at the windscreen, see where the glass is chipped. Voices come from up on the road. Turning to look back through the front door, I see the kitchen is empty. I walk slowly up the driveway.

On the road, a man is riding past on a horse, leading another horse by a rope. He is tanned, despite its being winter, with curly hair and a polar fleece top. He turns toward me. I am poised, ready to run back down the driveway. Closer still, walking along there are three boys. One points at me and nudges another with his elbow.

"Oi," the shortest boy says, grinning like a hyena. "Are you a boy or a girl?"

Huh-huh-huh, the others laugh. One of the boys has his arm in a sling.

I look down, stepping backward toward the house.

"Eh? I didn't hear you. Is this where you live?"

I just swallow.

"Eho, don't be nasty," the rider calls. He trots up beside the boys and looks down at them fiercely.

I try to keep my eyes averted, but as they continue on past the letterbox I steal a glance. One of them is watching; there's a threat in his look.

"*Pakehas* all stick together, eh, bro?" another boy says without turning around. "Now I know." They're just boys but they seem so fearless.

"Hi," the rider says as he passes by the top of the driveway. I see now that he's only a couple of years older than me. "They're pretty harmless, don't worry."

"Thanks," I reply, thinking of the stone that hit the back of my head. I go back down the driveway and inside.

Jim has his feet up on the couch and a glass of wine in his hand. The television is off. The classical music unwinding into the room from the stereo is vaguely familiar. I notice then that the home phone has been unplugged and taken away. I step closer to him.

"Why didn't you chase them away?" I say.

"Who?"

"The kids that threw the stones."

"That wouldn't be the best idea," he says, taking a sip of wine. "Just imagine what I would do to them if I caught them."

Seventeen

That evening from my bedroom window I can see a bar of light escaping beneath the steel door of the shed. What could he be doing out there this late? I climb down the back steps in my pajamas and cross the yard. I stand close to the door for some time listening to him tapping away on his laptop. He sighs and a chair squeaks. I could run now and try to escape but how far would I get in the cold? He would only need to check my room; then what would happen? I hear his voice. It's just a murmur from within the steel. I can only make out a few words.

"... it's my mobile number ... she was listening, that's why ..." The door swings open suddenly and light leaps out into the night. I shift around the corner of the shed, pressed up hard against the cold steel. Bile slides up my throat. The chill spreads down my body like a rash. I stay dead still, my heart thumping.

"Is that better? Can you hear me now?" he says. "Look, I just want to know if there's any news ... you broke up there a bit ... you don't like his chances, is that what you said?" He lets his breath out. "It's the reception out here, let me try to find a better spot," he says as he walks up beside the house toward the road.

I let my breath out. That was too close. I rush up the steps; the grass is icy beneath my feet. My jaw trembles with cold. I step inside, gently closing the back door, and creep down the hall to my room. Then I fall back into bed, waiting to warm up, thinking about what Jim just said. *You don't like his chances.*

In the morning Jim wakes to find the words "Fuck Off" spray-painted across the windscreen of the car. He simply clucks his tongue, goes out to the shed, and finds a blade to scrape it off with as if this is trivial, like finding a blown bulb in the lounge room, and yet small things—when I spilled a pot of water, when I let the fire go out—have made his face parboiled red and veins rise in his throat. In the afternoon, after he has cleaned off the red spray paint, we take a drive out of town.

"Where are we going?"

"Tauranga," he says. "For lunch."

As the noiseless sedan rolls along, I gaze through the windscreen, marked by five chips in the glass, although most of the paint came off. Out here, it's not like Melbourne, with all that concrete, all those cars stopping and starting, trailing exhaust fumes. Beside the road there's nothing but emerald paddocks and sheep with their heads bowed. He's constantly frowning at the rearview mirror and doubles back around a block on the way out of town. Does he think someone is following us?

He wants us to escape Maketu for an hour or so, to leave it behind and spend some time together. To be happy in each other's company again. We drive for forty minutes farther along the coast, stopping eventually to have lunch at a café overlooking the beach.

He says the café has *Melbourne food*. I guess he thinks it will be a comfort for me, but it's not the smashed avocado I miss most.

"We need a proper lunch, like in the old days. Just you and me."

The modern-looking café is almost empty. We find a table outside and sit for a while without talking, which suits me, because when I block out the engines of passing cars and the whirl and hiss of the coffee machine, I can hear the calming sound of the sea.

A pretty waitress wanders over. She's all smiles, pouring our water and setting out cutlery. I order a latte, noting the way his eyebrows converge. He leans forward a little. "Darling, it's almost two o'clock, are you certain you want caffeine?"

"I think so."

"You already have chemicals in your system, Evie. You don't need caffeine. No wonder you can't sleep. Why don't you get a cup of herbal tea or something instead?"

I don't answer. When the waitress passes by again, he reaches out and touches her forearm. She turns and smiles, charmed by him, I suppose. I can't help but stare at her hair. I could reach out and grab it. Then what? Maybe I could tell her he locks me away at night, that he tells me lies and hurts me. Even if she believed me, the only thing she could do is call the police.

"I think we will cancel the latte, please, if it's not too late."

"Sure," she says. She glances at me. "Did you want something else instead?"

"Hot chocolate," I say.

"Good choice."

When she leaves, I say, "If I want a coffee, I can have a coffee. You can't just control everything like that."

His expression is blank as a doll's. "That's not a decision you get to make."

When my hot chocolate comes I push it away.

"God, does the coffee mean that much to you?" Jim snaps. He leans in, speaking in a voice so low I find myself straining to hear him. "After everything we've been through, it would be a shame if that waitress saw your face on the news and remembered you as the girl that had a tantrum over a fucking drink and next thing we know you're locked away. Think about that, next time you want to make a scene."

A pair of old women sit nearby, squawking like geese, their voices too big for the small table. They glance at me, then lower their voices.

The waitress strides past. Jim's eyes follow her. *He does have a taste for younger women.* Then he turns back and pats my hand once.

I can see him thinking; he rests his chin on his knuckles. "If you could live anywhere in the world, where would you choose?" he asks.

"Melbourne," I say without hesitation.

He makes a frustrated sound. "What about somewhere you could start afresh, somewhere no one knows you?"

"I don't know."

"What about somewhere on the other side of the world?"

We had that choice, we could have gone anywhere, but he dragged us to Maketu. I think of Awhina, the small girl from the bus shelter, who doesn't have a choice. I feel a narcotic heaviness in my bones. "No. If we leave here, I want to go home to Melbourne."

"There's nothing for you in Melbourne, *Evie.* Can't you see that?"

I glance back at the women. Their eyes are on me. Their latte glasses are stained with crescents of mauve lipstick. I wonder if they recognize me. The video is still out there.

The waitress returns with a sandwich for Jim and eggs Benedict for me. I can hardly eat any of it. All I wanted was the coffee, something from the world *before.*

"... doubt it's cancer, might be a trend," one of the women says, just loud enough for us to hear. The other slyly shifts her gaze toward me.

I slide my palm over the tabletop. My water glass tips, falls, and explodes on the cobblestones.

"Jesus," Jim says. "Careful."

I watch their faces, the subtle disgusted look they exchange. I fix them with my most intense stare until I am sure they have both seen me. One of them gives a nervous laugh.

The waitress hurries out with a brush and dustpan.

"I'm sorry," Jim says with a *silly me* expression. "I bumped it with my elbow."

He shifts his gaze on the women. I turn my head so they can see the scar, the inch-long crease above my right ear where hair will never grow again. He is back, facing me, letting out his breath, blinking slowly. Then he places his hand on my wrist and rubs it back and forth until I am calm once more.

We roll past the abandoned surf club. In the car park a group has gathered. At least twenty people—kids with skateboards and rugby balls, and adults of all ages holding tall brown beer bottles—are standing around. Smoke rises where the heat swirls off the grill of a barbecue on the grass near the picnic area. Music thumps from a car with its doors and trunk open. It's as though the entire village has gathered. I see Tiriana from the shop among the group; she watches our car pass. Sitting on a man's shoulders is Awhina. The man has short hair on top but a long black mullet down his back. The child, too, looks over as we pass.

The bottom of the car scrapes as we go over a speed bump. As if on cue, all eyes swing to us. *Way to stay inconspicuous, Jim.* There's a stillness about the crowd. A man with thick dark hair and faded green tattoos on his face looks over. He taps the chest of the man beside him, then points at us. I feel a twinge of panic. I look over at Jim to see if he has noticed. His hands are tight around the wheel.

When I wake the following morning, Jim is out. I read the book I started at the airport, wondering if it has any more secrets for me. I find myself falling into the story and have read sixty pages before I find something else. No underlined letters but words written into the margin, pressed hard with an angry fist.

Death is the only escape.

I can hear my breath growing louder. *Don't trust him* and now this. Is it a threat? Perhaps he found the book and put these words in here to warn me about attempting to escape. Is he saying if I were to escape I would die? The handwriting is not so different from mine. The t's look like my own. These pages may hold more clues but I'm afraid to continue reading. My hands tremble thinking about what else I might find. The book is old and dusty, the pages yellowed and stiff. It closes with a thump and I slide it beneath my bed.

Out on the kitchen island, he has left a pile of seed packets.

It's been ten days since I quit taking the pills and the headaches have stopped. I feel like I am getting stronger and more lucid. I feel like when the time comes I will be able to escape, I will be able to get back to Melbourne to find out the truth. *Death is the only escape.* Those words are an icy hand on the back of my neck. Death is not my only escape. I can get away. I must get away.

Out in the garden I go to work thumbing carrot seeds into the soft soil. I am on all fours with the last few seeds in the palm of my hand when he returns. "Kate," he says, "come and have a look at this." He is actually smiling.

"What is it?"

He gestures for me to follow.

I clap the soil from my palms and climb up the steps to the house. Jim leads me through the kitchen and out the front door to the driveway. I hear it before I see it; tied to the tow bar of the car, emitting a low, excited whimper, is a black dog. Its tail flicks. Its mouth hangs open with a flat pink tongue lolling to one side.

"Welcome home, boy," Jim says, unclipping the leash. The dog rushes toward me, his tail swinging deliriously. He sniffs my feet and circles me. When I reach out to pat him, he leaps up and licks my fingers. Then he sprints up the driveway and back. His mouth is wide open in a perpetual grin. It may be fleeting but right now I am . . . happy. It's been so long that I forgot what it felt like.

"Can I name him?"

"He's already got a name," Jim says, reaching down and scratching the dog behind the ears. "Beau."

"Beau," I repeat.

"He's a staffy. A guard dog."

To me he looks far too cute to intimidate anyone.

After spending some time exploring, sniffing, licking, he drops to his belly in a square of sun near the back door.

"Is he ours?" I say.

"Well, yeah. But if he doesn't fit in, I guess we can always take him back to the SPCA."

A dog is a commitment. Does this mean we are staying here for good?

Jim lugs in a sack of dog biscuits and a square of lamb's wool for Beau to sleep on. He puts the biscuits beneath the sink and lays the bed in the corner of the lounge near the sliding door.

That evening after dinner, Beau lies on his bed, staring up at me with a mopey look.

"Come on," I say, coaxing him closer. Eventually he rises, stretches, and wanders over. I scratch the prickly fur between his eyes, feeling the bone beneath.

"You can feed him if you want," Jim says from where he is seated at his desk. "Just a scoop."

In the kitchen, I take a scoop of biscuits from the sack and tip it into the steel bowl Jim bought for Beau. Beau dives in snout first.

When he's finished eating, he comes back to the couch and looks up at me.

"Is he allowed on the couch?"

"Sure," he says. "Why not?" Soon enough, Jim turns from the desk and begins running through the same series of questions he always asks, while I stroke Beau's back.

"What do you think of when you think of Melbourne?"

I imagine the splitting sound of a human skull. "I think of school and my house."

"Who do you remember seeing, when you drove the car?"

"I don't remember."

Beau has returned to the kitchen, has his head in the cupboard beneath the sink. Jim rises to pull Beau away and closes the cupboard. "Make sure you leave this closed so he doesn't get into the bag."

"I'll be more careful."

"Okay," he says. Then he continues asking questions. "What was I doing on the street that night?"

"You were running along."

"And what was I carrying?"

I squeeze my eyes closed, concentrating to remember. "I don't know."

"All right, why don't you head to bed and get an early night."

I brush my teeth and go to my room. *Don't trust him. Death is the only escape.* I reach for the book but before I can read more than a few pages I'm dozing off.

Eighteen

dream a familiar dream. I'm driving and I hit someone but this time it's Thom. He raises a bent finger, pointing at me as I approach, and lets out a howl of laughter. His body flips over the car and flies up over the power lines, crashing down on the curb. His skull opens to reveal what looks like a soft-boiled egg. A dog is barking, the sound ripping me from the dream.

I lurch upright, breathing hard. The knocking in my chest is like a loose bolt in an engine. Was it Beau barking?

The house is quiet. But I heard it; a low bark. I open my curtains and look out over the moonlit lawn, toward the sea at the bottom of the hill. I feel so lucid and energized. This entire town and the man in black will be asleep. The ladder is still outside. I open my window and cool air rushes in. I climb up to sit on the sill and then, turning, extend one leg toward the wooden rung, then the other, and clamber down.

The frozen grass at the base of the ladder numbs my feet, and my pajama shorts and the wisp of a top are hopeless against the breeze that grabs at every part of me. I take in my surroundings:

the moon-shadowed lawn, the stars layered and sweeping all the way to the silhouette of the hills at the distant horizon. The night is a wonder; this night is mine.

Walking up beside the house, I hear the occasional rustling of the leaves, the movements of unknown animals in the trees and grass. The sea, too, seems louder, bigger, at night. When I reach the road I see a three-legged white dog—the same one I saw by the beach the first time I walked down the hill on my own. It is ghostlike in the moonlight. Is it waiting for me? For a second we are both still. Then it turns and continues along, its irregular gait mesmerizing.

I am shaking with cold and wish I'd thought to pull on my hoodie and track pants. I stop and the dog swings its head back once more. *Come on*, he seems to say, *I have something to show you.* I cast my gaze out over the village; there's nothing but shadows in the grass and pale ghosts in the paddocks. Nothing but shacks with cracked paint. Newer houses, the holiday homes, are all empty, with their curtains glaringly open.

The road knuckles the thawing meat of my bare feet. Am I following the dog or pursuing him? When we reach the bottom of the hill near the beach, he bolts off. I walk faster. By the time I get close enough to see him, he is sitting on the other side of the car park near the surf club.

Beneath the lone streetlight in the car park is a red station wagon, its engine murmuring. There are two people inside. I ease back, beneath a tree. Its shadow expands and contracts in the breeze like a lung. *I could run. I could run back.* Before I can make the decision, the passenger-side door opens. I am trapped. If I run I'll be seen; if I stay where I am I might be grabbed.

As a man gets out I see the dog has risen to its feet and is running toward me. *No, go away.* I make a shooing gesture. The man tilts his head and swigs from a bottle. The dog veers away from me and approaches the man, who aims a kick at it, but the dog scampers out of reach before the man's foot can connect. Someone in the car lets out a rip of laughter.

The man stands in the center of the car park swaying. My body feels as if it is nailed to the tree. The slightest movement might draw his attention.

"What's the time, bro?" a voice asks.

I hear a muffled response, and then the sound of a car door opening and closing. The car reverses before turning in a long, slow arc, the beam of the headlights washing over me.

My jaw is rattling now. Despite what many people think, the jawbone is not the hardest bone in the body. It is not even the hardest bone in the skull. The petrous parts of the temporal bones on the sides of the skull, near the ears, are the densest bones found in the human body. Although, as with all bones, under enough stress they too will crack. They too will chip and buckle.

Slowly the headlights wheel out over the ocean and then swing up to the road. I watch as the car passes, and then I see him, staring out the window, a fearful look on his face. It's Thom. The driver is Thom. I sprint out from my hiding place. I chase the car, stumbling as a sharp stone bites into my foot. The car is already climbing the hill. But I sprint hard, with my arms swinging. "Hey!" I scream. "Stop! Wait!" The taillights grow smaller and smaller until finally they disappear around the bend. I drop my hands onto my knees and suck in breath.

My heart is thumping. *Thom,* I think. *It was him. He's come for me.* But as quickly as the thought comes, it's gone. Thom hasn't learned to drive. And it's not just that; Thom couldn't be here. It's impossible. Maybe I really am losing my mind? Maybe Jim has been telling me the truth all along? I'm too frail, too damaged to face reality. Looking up, I notice a light is on at a nearby house. The curtains move. Someone was watching me. I start back toward the house.

The dog is a fading apparition in the black of night, creeping away along the stones of the beach, a silhouette in negative before the spilled ink of the black sea.

The moonlight is enough to see by and the stars are out between the translucent sails of clouds. When I get home, my heart chases me up the ladder, through the window, and into my room.

Nineteen

When I wake, the previous night reels in my mind. I reach down and itch the island chain of sand fly bites at my ankle. *I saw Thom.* But in the light of day, I realize that I didn't; it was one of the delusions Jim once warned me about.

It doesn't make sense, and yet I can't move beyond it, seeing Thom's face in the car as it sped past. Jim can't be telling me the whole truth about that night and I know not to trust him. I know there is more to it than simply my driving the car; there has to be more to it. He has always asked me if I remember him there, if I remember his holding something in his hand. The truth must exist in the gray area between what I sense to be true and what he has told me. The truth is in Melbourne.

As I brush my teeth after breakfast, I notice sómething different in the bathroom. Beside the sink there are only toothbrushes and soap and Jim's shaving cream. I cannot see his razor. I, open the cupboard beneath the vanity and find the first-aid kit. Unzipping it, I see the scissors are gone. In the kitchen, the steak knives have vanished from the drawer. Jim doesn't turn away from where he sits at his desk, but I see then his letter opener has vanished from his penholder. Just like the home phone, these things have disappeared without any word from Jim. One day they're there and the next they're gone. Maybe I really am insane.

I need a walk to clear my head.

I go to the door, then turn back and head toward Beau's lead, hanging up in the kitchen. The dog begins to whine.

Jim turns around from his computer. "Beau," he says sternly, "get on your bed."

Beau does as he is told, but he sits up ramrod straight, alert. If I do it enough Beau will get worked up and someone will need to walk him. When I go to the door once more he barks.

"Fuck me, I can't concentrate with that dog."

"He needs a walk," I say.

"Well, I don't have time to take him," Jim replies. "I have to find somewhere else for us to stay. I don't know if this house is helping with your mental state."

"My mental state?"

"I mean, you were doing well at first, but I think it would help if we had a change of scene. Somewhere more remote. I mean your agitation . . . it's grown."

More remote than this?

I should be relieved—more remote means less chance of being found—but I'm not. "Where?"

"Not too far. If I can't find anywhere suitable, we'll stay here. I just want to check our options."

"Can I take Beau for a walk?"

Beau fires off a volley of barks. He circles his bed, standing, looking at me.

"Don't say that word, Kate," Jim says wearily. "He gets excited when you say *walk*."

More barks, and then Beau rushes to the door and sits by it, looking up at me expectantly.

"I'll just go along the path," I say. "Where we used to walk."

"Oh, all right. But be careful." Jim gives me a set of house keys on a thick white key ring.

I put the keys in my pocket. Jim showed me the route I should take, along gravel paths and dirt trails across paddocks. Places where I'm not likely to see other people.

Beau tugs hard on the leash as we walk up the driveway. When I get to the road I listen for cars before unclipping him. In a flash he is off, racing down the hill to the bend before turning and sprinting back to me.

Beau rushes off again, this time rounding the corner. I pick up my pace. When I pass the bus shelter and the spot where Jim almost crushed the boy on the bike, a chill runs through me. "Beau," I call tentatively as I round the bend. "Here, boy."

Beau is there. But he's not alone. A group of boys in baggy pants, caps, and hoodies have gathered around him. They're stroking his back, touching his head. Beau is clearly relishing the attention. I stop walking. They are still thirty meters away, yet I feel too close. What are they going to do to him?

At once they seem to notice me and turn to look up like three heads of the same beast, fixing me with their dark eyes. They're young—eleven or twelve. *Old enough for cruelty.* I can't read their expressions from here, but I realize I'm squeezing the clip of the leash too tight. I pat my hip gently. *Come on, Beau.*

Beau doesn't move, looking up at the strangers for more attention, but their eyes are on me now. Finally, Beau bolts back to me. I squat down, grasp his collar, and clip the leash in. Rising, I start dragging him back to the house. After a few steps, I break into a run. I don't turn back to see if they are following.

I head inside, unclipping Beau's leash.

"What happened?" Jim asks.

"Nothing, I just don't feel like walking anymore."

"I have to go out to see a man about a potential place to stay. I don't know how long I'll be, but we can go out together later. It's good to exercise, Kate."

"Maybe."

"Why don't you heat up some soup for lunch?"

I put the soup on, then go to my room. I sit on the bed and pick up the book. I've only read seventy pages since I found it, because my mind refuses to stay focused. The words are always evaporating between my eyes and my brain. I think again about the night before, when I thought I saw Thom; that night in Melbourne comes to me, and I clutch at the short threads of memory, trying to plait them together.

In the middle of the book I notice a page is loose. Tearing it out, I realize the page is not a page at all. It's a photograph. Sun-faded, one corner torn away. It's a photo of a baby in a bassinet, mouth open and a fat starfish hand raised, clutching at nothing. The baby is me.

I turn the photo over. There is a date scrawled in the corner beside my name. Beneath that is written: *I never meant to hurt you.*

I glance up at my door instinctively, then back to the words. The handwriting is neater this time. Again I recognize the t's. I write one myself for comparison. Flipping the photo over, I stare at my button nose, cherub face.

"Soup's ready, Kate," he calls from the kitchen.

"Okay."

"I'm off now. I'll be back later on." When I hear the front door open and close, I go to the wardrobe and grab my escape bag.

The engine grunts into life and accelerates up the driveway. The sound fades as he rounds the bend.

I go to his room and search it, pulling back his sheets, peering under his bed, emptying his drawers. Surely he can't have taken our passports with him? I'll deal with that problem at the airport, I decide. Ready to scream with frustration, I head back up the hall. Tearing the flap off a cardboard box near the fire, I take a black marker from his desk and write AUCKLAND on the cardboard in large block letters.

Two big scoops of dog food into the bowl for Beau, then I scratch his head and squat down to let him lick my face. "Be good, okay?"

I draw one long breath to calm myself and set off.

Thankfully I find the boys are not at the same stretch of road as I trek down the hill to the beach. I am nearing the edge of town when I see the shop and realize I didn't eat the soup. I should get some supplies, something to snack on.

Tiriana is serving a customer when I enter, but she raises her eyebrows in my direction.

I recognize the customer from somewhere, cheeks patchy with stubble, tanned skin, coils of blond hair.

"Hi, Evie," Tiriana says. "Have you met Iso?"

"Hi," I say, realizing when he turns to me that he's the horse rider.

"Hey, Evie. You're up on the hill, right?"

"Yeah," I say.

"Cool, well it's nice to meet you properly. Tiri's told me all about you."

Has she? "Nice to meet you too."

"Sorry about those kids giving you a hard time. This really isn't such a bad place. How are you settling in?"

I don't have time to chat. "Fine, thanks. I'm in a bit of a rush, sorry. I just need a couple of things."

"Where you heading?" Tiriana asks, eyeing my backpack.

"I'm—I'm going away. Not for long. . . . Just out of town for a night or so."

Tiriana looks over my shoulder and out to the car park. "Where's your uncle?"

Iso's eyes are on me.

"My uncle? Oh, he's coming with the car now."

"Is that right?" She looks dubious. "Well, why don't you wait in here?"

"No need," I say, walking to the back of the store.

"Where you meeting him?" Iso asks. "I'm heading out of town, could give you a lift if you like."

"Oh thanks, but I told him I'd meet him up the road." I pull a bottle of Coke from the fridge and a bag of chips from the shelf, then I grope in my backpack for some cash.

"No, it's on the house this time, Evie."

I look up, meet her eyes. "You sure?"

"Yeah," she says. "But just sit with me before you go."

Iso unscrews the bottle of water he bought and puts it to his lips; his eyes don't leave me as he drinks.

"Thanks," I say. "But he'll be waiting, so I'd better get going now." I wonder if she notices the piece of cardboard folded under my arm.

"It's really good to meet you, Evie," Iso says. "Hope to see you round a bit more."

Tiriana comes forward and I throw my hands up in defense, but before I know it she has her arms around me. I squirm in her grip.

"Relax, girl," she says, "it's just a hug." Then she adds, "Listen, I heard the kids have been giving you guys hell. I've had a word with them—they're all right."

I think of the mean, ugly faces they made at me, the stones they threw, the words spray-painted on our windscreen, and I doubt it. But I let her hold me before I say, "I've really got to go."

She releases me and steps back.

"Right, well, I'll be seeing you again." She's frowning as I turn to leave.

Pausing at the threshold, I turn back. "There's a girl—Awhina. I think her dad has been hurting her. Someone should help."

"Yeah, I know the family, Evie. Not much anyone can do from the outside, you know?"

"The police?"

"You think they give a shit? Awhina is going to be a lot worse off if they get involved, trust me."

I turn back one last time as I step through the door. She's still watching me, but now she's holding a phone up to her ear and is speaking into it, her voice low and urgent. Iso is looking down at the screen of his own phone.

I resume walking, focusing at each intersection, taking the turns that I memorized. *Left, right, straight, right.* The gravel on the shoulder of the road slips beneath my feet, but I must be prepared to drop from sight if I see his car. *Don't trust him.*

Soon the houses, with their peeling paint and windows creeping with moss, are replaced with paddocks. Sheep stand nearby picking at grass. A wind comes, hitting me like a wave, but I am warm from the walk, charged with purpose and energy. Cars roll past in ones and twos. Occasionally a cattle truck rattles by, dragging the stench of shit and piss, and for just a second I can see terrified eyes staring out between sheets of steel.

It takes a couple of hours of walking up and down hills and along vast straight stretches, but finally I reach the highway. My feet are numb but my heart is pulsing. I've done it. How easy it is to escape; easier than I could have imagined. I think about returning to Melbourne, the surprised faces, but then I think about the tape, what we did, Thom and I . . . who would have seen it? And there are bridges to cross before then. I will need to organize an emergency passport at the airport. Will they believe me? Will they believe I am stranded in this country? Perhaps the police will be waiting for me in Melbourne.

I hold up my sign and thrust out my thumb.

Cars pass without stopping. The clouds darken and thunder follows; the air is cold and damp. Fog rolls in over the hills, and soon I can no longer see my surroundings. Headlights herald new sets of passing cars. The rain starts, light at first, then getting heavier, and it's not long before I'm wet through, trembling with the cold. A truck slings a wave of spray off the road that bends the cardboard in my hand. I keep my thumb out and the sign held against my stomach. What if this was the wrong time? The wrong decision? I force the thoughts out of my head. There's no room for doubt. I'm here now. I can't give up. But still, moths of anxiety fill my chest.

Cars approach. *Please stop. Please.* They pass. I drop my head, retracting my hand into the warmth of my sleeve. Then I hear a sound behind me. A car horn. I turn. Up the road a car has stopped and its red taillights are approaching. *It's reversing.* I run toward it, my bag bouncing against my spine. Relief washes over me; I could collapse beneath the weight of it. The passenger-side window is lowered and I see the driver: a lady with blond-gray hair pulled back in a low ponytail. The air coming from inside the car is tangy with stale cigarette smoke.

W hen the doorbell rang I leaped from my bed and didn't even stop to look in the mirror. My ponytail was too tight, and I wore a little makeup for Thom, but not too much for Dad. *Will he notice that I act different around my dad? Will he see what I'm really like?*

I ran quickly downstairs and got to the door first. Dad, arriving from the kitchen, made a *go ahead* gesture.

On one of my driving lessons a week earlier Dad had insisted I invite Thom for dinner.

"I knew the day would come when you would have a boyfriend. Fortunately you got your mother's looks," he had said.

It must have been the flowers in a jar on my dresser from one of our *anniversaries* that tipped him off.

"What are you *talking* about?" I said.

"I want to meet him."

I reached with my index finger for the indicator.

He was not mad or annoyed, but the tone of his voice knotted something within me and the words wouldn't come.

"Thom," he said. "That's his name, isn't it, Kate? Didn't you used to swim with a Thom?"

Another knock at the door. I reached for the handle and turned. Black jeans, but not the ones with holes at the knees; a faded plaid shirt; hair neatly combed back.

"Hey," I said, bubbles expanding and bursting in my stomach. More quietly I added, "Sorry if this is awkward."

"Wow," he said, stepping inside. His eyes roamed the walls. "This place is a palace."

In a second Dad was striding across the room, hand outstretched.

"Dad, this is Thom."

"G'day," Dad said, pumping Thom's hand.

"It's so nice to finally meet you." Thom spoke like he had something wedged in his larynx. A flush crept out of the neck of his shirt yet he stood tall, his spine straight and as taut as a guitar string, his chest thrust out. Dad, too, was stiff and overly formal. "Welcome," he said.

It's a strange thing seeing two people you know so well suddenly acting differently around you. I only wanted Dad to like him, that's all.

"Come on through to the lounge—dinner won't be far off."

Dad got himself a beer, offering one to Thom and asking me if I'd like a glass of wine. I was grateful that he wasn't treating us like little kids.

Thom and I sat next to each other on the couch, our legs touching at the thigh. Embarrassed by the intimacy, I shuffled over a little.

As Thom grew more comfortable in Dad's company, he started to ask him questions.

"So you're retired now?"

"No, not entirely. I stopped playing rugby but I've been working. What about yourself, Thom? Any plans for the future?"

Thom shifted in his seat. "I want to be a photographer."

They seemed to be getting on, yet still the silences filled the room like rising water.

"I'll put some music on," I said, standing up from the couch to put on the playlist Thom had made me for our four-month anniversary.

"What's this crap, Kate?" Dad said, and Thom blushed.

"It's my playlist," I said. "I love it."

Dad raised his eyebrows at Thom.

When we ate dinner, Thom led the conversation, asking questions and following up the answers with more questions. Dad asked him if he followed rugby at all.

"Yeah, I kind of do. But I'm not that big on sports in general. I like to watch UFC."

A small flicker of irritation behind Dad's smile. "The blokes trying to kill each other in a cage? That still counts as a sport, Thom."

"Well," Thom began, looking to me for a second, then back to Dad. He seemed embarrassed. "I mean, it's not really a sport. I'm not that big on it anyway."

"You don't participate in any combat sports, do you, Thom?"

"No," Thom said with a small smile. "I don't have it in me."

"Too bad. You've definitely got the build."

Dad looked down at his plate for a second, then, looking up, he studied Thom's face. Thom, busy helping himself to more salad, didn't notice the way Dad's stare lingered.

Dad washed up the dinner dishes. Thom offered to help but Dad waved him away. "No, you kids do your own thing," he said.

I showed him up to my room for the first time, leaving the door open behind us. We stood close, leaning in, and Thom draped his arms around me, his fingers laced at the small of my back. Then I kissed him softly with my eyes open, watching the door.

"Remember when your dad used to confiscate your phone? I can't even imagine it. He's a nice guy."

"Yeah, he is."

"He likes me, I can tell."

"Yeah. You were great." *But you're wrong.*

"I was just shooting the shit with good ol' Bomber Bennet."

He wandered around my room looking at the photos on the walls, running his hand along the top of my dresser and touching all the trinkets and seashells I had carefully lined up. The post-card he took from the art gallery, the saltshaker from a café, a small crystal from a store in Fitzroy, a flashlight, a yo-yo. All those pilfered keepsakes that were special because Thom had stolen them for me; he had risked something for me. Those otherwise meaningless items were freighted with memory.

I had a few other keepsakes on my dresser. A mini Statue of Liberty Dad had brought back from a trip to New York when I was a baby. Mum's wedding ring strung on a silver necklace. The photo of me as a baby in Mum's arms.

"Seriously, Kate, your dad is fine. I don't know why you made such a big deal of introducing me."

I closed the door a little further. Clearly sensing I didn't want to talk about it, he smiled and took my cheeks in his hands, kissing me again. It felt like burning where my chest touched his. He ran his hand down my back and around my waist, unpicking the front button of my jeans.

"Don't, Thom." I placed my hands on his chest, pushing gently. He grabbed my wrists and made a noise in his throat like he was holding back a sneeze. He gripped with such force I felt a sort of ache where his thumbs dug in.

"My dad's downstairs," I reminded him.

"Okay," he said, still with that intensity in his eyes. Then abruptly he let out a laugh. "Relax, Kate. I wouldn't do anything— *we're not ready*, remember?" He was repeating my own words back to me. We had been going out for five months—from September through most of summer. We were both sixteen. He had presented so many clever arguments but still it didn't seem right yet.

I felt bad, like it was my fault and I should somehow be different. And that's how they get you, boys like Thom. The obligation to protect them from their insecurities by conceding, bending. I leaned in and kissed him gently on the lips.

I thought about one time when I had been at Thom's and, while he went to the kitchen, I opened his laptop. The screen had filled with naked flesh, a manufactured sensual whine issuing from the speakers. I knew most guys were into porn, but until then I'd thought Thom was different. There was something almost forceful about it. I had watched for a few seconds, curious.

That afternoon we'd had our first fight. I could tell he was embarrassed by what I'd seen and that his embarrassment made him angry. He told me never to go through his things again. He said if I did, we would be through. I cried and he didn't apologize, but eventually we swept that episode aside, never mentioning it again.

"It'll happen soon," I said now.

. . .

Later that week Willow texted me.

> It has literally been a month since I saw you. Please can
> you visit me soon?

I thought for a moment. She always had lots of friends. Basically all of my friends were her friends first. At least Thom was all mine. I suppose he was the reason why Willow and I hadn't been seeing much of each other, that and the needling fact she had lied to me about him.

> Not a whole month but we've been slack. We should
> hang soon?

> We've been slack? Not we, Kate. You. But I'll forgive
> you if you come see me soon. I'm dying for the goss.

After school I walked the long way home, stopping in at Willow's. We lay on the rug in the lounge room in front of the television. Sensing eyes on me, I glanced over my shoulder. Her dad was watching us. Or perhaps he wasn't actually *watching*. Perhaps he'd glanced up from his iPad at the same instant that I'd turned around. Whatever the case, our eyes met briefly.

Willow asked me something about Thom and I directed my attention back to her. We were talking quietly, but I could tell that he was listening. I liked that he knew how mature I was, that I had a boyfriend. When the conversation edged toward sex, Willow jerked her head toward the stairs and we retreated to her room.

"We're still waiting," I told her.

"Right," Willow said, quirking an eyebrow.

"What? That's normal. It'll happen."

"Well, there's no point waiting forever. I mean, it's not like you're going to marry Thom."

"Why do you say that?" I didn't want her to know that I had fantasized about just that, but I couldn't keep the prickle of annoyance out of my voice.

"Relax, it's just not likely. Like, statistically or whatever. I mean I've been with four guys now."

"Well, that's you."

In the silence that followed, I could hear our breathing.

She swallowed before speaking. "So that makes me a slut? Is that what you think?"

"No," I said. But I couldn't meet her eyes.

She let out a huff of anger that spilled into laughter. "You don't get it, do you. You just don't see it at all. You've turned your back on me and probably all your other friends for a guy you've been with for ten minutes."

"You don't make an effort with me either. *And* it's been five months."

"It won't last another five."

"Admit it, you never wanted us to get together. You tried to ruin it from the start."

"What are you talking about?" she said, eyes pinched, lip curled in a snarl.

For a single heartbeat I had the sinking feeling that I had read it all wrong, but then I remembered what she had texted me. Perhaps I still had the messages. *They like each other. A lot.* "You told Thom I had a boyfriend and you told me he was going out with Sally."

"Okay, firstly, Sally told me he was texting her and I told you because that's what *real* friends do. I didn't know she was lying. Secondly, I never told Thom you had a boyfriend. Thom's either lying or not remembering it how it happened." She flicked her hair away from her face. "It won't last anyway. Trust me."

Doubt rinsed over me like icy water. She was just causing trouble, like usual. Willow loved drama and was always ready to poke at sore points. She carried those sly jibes around in her pocket like thumbtacks.

Twenty-one

A continent of cloud edged across the sun, darkening the sea from cobalt to gray. The waves were high, crashing close to shore. I'd always been drawn to the beach, remembering those days with Dad down at Torquay and the time Mum, brittle in her two-piece bikini, had lifted me by the hands and carried me out into the shallows down near the house in Portsea. That's what it was like when I was young—so happy. The sky was always an unbroken blue in those memories. Mum was always smiling. The beach was a magical place.

But now I was at the beach with Thom's family, not my own. Thom and I walked out into the surf, diving into the first wave. The water was cold until my head went under, then it felt almost warm. The sea grabbed my ankles, pulling me back with the rush of the swell. Thom dived under and lifted me up over his shoulder. A squeal tore from my lips as he carried me forward and tumbled into a wave. The saltwater drilled up my nose into my sinuses.

When we headed back in, we sat on our towels beside his

parents, me reading a book, Thom on his phone, scrolling through Instagram, taking snaps. At one point we tilted our heads toward each other and Thom took a selfie, posted it to Instagram. Another image that would eventually become newspaper fodder.

After a while Thom got up and began walking along the beach, hunched over, scanning the sand for something to shoot with his camera.

"I hope you've got plenty of sunblock on; skin like yours will burn in this sun," Suzie, lying nearby, said.

Skin like mine? I looked down at the pale, freckled plane of my stomach, then my eyes traveled farther, coming to rest on the pink scars covering my thighs. Thom would kiss the scars on my legs; he told me he loved them. Maybe it was true. Maybe he was the only one who saw them as something other than a disfigurement. When we were alone with his camera, he took photos of me—I had never felt truly sexy until then.

I rose and walked down along the beach. The stretch of sand was almost vacant except for a few couples and a small group of guys. I wanted to check out the point at the end of the beach. I walked toward it, picking up a knotted piece of driftwood on the way, thinking it might make a nice photo for Thom. I hadn't gotten far when I heard something sprinting on the sand, and I turned back just in time to see a dog leap up, printing two sandy paw marks on my thighs. A golden retriever stood, eyeing the driftwood in my hand, its long fur shaggy from the seawater.

"Sorry about him," a voice said. I looked up and a guy in just his board shorts was rushing over. He seemed only a couple of years older than me.

"Oh, he's fine. He just wants my stick, I think."

"Come here, boy," he said, but the dog stayed sitting there, waiting for me to throw it.

"Can I throw it for him?" I said.

"Sure."

I tossed the stick away and the dog sped off after it. When I looked back, I could see Thom down the beach watching me. I dusted my thighs off and walked toward him.

"What was that all about?" he said when I got back to him.

"What?"

"Who was the guy with the six-pack?"

"The six-pack?"

"Macho man, down there," he said, pointing.

"Oh, him," I said, warmth spreading in my cheeks. "His dog jumped up and scratched me."

He looked uncertain for a moment, then a smile broke. "Want me to kiss it better?"

That night we had a barbecue and played Scrabble while the kookaburras cackled out in the bush. At bedtime, Thom and I went to different rooms. We said good night, knowing when the lights had been out long enough we would end up in the same bed. Soon enough my door whined open and Thom slipped in beside me. His body relaxed against mine. I sensed him smiling in the dark.

I turned and pressed my lips against his cheek.

"Maybe one day we could just quit school and move here. You could catch fish and I could plant a big garden full of vegetables."

"So you can be close to your new boyfriend?"

"What?"

"Never mind."

"Oh my God," I said. "Are you talking about the guy at the beach?"

"What? No."

"You're *jealous*," I teased. I kissed him again, resting my hand on his warm chest.

"I was joking, Kate."

"I didn't know you were the jealous type," I said, climbing on top of him. "Lucky I only want you." He pulled me against him. I wanted to show him what he meant to me and crush the seeds of doubt Willow had tried to plant in my head. Our bodies pressed together, bones on bones, squeezing each other like we were drowning.

"Kate," he said in the dark. "I . . . I think I love you."

I wanted to say it back, desperately, but I couldn't get the words past my throat. I felt his body tighten with anger or embarrassment. Until that moment, the day, the evening, had been close to perfect.

"Then maybe I'll let you prove it," I said at last, and lowered my face to his.

AFTER

Twenty-two

Who—who are you? How do you know my name?"

     - Her face is sun damaged and it is hard to guess her age, but the brightness in her eyes suggests she is not an old woman. The car is muttering under its breath at the road's edge.

"I'm here to help," she says, smiling pleasantly.

"Can you take me to Auckland?"

"Auckland?" She laughs, shakes her head. "Not today, doll."

I look back at the spot where I stood for so long.

"Where are you going?" My words are unraveling at the edges.

"Why do you want to go to Auckland?" she counters.

I don't answer, just stare straight ahead.

"Look, I'm not taking you anywhere you don't want to go," she assures me. "I just wanted to get you out of the rain before you catch your death."

"How do you know my name?"

She grins at me again. "My son, Iso, said he saw you walking out of town. I'm Donna."

Clearly he didn't buy my story about meeting Jim up the road. He and Tiriana must have seen my sign and known I was hitch-hiking. Or is it possible Jim knows this woman?

"I'm leaving here," I say.

"Evie, dear," she replies, "whatever you are running from, surely it can wait until the rain has cleared."

"Do you know him? Do you know Jim?"

I can't read her expression.

Turning back to the road, she sniffs, then winds the window down a little and spits out into the rain. "Jim? That's your uncle, is it? Never met the guy. I've seen him about, though." She winds her window back up. "People take notice when outsiders start showing up, you understand?"

She does a U-turn and drives back the way I walked.

"Let me out."

"Evie, it's not safe out there in this weather. I can drop you back here later, or we can pull over and you can wait in the car for it to clear up. But one thing I'm not going to do is let a skinny little thing like you get sick out in this weather."

I stare at her. Tiny feet of rain are dancing on the roof. A sixties melody unwinds from the car's tinny speakers.

"I can take you back up to my place, get you in front of the fire so you can warm up, dry your clothes."

"Do you know?" I ask.

"Know what, dear?"

"Do you know who I am? What they think I've done?"

No confusion or alarm, just sorrow. Smile inverted, eyes shining blue. "What have you done?" An asthmatic laugh. "You're acting like I'm the one who should be afraid."

What does she mean? *Is she helping Jim manipulate me?* I don't remember agreeing to go back to her place, but it's too late now. As the car speeds up I begin to hyperventilate. I can't get enough air, my vision blurs.

Donna slows the car, glancing over with concern. "What is it? Are you all right?"

I reach for the door handle and yank it. I push the door open and tumble out. The gravel hits me like a sledgehammer. I roll and roll. All the clothes around me catch and twist. The car slides in the wet, hurling a wave of stones. A sharp pain stings my elbow. Before I can get to my feet, Donna is there, lifting me up. She wraps her arms around me.

"It's okay, Evie. It's okay. I've got you. What is it, darling? What are you afraid of?"

"I need to go home."

"I can drop you home—that's fine."

"My home is in Melbourne."

Her eyes are glossy and her mouth is turned down. I can see she is shaking. Before I know it, she has guided me from the rain back to the front seat. I sit there while she squats down on the gravel, looking into my eyes, holding my hands in hers. A truck passes and the gust rocks the car.

"We need to get you somewhere safe and warm. Do you want me to call someone, maybe your uncle?"

"No."

"Well, I'm here to help. Is it okay if I drive you home?"

I just shake my head and begin to cry.

"It's okay," she says, closing my door and moving around the hood of the car back to the driver's seat. "We can sit for a while until you decide."

She cranks the heater and turns the radio up a little. The air from the vents blows the tears back down my cheeks. A woman's voice tells us we are listening to the Breeze. Eventually I turn to her. "Please just go slowly, okay?" I say.

"Of course." She tilts her head. "Is there anything happening at home, Evie? Anything you want to talk about?"

They could be anywhere. "No," I say. "No. I just need to get to Auckland. That's all."

"Well, let's focus on getting you warm and dry first. Now, *Evie*, is that short for Evelyn?"

Why is she asking me this? The car eases onto the road. "Just call me Evie, please."

Soon enough we are back in Maketu. We pull over into the car park beside the fish-and-chip shop and watch the sea through the fog and the windscreen wipers go *zombp-zombp-zombp*. "So you're up on the hill, right?"

"Yeah." I hold my elbow. The pain still sears from slamming it against the road.

"Which street?"

"I don't know." I can't go back there. I can't face Jim.

"Well, I'll take you back to our place and then I can drop you home when you're ready."

She drives out around the estuary, turning into a road I've never been up. A goat lifts its head from a nearby paddock as we pass. I realize, as the car climbs and the properties become more rural, that we are on the opposite side of the hill from our house. Soon Donna pulls over and climbs out into the rain. She opens a gate fastened to a post with wire. She gets back in and the car rattles down a potted driveway.

"Come on," she says when we have parked up beside the small pale house.

The yard is flat and unmowed, dotted with plastic flowers staked into the earth, chipped clay enamel sculptures, and a rusty old swing set. Around the front door, wind chimes tinkle, closing in on me like a flock of panicked birds.

She opens the door and I step into the house. The door slams behind me.

Inside, the place is small and dark. Along the hall photos are pinned to the yellowed floral wallpaper. I stop before one—a photo of Iso as a child. He holds the hand of a more solidly built, older version of himself, who I assume must be his dad. Which makes me think about my own dad, how much I miss him.

In another photo, he is holding a fish to the camera. There are photos of his mum too. Leaning on a shovel in the garden, caught mid-laugh at a restaurant. She looks younger, her features less pinched and plumper. I turn my gaze to another picture: Iso on horseback with a surfboard under his arm, riding away from the camera.

"Always been a good-looking bugger," says Iso, coming up the hallway. He points to a photo of himself as a child, eyes closed, wide grin, proudly showing off a missing front tooth.

"Go on," his mother says. "Get the poor girl a towel and run her a bath."

"I'm fine."

"You've damn near got hypothermia and those bones would be sore after your fall."

"Fall?" Iso says. "Jesus, Ma. What have you done to the poor girl?"

"Oh, don't you worry. She had a wee knock is all." Then she turns back to me. "Look at you, shaking like a leaf. Give me your clothes, I'll spin them in the washing machine, then chuck them in the dryer."

"My uncle——" I begin, but she cuts me off.

"Your uncle will have me guts for garters if I send you home looking like a drowned rat," Donna says, then comes that racking asthmatic laugh again. Iso shows his white teeth but I can barely muster a smile.

"Don't worry, we'll get you home safe. If you were worried about him, you wouldn't be out there alone." There's a thorn in her words now. "Come on, this way." She leads me up the hall.

Glancing into the lounge room as we pass, I see a fire blazing. A cat is stretched out before it. Where a tail should be there is only a knob. The smell of soup fills the narrow hall, and as we enter the kitchen I see pots and pans hanging by their handles over the stovetop, a fridge cluttered with magnets and stickers. I hear the sound of water running. A bath. I can't do it. I can't have a bath. I haven't been able to since I was little.

"No bath," I say. "I said I didn't want one."

She leans over the bench. "Well, why don't you take a shower instead?"

I search for an excuse.

"Chester!" The woman makes a clicking sound with her tongue, empties a container of ambiguous and bloody meat into a dish on the floor. The cat rushes in, its bell tinkling.

"Iso," Donna calls. "Forget the bath, Evie here will have a shower."

Iso enters the kitchen and hands me a towel.

My guts churn and squeeze. Something is off about this. What if they're just keeping me here until the police arrive? Or something worse. "I'm not so sure——"

Donna makes an irritated noise, cutting me off. "Don't be silly, Evie. Get in the shower and by the time you're done your clothes will be almost dry. I'll drop you home after."

Iso shows me to the bathroom and I enter, closing and locking the door behind me. An old claw-foot bath, half full, steams beneath the fogged windows. In the corner a candle burns. As soon as I've stripped off, there's a knock at the door. I wrap myself in a towel, unlock the door, and open it. Iso's mother steps in and scoops up my sodden clothes. "Let me take these. You want a cup of tea or anything? Maybe some soup?"

"I'm fine, thanks. You've done enough already."

The door closes. Now I don't have any clothes. I hear a muffled exchange between mother and son.

I wait and wait until the water is hot. The shower burns. It's a good burn. The water runs down my legs, over the pink of my thighs, heating my stomach. A bruise is already darkening around my elbow. It hurts to touch.

The scented candle issues a cloying fragrance. Stepping from the shower, dripping, I lean forward and blow it out. I have escaped, but I'm still in Maketu. Maybe Donna will take me back out to the road. I could try hitchhiking again. But the fear I felt when I got into her car and we sped away was overwhelming. Would I dare to get in a stranger's car again? A flash of memory: driving the car, then I'm outside and someone is lying flat, blood pooling around their head. But in this memory Jim is standing there with something in his hand. *Don't trust him.* Dread clogs my throat.

I step back into the hot shower, and almost immediately the lights go out. Darkness swarms the room, then thunder sounds outside. My heart slams, my breath quickens.

"What's going on?" I call. So frail, so pathetic. "What's happening?"

"You all right in there?"

"The lights . . . I can't see."

"Power's out."

The wind screams. A knocking sound comes from up the hall. I kill the shower, get out, and wrap the towel around me.

The darkness fills every corner of the room but for the glow of the frosted window. Night has almost come and the storm is growing and growing. I open the door and leap back in fright. Standing with her face lit up by a candle is Iso's mum. "I can't use the dryer," she says. "Power's out. But you can wear these for now." She holds out a gray sweater and a pair of navy pants.

Something touches my bare leg. I rear back, then look down to see the cat. I stifle the impulse to kick it away.

"Shoo, Chester."

The cat twists away and rubs its body against Donna's leg.

"I want to leave," I say.

Her expression changes, a slight adjustment of her features. "Of course. Well, put these on for now."

I wait till she has gone, then close the door and pull on the pants and sweater. When I open the door she is waiting again in the hall.

There is the sound of a car crunching along the stones of her driveway. Her head turns toward the door, then she looks back into the kitchen.

"Wait here," she says.

She moves surprisingly swiftly down the hall to the door, whips it open, and steps outside, pulling it half closed behind her. I hear voices. It could be anyone.

I go into the lounge. There's no sign of Iso. I pick up my bag and throw it over my shoulder, then creep back down the hall past the bathroom. I find the laundry off the kitchen, near the back door. The dryer is full of my still-damp clothes. I cram them into my bag, then burst out the back door.

I'm outside and running before I have time to think where I am going. I scramble over a fence and rush across a paddock, sliding in the mud. Over another fence and then I'm at the road. Nearby there's a man in a flannel shirt digging a hole in a paddock; he looks up as I pass. I could be a wraith gliding by, barefoot and wild-eyed. I don't turn back; my feet hit the gravel and I run and run.

Twenty-three

The lights are off inside and Jim's car is not in the driveway. I try the front door; I had left it unlocked with my keys on the kitchen counter, assuming I wouldn't be coming back. It opens.

Beau starts up his yapping from a dark corner of the lounge as I enter and jumps up to greet me. I creep on the balls of my bare feet, numb and muddy from the walk, checking each room. There is no sign that Jim has been home. I hang my damp clothes on the curtain rail in my room, then return to the lounge and light the fire. Shucking off the clothes Iso's mother lent me, I pull on clothes of my own from the dresser, then I quickly tidy Jim's room, remaking his bed and pushing everything back into place.

I feed Beau before returning to my own room, climbing into bed, and pulling the covers up to my chin. The book I was reading is still sitting on the bedside table. *Don't trust him.* The storm rages outside.

I believed everything he said the day we arrived. On the drive from the airport he told me he would do anything to change how

I looked, make me unrecognizable. *The most important thing, Kate, is to stay hidden and anonymous.* That's why I took the scissors. That's why I started hacking at my hair.

He didn't need to scrape the last of it off, though; part of him must have wanted to make me suffer for what I had done, to punish me, even if he didn't know it. As usual, he would form clever arguments to justify his actions. He would find gaps in the meanings of words to stash his lies.

I wake in the dark of my room, unsure how much time has passed. I switch on the lamp but nothing happens. The storm has died down but the power is still out. I pull back the curtains and see blue evening light, bright enough to open the book and scan through the pages, searching for any other messages. I flick through slowly and reach the end without finding anything else. I take up my journal instead. I open it and read through my words but there are gaps like missing teeth where pages have been torn out. The blank pages are embroidered with letters punched through in rage. Two sets of words, one in ink and one indented. The leaning scrawl fills the page. All those angry words. *He betrayed me, he ruined my life, I'll never trust him again.* I shove the journal back under my bed and look out the window over the town, to the sea sparkling beneath those few stars bright enough to break through the skeins of cloud.

Quietly I cross my room, ease the door open, and pad down the hall to the lounge room. Jim has been back; his laptop is on the desk. I stand and listen. From his room comes the sigh of a man in the soundest of sleeps. I walk over to the sliding door, press my nose to the cool glass, and stare out into the night.

I have never felt so alone. I had Thom to fall back on when we were together. I think about Thom's family. *What do they think of him? And me? Are their lives different now?* I imagine them all moving on. People are not frozen in time when you leave them behind; they keep changing and living. I wonder what Willow is doing too.

At Jim's desk, I lift the lid of his laptop. The screen lights up, blue and ghostly. A small square image of his face stares out, but I can't get any further without a password. It will surely be complex, something long with capital letters and symbols. I remember a P and an E from when I watched him type the night he showed me the message boards. I can't think of anything it might be. I try to remember the shapes his hands made as he typed. Something on the desk catches my eye, illuminated by the computer's glow. It is his diary, open to today's date. It's cold in the lounge but my shirt is dampening with sweat. Is this a manipulation or clumsiness? I read the entry; brief, clipped notes, as if written in code.

> *Wednesday 22nd August*
> *Breach of privacy, e-mail Paul.*
> *CBT for trauma*
> *Anger blackouts/IED*
> *Credible defense?*

I flick back through the pages, scanning the dates. There are references to things we have done—chopping wood, planting vegetables—but nothing else, nothing unusual. I go back to the week we left Australia.

> *Things that could cause head trauma, skull cracked in three*
> *places, bruises around collarbone and right shoulder:*
> *Car accident.*

A fall (no drugs/alcohol).
An attack.
Media reporting suspicious fall day one. Day two attack. Car involved.
Brick dust in/on Mercedes? Blood splatter? DNA.
How to link Kate to scene, phone record, camera?

I search the desk for anything else. His laptop bag is near my feet. I grab and open it in the light of the laptop. Letters, sheets of paper, pens. Nothing of any significance. Then I find something. It's a short handwritten letter. I scan to the bottom to see who it's from: *Thom*.

> *Dear Kate,*
>
> *I know you're still angry and afraid and you don't want anyone to bother you but I'm worried. You were so mad the last time I saw you and I just want the chance to talk to you about everything and to help you through it. We're both in trouble but you can't just close yourself off to the world and expect this to go away.*
>
> *Please answer your phone or text me. Or at least post something online so I know you're okay. I'm worried.*
>
> *Thom*

Where did it come from? Jim kept this from me? Why didn't he show it to me when it arrived? I'm startled by a crash outside. I look up. Was that glass shattering? Beau starts barking, and I hear Jim's door open. I jam the letter back in his bag.

"Fuck's sake," he mutters under his breath.

I slip from the chair and curl myself up into a ball beneath the desk. Fear wraps itself around my organs. Footsteps are coming down the hall, and in the dim light I see him pass through the kitchen carrying something in his hands. The light switch clicks on and off but no light comes. He opens and closes drawers, finally finding the flashlight. He shoots the beam toward the door. I almost gasp when I see what he is holding in his other hand: the long barrel, the thick stock.

Beau comes over to me. *Go away.*

"On your bed," Jim says to Beau, who is blocking me from Jim's view. Does the dog realize he's protecting me? I dig my fingers into my arms, holding my breath. The front door creaks open. He aims the flashlight beam into the fog.

"You just going to hide in the bush like a dog?" he says, his voice loud in the silence.

There's no response. I can hear my heart beating.

"Come out here, right now." His voice is getting farther away.

I could make it to my room if I ran now. I push the computer chair back gently and scramble up from under the desk. *What if they get him? What if they hurt him?* I sprint up the hall.

"Leave me alone, this stops tonight."

Did I leave my door open? I pull the door closed gently behind me, holding my breath. His voice still reaches me. Incoherent murmurs. Are there other voices, or just his?

I hear the low, flat pop of a gunshot. Then another one. "Don't come back," he calls.

A scrape as a bin is turned upright. *That's what the sound was, a bin falling.*

I lie in the dark with my eyes wide open, waiting for the creak of the front door. Eventually I hear it open and close, hear each bolt slam home. The chain lock rattles into place. His footsteps up the hall. Two thoughts chase each other around my brain. The first: *He kept Thom's letter from me.* The second: *He has a gun.*

In the morning, I wake to a throbbing elbow from yesterday's tumble out of Donna's car. Jim wrote about blood splatter and DNA. He wrote about ways he could link me to the scene. He has a letter to me from Thom. The evidence is stacking up; I know I can't trust him. I know he is playing games with me.

As I eat breakfast I can barely bring myself to look at him moving around the kitchen, his mouth a terse line. There's an ax leaning beside the door; I'm sure it wasn't there the day before, and still there is no sign of the home phone, the sharp objects. I finish my breakfast, then pull my sleeves up and wash the dishes in the sink. Like a sharp prickle I suddenly remember something else.

He has a gun.

He walks to his desk. "Kate," he calls. "Come here."

What does he know, that I escaped or that I was snooping?

I creep over. "What's up?"

"How are you feeling these days?"

"I'm good," I say, forcing a smile.

"Every day it's a different answer. But *generally* do you feel better?"

"Yes, I . . . I feel fine." I try to keep my smile steady.

He nods, then notices my arm. "Shit, what happened to your elbow?"

A purple swirl has blossomed. I pull the sleeve of my hoodie down. "I slipped coming out of the shower."

He bites his lips and taps a finger on his chin. His eyes bore into me. "Is that really what happened? You fell getting out of the shower?"

"Yeah," I say. "I didn't put the mat down and the tiles were wet. It was stupid."

"All right. Be more careful." He steps forward and kisses me on the forehead. I stiffen but don't push him away. "I've confirmed that they've found us. It's just one man, though. I think I can deal with him."

"How do you know? How can you be sure?"

"I saw him."

"Who?" Short urgent breaths. "Who is it?"

"No one. Jesus, Kate. This is why I kept it from you. Trust me, he's harmless, he'll be out of the picture soon enough. But I want you to be extra careful out there in the meantime. Try not to leave the house and don't speak to anyone you don't recognize."

"Okay," I say. "Are we safe?"

"Of course," he says. "I'll always keep you safe but I can't say that about anyone else in this town."

Now he steps back and holds me by my arms. "There's something else, Kate."

"Wh-what is it?" I brace as if for a coming blow.

"Last night"—he swallows—"they turned the life support off."

A black hole opens inside of me. I buckle against him.

I have been crying all morning and most of the afternoon. Nothing he does could possibly console me because when the grief fades it's anger I feel—anger at him.

Balled up on the couch, wrapped in a blanket with Beau beside me, I've stopped weeping. *Don't trust him.* I have to accept the possibility that this is just another one of Jim's lies. He wants me to believe I'm a killer. He stands nearby staring out the window over the bay. Then he comes near me and sits on the arm of the couch.

"You feeling okay, darling? We knew it was only a matter of time, didn't we?"

I nod. "I'm okay now. It was just a shock."

"Good girl," he says, turning his gaze back outside. The day is clear, the fog has lifted. "I know you probably don't feel up to it, but there's a spade out there and you could make a start at extending the veggie garden. The exercise will help."

"Maybe," I say.

"Okay, well, I'll be back soon. Just come knock if you need anything."

Without another word, he rises, opens the back door, and crosses the yard, disappearing inside the shed.

I think of the key in the cavity beneath my drawer; if I could drive, I could go anywhere. The rental car is not so different from the Mercedes. But next time I escape I will be prepared. I will have my passport and enough money, with an actual plan.

After glancing once out at the shed to make sure he's still there, I rush to his room and search it again. Opening drawers, carefully lifting his underwear and socks away, unstacking and restacking his shirts and pants. Then I go to the wardrobe and swing the shirts out of the way, rummaging among his shoes. I listen for the back door opening while I search. Under the bed, I find nothing. Scanning the books on his bedside table, I find: *Psychology of Choice, Understanding and Helping Troubled Teens, Cognitive Behavioral Therapy, The Myth of Repressed Memory.* I open one book, *Thinking, Fast and Slow,* and skim a few pages, but I can't make sense of it. There is a slim volume tucked in among the weightier tomes: *Inducing False Memories: On the Fallibility of Memory.* It is the only book with a bookmark in it. This is the book he has been reading. I take it from his room and stash it beneath my bed, glancing once more at the shed before returning to continue my search. There is nothing else to find. I can't see the gun, or find any cash or credit cards, and my passport is not in his room either.

I straighten the bedcovers, push his shirts back to the middle of the wardrobe, then walk down into the garden. Taking the spade, I begin to dig.

The digging is a kind of meditation: pain, repetition, breathing. It's the sort of work that untethers the mind. Beau watches me from the deck as I continue cutting into the soil, slowly moving around in a square. A blister is rising at the base of my thumb and a callus has torn off, causing blood to trickle into the creases of my palm.

I think about everything that has happened since we arrived: the children throwing stones, the three-legged dog, Jim almost hitting a boy with the car, the man in black, and Iso's mum leering at me when she picked me up. Then I think about the things that happened before: falling for Thom, hurting Sally, Dad meeting with Thom's parents, afternoons at Willow's, the video . . .

A new blister swells, opens, seeps. My hands are numb; pain throbs in my back, my shoulders. Adrenaline rises. I'm angry. I tremble with it. I remember the betrayal and above it all are Jim's words. *They turned the life support off.* Focus, Kate, just remember. I see the shape in the headlights. It was a man. A man rushing out of the way of the car. The man tripping, his head striking the curb, snapping back . . . No, it's my imagination inventing things. I know somehow Jim is responsible, I just need to find a way to prove it.

. . .

By the time Jim emerges my muscles are aching with fatigue. The tightness feels good.

"What the hell have you done here?"

"I was digging."

"You should have stopped."

I just shrug. There's something addictive about the work. I take the spade up again.

He moves quickly to snatch it from me. "Stop now."

"Do they think I killed him?"

His face falls. "Oh, Kate . . ."

"Tell me exactly what happened. I can handle it. Do they think it was me?"

"Oh, shit, what are you remembering? It wasn't your fault. You need to understand that."

"It's true, though, isn't it? They're after us because you let them believe I did it." The words don't sound like mine, they're bitter and accusatory.

We stare at each other, then the silence is broken by a knock, and Beau begins to bark. There's someone at the front door. He nods toward the house and I quickly climb the steps ahead of him, rushing to my room as the tears begin.

The door opens.

"Hello?"

"Hi. How are you doing?"

"I'm okay." Then quietly: "What are you doing here?"

"I wanted to see Evie. Is she about?"

"Evie?"

"Yeah." It's Iso, I realize. They speak to each other with an unsettling familiarity. *Fuck. Please don't tell him. Please don't let him know I was running away.*

"Evie," Jim repeats. There's a long pause. "Look, ah, let's talk outside, all right?"

The door closes but I creep down the hall and press my ear to the wood. The murmurs from outside are barely audible—not loud enough to drown out the words reverberating in my skull. *They think I'm a killer. The world thinks I am the killer.*

They're out there for some time, still talking. Five minutes, maybe more. What are they saying about me? The door opens so abruptly he catches me standing there.

He raises his eyebrows. "Friend of yours?"

I shrug one shoulder, feigning nonchalance.

"I'm not mad, Kate." Now he shows me his teeth. Despite everything, it makes me feel a little normal. He fetches the first-aid kit and begins carefully cleaning and bandaging my blistered, weeping hands. "You've been a little erratic lately. Have you been swallowing your pills every time?"

With my forearm, I scratch my head through my short hair. What does he know?

"Yes, I have."

"Are you certain, Kate? Don't lie to me."

I nod.

"Well, I'll be making sure you are."

That afternoon we walk together to the headland. Beau sniffs at patches of grass, stopping frequently to cock his leg against a fence post or power pole.

On our way back we see two children coming up the track from the beach, each carrying a plastic bag full of sharp green mussels. The elder of the two is a boy with a faint scowl. He doesn't say anything as we pass each other. Then I hear the smaller of the two speak. "Hi, Kate."

I look back. It's Awhina. I notice that her right eye is bruised. She gives me a small wave, then continues on her way.

When I turn back I see that Jim has stopped and is staring at me. "Kate," he says quietly, his eyes fixed on the children. "That child just called you Kate."

I resume walking but he snatches my wrist.

"How does she know your name?"

"I accidentally told her."

"When?"

"I don't know. A week or so ago."

His lips tighten to a white line and he shakes his head. "Jesus Christ. Use your fucking brain, won't you? I'm busting my arse trying to plan my way out of this mess and you're being careless."

"She's just a child."

"Children have big fucking mouths, Kate. In case you hadn't noticed. What if she tells her parents your real name? What if they're curious why you're calling yourself Evie?"

"I'm sorry."

He sighs, anger ebbing, and we start walking again. "Did you see her eye?" he asks.

I don't say anything but I know already where the bruise came from: her father. Maybe when I go, I could take her with me?

"Someone has been hurting her," I say.

We have reached the fence, and he opens a gap between the wires for me to step through. "I think that's pretty obvious, Kate."

"Maybe someone should help?"

"It's not our business."

"But—"

"That's enough, Kate. I don't want to hear it. My only concern is keeping you safe—and that should be your only concern too, quite frankly. Someone died, do you think this is going away?"

. Back at the house, he pauses at the front door. "Shh," he says, suddenly alert. Beau whines on his leash. Jim pushes the front door; it creaks open. Signaling with his palm for me to stay where I am, he slips off his shoes and creeps into the house, stopping to pick up the ax from beside the door. From the driveway I can hear him moving about, opening doors and checking rooms. I wait for a new voice, or the muffled thuds of men fighting, but there is nothing. Finally, he comes back.

"What?" I say. "What is it?"

"The door was ajar. And . . ." He pauses. "Here," he says, gesturing. "Look at this."

He points at marks on the linoleum in the kitchen. Partial footprints, two or three of them. Could they be from my muddy bare feet when I fled Iso's?

"Did you leave the door unlocked?" he asks. "Was the house unlocked when we left?"

"I don't know."

His face reddens; he grits his teeth. "You were the last one out, Kate. Try to remember."

I want to protest: I wasn't the last one out, he was. If anyone left the door unlocked it was him.

"Check your things, make sure nothing is missing."

I can see his nerves are fraying; it's only a matter of time until he snaps. *Who is the mad one, me or him?*

My room seems the same, but I can't tell for sure if anyone has been in here. The floor is clean, the bed made. My book is where I left it on the bedside table. I open it at the marked page, then close it again. Who would send me this message? *Death is the only escape. I never meant to hurt you.* I lie on my bed and stare at the ceiling. Jim handed it to me at the airport to read on the flight. But I've seen it before, somewhere. Maybe in Dad's collection of books? Then I found it again in my wardrobe in this house. Jim must be sending these messages; perhaps he's trying to express himself. Perhaps the old Jim is in there, trying to tell me something.

I can hear him making a phone call out in the lounge room.

Eventually he comes down the hall to my room. "Good news," he says.

I turn my head to look at him.

"I just called Terry from next door and told him I was worried someone has been breaking in here. He reckons it's the old bloke that used to rent the place. He's done something like this before, apparently. Has dementia and has probably forgotten he doesn't live here. He might even still have a key."

As he walks back up the hall, I whisper to myself: "Don't trust him."

A couple of hours later a locksmith arrives. I stay in my room until he's done. After he leaves, I go out to the kitchen. A shiny new set of keys waits on the counter. Jim has put the white key ring on my new set. Also on the counter is a series of identical white boxes.

"What are those?" I ask.

"These," says Jim, "are surveillance cameras."

"Cameras?" I pick up one of the boxes. "What do we need cameras for?"

"I'm installing them to keep you safe. Turns out this guy here"—he nods at Beau, who is sleeping on his lamb's wool bed—"is a better companion than guard." He takes the box from my hand. "They run twenty-four/seven. State-of-the-art, night vision, motion detection, completely wireless. I can patch the feed through to my phone so I'll know exactly what's going on at the house, even when I'm out."

"Where will you put them?"

He opens a box and pulls out the black tube. "I'll show you once I've installed them."

I think of the man in black who I saw up at the top of the driveway. "What happened with the guy who found us?"

"Don't worry, I'm on top of it. There were some photos. I think they came from him. But I'm sorting it all out."

"Photos?"

He just shakes his head. "Don't worry—it's nothing, really."

"Do others know where we are?"

"So far it looks like he's the only one. But if he found us, others might. It's just a matter of time and we better be prepared."

As afternoon fades into evening, he drills the camera mounts into place and installs them while I begin emptying the soil into the garden boxes I dug. My hands still burn beneath the bandages and the gloves but it's bearable. I feel the eye of the cameras as I work. Eventually he walks down into the backyard, staring into the screen of his phone.

"You want to see?" he asks.

"Yeah, okay." I drop the spade and the gloves and move in beside him.

He switches between the cameras. First we see the driveway, looking up toward the road. He touches the screen. Next we see ourselves standing in the yard, hunched over his phone.

"Watch," he says. He lifts his hand toward the camera and the man on the screen does the same.

The third camera is in the lounge room. It is placed at an angle so you can see into the kitchen and the front door. The final image is of my unmade bed, my pajama bottoms twisted on the floor, and my open door.

"That's my room." I look up at him.

"You can never be too careful," he says before putting his phone in his pocket and walking back up to the house.

BEFORE

Twenty-four

Why don't we play spin the bottle?" Thom's friend Rick suggested. He was pimply, with a belly that poked out of his T-shirt.

"That's fucking lame," Willow said, not even looking up from her phone. She took a sip from her cup. "Is this the best you got, Thom? I might have to find us some others, hey, Jodie?"

Rick looked hurt.

"Put some music on," I said to distract Willow. She had, after all, organized this gathering. I thought it was an olive branch, a way for her to hang out with Thom and me.

"You do it," she responded.

I got to my feet and plugged my phone into the speaker in the corner of the room.

"Why don't we go to that party in Elwood?" said Jodie.

"How would we get to *Elwood*?" Andrew asked, draining his cup of wine and reaching for the bottle to pour another.

"We could walk," Willow said. "It would take half an hour."

"Do you plan on running? Because that's the only way it would take anywhere close to half an hour."

"You're an idiot."

"It's more than half an hour, Willow," I said. She threw a fierce look in my direction.

Willow jabbed at her phone screen with her finger. "So, according to Google, it will take thirty-eight minutes to walk."

"That's not half an hour."

"Fuck off, Thom," Willow said. "It's always slower on Google anyway."

"I think I know which party it is," Thom said. "Footy boys, right? So basically, a room full of gorillas drinking each other's piss."

"Not all of them," Jodie said.

Thom snorted. "Not all of them will be drinking each other's piss? Well, that's reassuring." I laughed; we all did. All but Willow, whose eyes stayed on me.

"And what do you propose? Go on, Thom. I'm sure you've got loads of other parties to be at?" Willow said.

"Why don't we vote?" Jodie suggested.

"No point, Thom wants to be boring and sit here all night because he doesn't let Kate have any fun and Kate will just do whatever Thom says," Willow said. "So they'll just vote no."

"I vote no to a vote," Thom said.

Willow tipped her head, raised her middle finger at him.

Thom rolled his eyes, then said, "All right, show of hands, who wants to check this party out?"

Everyone, including me and Thom, raised our hands.

"That settles that," Thom said with a smirk at Willow. "What were you worried about?"

We walked along, passing the wine between us, drinking straight from the bottles and keeping them hidden from the passing lights of cars speeding along the roads.

Jodie smoked a cigarette while she walked and pitched it into the road when she was finished with it. The boys trailed behind, talking about football.

Willow took a long suck of wine, then said, "Don't bring these losers to my house again."

"You told Thom to bring friends. And they're not losers."

She snorted. "Defensive much, Kate?"

With the booze thrumming in my veins and my body numb, I could feel myself letting go of any restraint. "You're jealous. That's it, isn't it. You're jealous that nobody wants you. Why buy the cow, right?"

"Oh my God, you're *such* a bitch," Jodie said.

"Just leave me alone," I said, eyeing Willow as her plump lips stretched into a tight smile. I dropped back and hung with the boys for the rest of the walk, taking longer and longer drinks whenever the wine ended up in my hands.

By the time we could hear the thumping bass of the party and see the spill of bodies stumbling out on the footpath, we were all drunk.

Despite not knowing anyone, Willow fit in naturally. Her long legs shrink-wrapped in black jeans, her dark chaotic hair and eyes thick with charcoal eyeliner. She spoke loudly, demanding an audience, demanding to be seen and heard. She abandoned me to Thom and left Jodie with the first group of guys we passed. They were crowded around the door, taking turns pouring beer down a funnel into their mouths, cheering each other on. She didn't look back once after she was inside.

The party was a whirlwind. Willow quickly found some

boy—a man, really, with a real beard—and before long their faces were locked together in the hallway. Thom and I stumbled out into the backyard but not before pilfering a bottle of beer from the fridge in the kitchen. A guy took it out of my hand to open it, but Thom snatched it back and twisted it open himself. He had shown his jealous side a little lately, but it was only because he cared for me.

Out in the yard I bumped into Tara, a girl from my school. Her blond hair was scraped back in a ponytail and her face was rosy with alcohol.

"Kate!" she screamed, throwing her arms around my neck. "Oh my God, what are you doing here?"

I could hardly string a sentence together. I just found myself back inside, swaying, trying to dance with Tara but barely able to stay upright.

"Let's do a shot!" she yelled over the music. Suddenly a cup was in my hand, and we were throwing them back. It scorched my throat.

I felt a rush of cool air on my legs, then looked down and realized what was happening. My dress flew up. Someone had ahold of it. Everyone looked over. "Show everyone those scars—freak." I turned back to see Willow's nasty smile.

Gasping, I pushed my dress down with both hands. I looked up at Willow's face. There was no regret. My gaze swung wildly around the room at all the staring eyes. Someone was holding a phone up, filming me. She wanted to show everyone my scars. She wanted to embarrass me. I reached for a cup and flung it to splash her in the face but she only continued to laugh. Others were laughing too. I realized her face was dry, the cup was empty. Hot tears stung my eyes. "Well?" she said. I stepped toward her, then felt Thom's arm wrap around my waist, pulling me away.

"You bitch!" I raged. "I hate you!"

Willow looked about her, shrugging at the others, that stupid smile plastered over her face.

The alcohol hit me like a wave. I was stumbling from room to room. Thom held me too close and I fell down. I tried to get up and realized I was weightless; someone had me by the arms and someone else held my legs. We were outside now, and the streetlights swayed above me. The hands helped me to my feet. *Show everyone those scars.* I was breathing fast. I wanted to rush back and snatch her hair but Thom kept me hard against him. We walked unsteadily through the streets.

A car, yellow, a light pinned to the roof. *She's not going to be sick.* Thom's voice.

It seemed a long drive. The taxi dropped us near the park, *the spot.*

"You need to act sober and be quiet, okay? My mum will kill us if she sees how smashed we are."

Thom gripped my arm to keep me upright, but he was tripping over his own feet too. We laughed and spun, our foreheads pressed together. As he twirled me, my hands slipped from his; I fell softly to the grass. He pulled me back to my feet. It seemed like we'd been there for hours, although it must have only been minutes. I was sobering up; my feet were beginning to follow each other.

"Dad," I said, slurring the word.

"What about him?"

"He thinks I'm at Willow's. I fucking hate Willow." The anger, now cooling, was morphing into something else, something cold and sharp deep inside of me.

"You can stay at my place."

"Hey, Thom?"

"Yeah?"

I could feel the tears building. All the people saw me. It wasn't like swimming, when I was younger and it was my choice to bare them. "My scars are disgusting."

"No, Kate. Your scars are beautiful. Like the rest of you."

"I hate her."

"You don't need Willow, you have me. I'll always be here for you."

We stumbled back toward the road. So close to his house. He dragged me inside, into his room, shushing me. His table lamp was aimed against the wall, muting the light.

"I love you." It was the first time I'd said it. I wasn't sure where the words came from, if it was alcohol or gratitude that formed them, but in that moment I meant every syllable. "Thom, I love you. Thank you for looking after me."

He had been taking off his jeans, but stopped then and stood swaying in the center of the room. "Really? You mean it?"

"Did *you* mean it? About my scars. Do you really think they're beautiful?" I looked down, examining my body through my clothes.

"Yes," he said, his eyes softening. "I meant it."

"She pointed them out to everyone."

He pulled his jeans off and stood straight again. "Who cares what everyone thinks? All that matters is what you think."

"And what you think."

"You know what I think, Kate," he said, stepping forward and taking my cheeks in his palms. "If you could see yourself through my eyes, you wouldn't have any doubts."

I could, I realized then. There was a way for me to see myself through his eyes. *You're beautiful through the lens.* Hadn't he told me that, the first time I went to his house?

"Shoot me," I said.

His eyes narrowed. "What?"

"Where's your camera? I want you to shoot me."

"Kate—"

I turned from him, bent, and dragged the black case from beneath his bed. "Show me what you see," I whispered, handing it to him. Then, closing my eyes on a deep breath, I pulled my dress over my head.

The silence ticked on between us. Then I heard the shutter click once, again. I moved to the bed, sank down on it, limbs splayed. The shutter clicked, then stopped. When I finally got the courage to look at him, his brow was lowered in concentration.

"Come here," he said.

"Why?"

"You'll see."

I slipped from the bed to join him in the middle of the room. He turned the screen to me, and I watched myself. A video of my legs, twisting and turning, striking poses. My scars could have been a map of the world; they made me different, like my own tattoos. *Maybe they really are beautiful.*

"Now you know," he said. "Beautiful Kate. And all mine."

I felt a surge of desire. "Do it again." I leaned forward and pressed my lips to his. "But this time I want you in the video too." The longer the camera was on me, on us, the better it felt. He held it steady as my confidence grew. The euphoria of the experience swelled in my chest. And the camera stayed with us, capturing the most intimate, the most perfect moment of my life.

I didn't know that something was changing. That we had reached the peak and the only way we could go from here was down.

AFTER

Twenty-five

When I open my eyes in the morning the first thing I see is the camera in the corner of the room. Did he watch me sleep? He must have discovered that I tried to run away. The cameras are here not to keep me safe, like he said, but to keep me under surveillance. He hasn't noticed his book is missing, or perhaps he has but doesn't care. So now I have two books plus my journal, which I'm writing in more. I'm writing to unlock those memories but I have only written about Mum and other painful days in my life. Some things scar the memory, some scars harden.

I'm getting stronger from working in the yard and am so hungry that I find myself eating whole chicken breasts, heaped scoops of mashed potato. Most meals I eat until I'm bloated and sleepy. Jim puts me on the scale; the numbers have risen again. It's been twenty-four days now and the weather has gotten a little warmer. But while I grow stronger, Jim seems to be deteriorating. He's up late every night. He takes more and more trips out to the shed and he is drinking more wine. Last night, as he sat on the couch, he said, without preamble, "You know, every day I imagine you dead. Think about that."

I can't even read the book I stole from his room for fear he will see me with it on the cameras. Maybe if I sit on the floor, hidden from the camera by my bed, I can read it. I reach under the bed for the book, then thrust it across the carpet so it slides out the other side. Then I walk around the bed and sit down, taking it in my lap. The book opens to a dog-eared page and I begin to read from where the text is underlined.

> *Memories change not only with time and perspective, but memory change can be induced.*

I scan farther down the page to the next part that is underlined.

> *Another study exhibits the power of suggestion. Employing a Socratic method of questioning rather than telling, scientists tested recollections of two groups.*

Why has he underlined these sentences? My door opens. I close the book, slip it behind me under the bed.

"Kate," he says from the doorway. "What are you doing down there?"

"Just sitting."

His eyes narrow in suspicion. "Your juice is ready."

I need to get away from the eye of the camera.

"Sure."

I follow him to the kitchen. "I'd like to take a walk today, stretch my legs a bit," I say.

"I'm not really in the mood."

I take the glass of juice, block my nose, and drink it all. I cough, then speak again. "I haven't been out much this week. Maybe I could go by myself?"

His expression is neutral. "Where do you want to go?"

"Just to the beach. I'll be careful."

"Just the beach?"

"Yeah." Then I pause, thinking about my dream, or is it a memory? If it happened the way I dreamed it, then why was I driving? But those underlined words come back to me. What if he's shaping my memories? I must read more of this book to find more clues as to what he is doing to me. "Can you tell me why I wanted to drive that night?"

"Well, there was the video. You remember that, don't you? He made a recording of you."

"I remember, yes." I think for a second. "But . . . now you are recording me too. And you took pictures of me. I wasn't wearing clothes."

He coughs into his hand to clear his throat. "That was different. I took pictures just in case we were caught, to show them how thin you were, how you had"—he pauses, as if struggling to put it into words—"how you had changed since it happened. And our cameras are to keep you safe, Kate. They're not to hurt you."

"The video . . . is it still out there?"

"No," he says. "No, it's gone now."

"But you said it will always be there, somewhere."

"I was wrong. It's all come down."

"Okay. So can I walk down to the beach?"

He sighs. "Take the dog."

I grab a plastic bag from the kitchen and go to my room. I stuff my sweater, my journal, and the two books into the bag. I'm about to leave when he stops me.

"One second, Kate. Arms up."

"Why?"

"I want to check something." I raise my arms. He pats me down, then plunges his hand into my carry bag, feels the books within.

"There's three books," he says, frowning.

"My journal, and the book I'm reading."

He snatches the bag and opens it, looking in. He pulls out my journal first. I brace, my entire body becoming tense. Next he removes my book. "You're reading this one?"

I swallow, nod. Finally he finds his book and his frown deepens. "You've been in my room."

"I just wanted to read something new."

A thick vein rises in his throat. "You *never* go in my room."

"I'm sorry, I—"

"Never."

I conjure a *sorry* expression. "Can I still go to the beach?"

He just stands there, watching my face. Finally when he points up the hallway, I flinch. "Put that book back before you go, and take these," he says, handing me my keys.

The walk to the beach is short. I sit on a bench looking out over the stones and sand, the fang of black rock rising from the water in the valley between waves. There's a surfer out there, past the breakers, waiting for a big set.

Beau is sitting beside the post he's leashed to, looking up watching the seagulls. I open my journal. Turning toward the back, I find a blank page. The pen hovers. I can't write. I read my words from Melbourne. The anger and fear from all the horrible things I read and heard about me. I close the journal and slap it down on the bench. I feel a burning anger inside. *Show everyone those scars.* The wind picks up and fingers through the pages. I take out my book but I know I won't be able to focus enough to read it.

I look at Beau, thinking about the words Jim underlined: *Memory change can be induced.* Everything he has said, everything he has suggested, could be a manipulation. It's possible I had nothing to do with any of it. It's possible my dreams and memories are fabrications. Maybe I wasn't there that night at all.

. Someone slides my journal toward me along the bench and sits down. I startle.

"Hey, stranger." It's Iso. He's in paint-stained shorts and a torn T-shirt. His work boots are untied. He's holding a meat pie; the minced insides drip down his fingers as he takes the first bite. I think about the night I ran away from his house.

"Iso," I say. "Hi."

He nods at the book in my lap. "Looks interesting."

"Oh, um, yeah—I'm just getting into it." I turn to see if there's any sign of Jim. I notice a gray sedan at the far end of the car park. It looks like his car, but I can't be sure.

"You a big reader?" he says.

"Not really."

He tosses the last of his pie to Beau, who snaps it out of the air. "I'm not trying to be nosy or anything, but you seem a bit down. I mean, when I see you, it always seems like you're having a hard time." He's got this expectant look, as though he actually cares about my answer.

"I'm sorry. I'm fine, really."

"Well, I know there's not much to do around here on the weekend, but a few of us are always going hunting or surfing. Or I could take you for a trek on the horse."

"That'd be cool," I say, turning from the ocean to him. "Have you always lived around here?"

"Yeah," he says.

"Do you ever think about going away?"

"I guess so. Got heaps of mates who worked in the mines over in Oz. But why would I? This is paradise. There's as much fresh seafood as you can eat, clean air, a million-dollar view, when the swell's up it's great surf. Sometimes I think I wouldn't mind moving up the coast a bit. But I don't really want to leave Mum on her own. Speaking of which, the old lady didn't scare you too much? She can be a bit full-on." He scrunches the pie wrapper in his fist.

"She was okay."

"You just disappeared."

My cheeks glow. "I needed to leave."

"Evie, why were you hitchhiking?" Iso is frowning at me, his blond eyebrows low over his blue eyes.

"I wanted to get out of town for a day."

He shrugs. "Sure, I get that. Mum said you wanted to go to Auckland."

I'm thinking of a plausible excuse when he speaks again.

"It's just I might be heading up there next week. Did you want to go shopping in the big smoke or something?"

I look down at the book in my hands again, then lift my gaze to meet his. I feel instinctively that I can trust him. "I know you met my uncle the other day, up at the house."

"Yeah, nice guy."

"He's not very nice, Iso. He's not a nice man at all."

"What do you mean?"

"I mean he can't find out that I'm planning on leaving. I think :.. I think he might be watching us now."

Iso looks uncomfortable, shuffling on the bench. "He's, ah, he's only looking out for you. It wouldn't feel right to keep him out of the loop."

"When you came over, did you tell him your mum had picked me up? That I was trying to leave town?"

He looks over his shoulder. "No, I was just dropping your shoes back after you left them at our place. Well, I said that you were at our house, but I'm pretty sure I didn't mention that Mum picked you up hitchhiking." He is looking at me closely now. "Are you okay, Evie?"

Can I trust him? I have started to doubt my impulse to confide in Iso. I slide my book back in my bag, leaving the journal sitting there.

"Yeah," I say. "My uncle's just a little overbearing."

"Well, that's what uncles are for," he says. "Still, I suppose it's always nice to get away. And it's safer getting a ride with someone you know instead of hitching. Most people around here are friendly enough, but there are a couple of rotten bastards in every town."

A breeze drives up off the sea. It whispers against my cheek, cools my scalp. I turn to look across the car park. The gray sedan is gone.

"Iso," I say, "could you do me a favor?"

"Yeah, sure thing."

"For some reason our mail hasn't been getting delivered. Would you mind if I had a letter sent to your house?"

"Sure."

I open my journal to a blank page and hand it to him. He scribbles down the address.

"Just let me know if anything arrives. Or I could come down and check in with you—that would be better."

"I'll keep my peepers peeled, Evie."

I make a mental note that if a letter comes back, it must be addressed to Evie and not Kate Bennet.

"Thanks for your help, Iso."

I turn toward the hill and look up, scanning the trees and houses. In the distance, way up the top, I think I spot our back deck. It may be a quirk of the light, a reflection off the glass of the sliding door, but from here it looks as though Jim is standing out there watching. It looks as though he is holding something up to his eyes.

"I've got to go," I say.

"Okay. It was good to see you, Evie. Come say hi soon—you know where we are."

I write the note on the way to the shop, scribbling as I walk, before Jim can sweep me up.

> *If you ever cared about me, you have to help me. He has me locked up, trapped in New Zealand. We are in a place called Maketu. He has told me that if I try to go back to Australia I will be put away for a very long time. But he has lied about what happened. He has changed. He's not himself anymore and I never should have trusted him. He has been manipulating me, trying to make me believe that I'm a killer, but I'm not. You have to believe me. I am not.*
>
> *Please send your message to the below address, confirming what is happening back there. Is it safe for me to come home? Are the police really after me?*
>
> *I'm so worried something is going to happen; this is bigger than any hurt we might have caused each other. He is becoming more and more controlling. Please address your return letter to "Evie," not Kate.*
>
> *Kate*

Tiriana isn't at the shop but someone else, a boy, sits behind the counter. I buy the stamps and the envelope. I scribble down the address I know so well on the front and hand it over. My letter is on its way. It won't be long now until I know the truth.

When I enter the kitchen, the kettle is on the burner. He takes his phone from the counter and slides it into his pocket.

"How's the weather?" he asks.

"It's nice, starting to cool down."

The kettle begins to rattle, with steam rising from the spout. He pulls it off the burner and fills his cup before stirring in a teaspoon of instant coffee. I sit down on the couch and turn the TV on.

"It's hard to trust you when you do things like that."

"Like what?"

"Take things from my room."

Has he been thinking about it since he found it in my bag? "Sorry, I just wanted something else to read. I didn't think you would mind."

"I need to trust you because I have to go away tonight."

"What?"

"I'm going away. I may be back tomorrow, or I might even be away another night."

He's going away—is this a trick? "Where are you going?"

"Not far." Irritation sits just below the surface. "You'll be on your own all day. I mean, you wanted me to treat you more like an adult, right?"

"I'll be alone?" This could be my chance for a clean escape.

He turns to me and places his palms down on the counter. "We've got the cameras now. You'll be safe."

I spend the remainder of the afternoon in my room, checking my escape, running through a getaway plan in my mind: search for anything I can take; passports, cash; then walk out to the highway again and hitchhike as far as I can. Those underlined words come back to me. It's so obvious; I should have known. We are here so he can keep me isolated from the truth. He has quarantined me to implant a false narrative, something close enough to the truth that it could form a memory in my brain. I hear him answer his phone. He speaks only three words.

"Two minutes. Fine."

I stay in my room, waiting in anticipation. I think I hear a car pulling up. The front door opens and thunks closed. Has someone arrived? Or is Jim going out?

I rush out the back door and down the steps and creep up the side of the house, ignoring the cameras. Jim is walking toward the top of the driveway. In the fading light, I can just make out the dark shape of another man standing, waiting. I recognize him; it's the man in black I saw here before. I think Jim is going to hit him, for just a single heartbeat, then I see Jim reach out and shake his hand. *What is he doing?* Jim hands him something. He knows this man? And what was it that changed hands: money, more photographs of me, or something else entirely? I'm trembling. Jim turns back, walking toward the house. I rush back inside with fear or anger or a combination of the two thrumming in my blood. *He's orchestrating it all.*

I sit on my bed and soon enough he calls me. "Dinner's ready."

At the table shepherd's pie is steaming on plates. He drinks wine from a coffee mug.

"I'll hold on to our important documents while I'm away, Kate. But the fridge is fully stocked and there's really no need for you to leave the house."

My heart plummets. *Important documents.* The passport, he must be taking it. A credit card and a passport; escape would be so much easier if I had these two things. There is a small amount of cash in my escape bag but not enough.

"I feel like I can really trust you again," he tells me, taking a forkful of shepherd's pie.

"Oh, ah, thanks."

He pauses with the fork halfway to his mouth. "Whatever happens, I just want you to be prepared. I want you to know that you can do anything, be anything, so long as you get through this. Do you understand?"

I twist my fork through the food. "What do you mean?"

"Well, this has been quite an ordeal. I'm sure it's all becoming clear in your mind, what happened. I think that's healthy. Eventually you will remember it all in full color." *But what I remember isn't what happened. It's what you want me to believe happened.*

"What if everyone finds out what I did? It will follow me everywhere."

He points his fork at me. "What did you do?" he asks.

"I hurt him. Didn't I?" I lie to please him.

He chews and swallows a mouthful of shepherd's pie. "Be completely honest with me, Kate. I have to make a decision tomorrow, and your next answer is ultimately going to determine what happens next. So tell me, is that how you remember it, or are you just telling me that?"

"That's how I remember it."

"Well, what did you hurt him with then?"

"The car," I say.

"Right," he says. "Was I in the front seat or the back?"

Don't trust him. "You weren't in the car," I say. "You know you weren't in the car because you were already there."

Something flares in his eyes. He sniffs, continues eating.

I have him cornered now. He's not denying it.

"You've lied to me since day one."

His fist hits the table so hard the plates jump. Slowly he lifts his knife and points it at me.

"Don't get fucking crazy now. You need to accept reality."

"I've accepted it. I know exactly what happened. Just take me home. Please?"

"Is that right?" he responds derisively. "You've accepted it, have you?"

"Yes."

He puts his cutlery down, rests his elbows on the table. "You don't believe a word I say, do you? I know everything that goes on inside that head of yours." Now he leans forward over the table and grabs my wrist. "Before you can even think about going anywhere, I am going to heal you. Do you hear me? I. Am. Going. To. Heal. You. You'd better start believing *that.*"

He drops my wrist and resumes eating. It aches where his thumb dug in.

I look down at my food. But what about the man at the road? I'm afraid to ask him. I'm afraid of what he will do to me if he realizes how much I know. "I'm sorry. I just get confused."

"The rules for while I'm away are the same as always, but the consequences for breaking them are much greater. Don't leave the house unless you absolutely have to. Don't open the door to anyone. Don't eat or drink something you shouldn't. Don't hurt yourself or anyone else. I've got the camera feed on my phone and I will be watching. I've got the police on speed dial, Kate. You fuck up this time and I will call them myself. Understand?"

"Who is the man?" I say. "Remember? You said someone found us."

He exhales. "He's an investigative reporter. He's been taking photos and selling them. He's trying to find other things out about us. But he's going to go away now. I've taken care of it."

He's lying again. He's paying the man to scare me, to keep me trapped. "Can I see them? Can you show me the photos online?"

"Not right now," he says. "There are things you still don't understand, so you will just have to trust me." He rises and takes his plate to the sink. Then he gathers the knives in a container, carries the container outside, and puts it in the shed, which he locks. Back inside, he strides up the hall to his bedroom. When he returns he's dragging a small suitcase and wears his laptop bag strung from his shoulder.

"Do I need to lock you in your room while I'm gone?"

"No, I'll be good."

"You promise?"

"I won't go anywhere," I say. "I'll just work on the garden."

"Leave the door locked at night and when you are out. Do not open the house for anyone. You should be safe, but please be good, Kate. Look after Beau, make sure you feed him. If for any reason you find yourself off the property, stay away from the roads and the village." He nods up at the camera. "I'll be watching. Make sure you always have your keys on you."

"Don't worry, I'll be okay."

He pulls on a beanie and comes back over to the table. "Come on," he says. "Give me a kiss."

I stand and hug him, feeling the muscles of his back stiffen as he squeezes me, then kiss him, but he turns his head so my kiss lands at the corner of his mouth.

"Before I go, I need to see you take your pills, okay?" He takes the bottle from his pocket and taps a couple into his palm. "Open." He places them on my tongue. This time I swallow. He pokes his finger into my mouth, feeling inside my cheeks, under my tongue. "Good girl," he says, taking another two pills from the bottle and putting them on the counter. "Take these tomorrow."

"Sure."

"One more thing before I go." He reaches into his pocket and pulls out a mobile phone. A wafer-thin amalgamation of glass and aluminum. I find myself listing toward it, tempted to snatch it from his hands. A portal to the unseen digital world.

He drops my phone back into his pocket and walks to the front door. "You can have it when I get back, okay?" There he turns. "Lock this behind me." Then he is gone.

I stand alone in the house, the night closing in around me. I can feel the pills slowing everything down.

The evening brings wind, pressing the windowpanes; the storm rises. Rain lashes the husk of the house. The wind wails like a widow and the old structure creaks. Beau barks at first, and then is reduced to whimpering. Lightning flashes outside, followed instantly by a concussive thump of thunder. I think I hear horses galloping, though perhaps it is just a quirk of the storm. I reach under the couch and place my hand on Beau's back and find he's trembling. The storm could strike us all from the country. This thumb of land could be sent sliding into the sea. Somewhere among it all is the endless lolling of the waves. Always folding over themselves onto the shore. One wave coming in while another recedes and the rain drills down. Between the two waves they make an ever-widening grin, some dark thing laughing in the face of the girl in the wooden box up on the hill. There's a loud thump against my window. It's too loud to be a branch, I think, but I can't summon the courage to look outside. It could have been a stone or a fist.

"Come on, Beau," I say. "You can sleep on my bed tonight."

BEFORE

Twenty-six

The bathroom door wouldn't budge. I could hear the hurl and splash of someone vomiting, so I went outside and squatted down in the backyard beside a bush, hitching my dress up to my waist. Thom found me wandering back toward the house. The music throbbed. He took my hand and guided me along. Thom liked to keep me by his side at parties. I'd learned he didn't like it when random people, especially guys, spoke to me.

His friend Rick was speaking to someone about the police, yelling to be heard over the music. "They were just doing their job." A girl, one of Thom's friends, had been arrested and charged with urinating in public on her way to the party.

I leaned close to Thom's ear. "Be right back."

I wanted to get away from the noise. I headed for the back yard. People were dancing as I passed through the lounge, while others sat around playing a drinking game with cards.

It was awkward, just standing there. I spotted a girl I'd only met once before and asked her for a cigarette. Willow was at the same party, but so far I had managed to avoid her. The morning after the party in Elwood, I'd woken up to five messages from her. She texted me about how sorry and embarrassed she was, how she was never getting that drunk again and regretted ever hurting me. I deleted the messages without responding. All she had ever done was try to create tension between me and Thom and try to stop us from getting together. Now, months later, she'd stopped reaching out.

The girl with the cigarettes went back inside, leaving me alone with a group of guys standing in the dark. Those were the only times when I missed Willow. If she had been there, she might have broken the silence with something ironic or crude or funny. She might have drawn the guys' attention away from me. But she wasn't there. I reminded myself of what she'd done and realized she would never be there again.

The guys were quiet; some were watching me out of the corners of their eyes as they put their beer bottles to their mouths and tilted their heads back. The music spilled from inside, growing louder in gasps as the back door opened and closed. This was where things happened at parties. Not inside, but out on the fringes, the places between.

"Shit music," one of the guys said, and they all laughed together. They were older, I realized. I was used to seeing guys awkwardly trapped between the soft edges of boyhood and the vastness of adulthood, old enough to be at nightclubs yet most weekends standing about at high school parties.

I soon realized that they were talking in a sort of code, a language I couldn't follow with the alcohol swirling in my blood. I just stood there swaying, drawing on the cigarette. The night was fading. I would go back inside and kiss Thom, then ask him if we could leave.

"A lot of pretty guys here, if you know what I mean," one of them said.

I leaned closer to hear, then stumbled. My legs ached from dancing. A murmur of laughter.

"What about the pussy?" another asked. "It's everywhere— take your pick, boys."

A couple of them laughed louder now and looked at me, then back to each other. There was something about the way they looked: like hungry dogs. Then the shortest one, with a shaved head and a tight white T-shirt, reached for my hand. I gave it to him and he leaned forward and touched my knuckles with his lips. His friends snickered at his audacity.

"What's your name, girl?"

"Kate," I said. I took my hand back and pulled on the cigarette coolly; I was growing uncomfortable but I didn't want it to show. If I just walked away now it would be awkward.

"That's a nice name. *Kate*." He said it like he was savoring something sweet on his tongue. "You got any more cigarettes, *Kate*?"

"No," I said.

"Trying to quit?"

"No."

"Oh, so you're the type who always smokes men's cigarettes at bars, never have to buy your own, right?" He turned to his friends, his eyebrows raised. "Don't worry, I'm only teasing." He shuffled a little closer.

I took a last drag of the cigarette, then dropped it on the grass and stamped it beneath my shoe.

"So what are you doing after this? You heading out?"

"I don't think so. I'm going home soon."

The man's eyes cut to something behind me. Another gasp of

music from the house, then footsteps, and soon Thom's muscular arm was resting across my shoulders. I took most of his weight as he leaned in in a drunken stupor. "What's going on, Kate?" His words were slurred.

"Hey, brother," the short man said. "Dean." He held out his hand.

Thom looked at it, eyes narrowed. I could hear a car horn sound from out on the road. Laughter came from inside the house. The guys around us had stopped talking. At last Thom took the man's hand and gave it a firm pump.

"This your girl?"

"What does it look like?"

There was a shiver of movement among the others.

"Hey, Thom, it's fine, relax," I said.

"Don't tell me to relax."

"Listen to your girl, *Thom*. Relax before you hurt yourself."

I could feel him tense against me.

"Please?" I said. "It's fine."

He ripped his arm from across my shoulders. He looked confused for a second, then he looked angry again. "Why are you even out here, talking to these creeps?"

"Who you calling creeps, bro?" one of them said. The air was charged with an invisible electric current. Dean grinned and dropped his empty bottle. It chinked softly on the grass. He was clearly not afraid of Thom, despite Thom's height and size.

"I was just talking," I said.

"*Just talking.*" Thom's voice was stretched as though it were going to snap.

"Thom, don't," I said. I hated how needy my voice sounded. Why didn't he realize that I couldn't just order people not to talk to me? Didn't he see how unattractive his jealousy made him? How it pushed me away?

"Plenty of other options over here, you know, if you get sick of white rice." It was Dean. He was talking to me.

Thom didn't look away from me. The anger, the embarrassment, burned in his gaze.

"Please don't make a big deal."

"Shut up, Kate."

Dean twisted the cap off a fresh beer and took a long swig. He smacked his lips and said, "Has anyone ever told you, Thom, that you've got a really bad attitude?" He was still grinning. Murmurs from behind us were growing louder.

"You're acting like an asshole, Thom, let's just walk away," I said.

Thom gave me an ugly look, then turned his gaze back to Dean. "You can fucking have her," he said, loud and cruel. He pushed me in Dean's direction. "You deserve this scum," he told me.

I wanted to cry, could feel tears welling in my eyes.

"Fucking creeps," Thom said as he walked away. Then, a little louder, "Can't find girls their own age, that's their problem."

Dean strode past me. "What's that, tough guy?"

Thom's school friends had come outside by now; voices were rising in argument around me. But I barely noticed; I was watching Thom as he stormed inside.

"Fuck off and leave, right now," someone said to the older guys.

And then it was on: people pushing, grabbing each other, the dull thump of flesh being struck, and me in the middle of it all.

I heard girls shrieking; someone bumped into my back. I stumbled forward and then a full bottle of beer exploded against my skull.

AFTER
Twenty-seven

The first thing I notice when I open the curtains in the morning is the sea. Sets of waves are sweeping. They look like ripples up here but down by the beach those ripples would be tall snarling things, peeling along, folding into the estuary. There are a few surfers out, more than usual. Then I realize it's Saturday; the weekend crowd must be in town. The second thing I notice is the havoc wrought by the storm: leaves, branches, strewn across the flood-swept grass in the yard.

I dress and go straight down into the garden. The garden bed I was working on yesterday is flooded. The green shoots that were beginning to sprout are leaning with their tiny roots exposed. The trellis against the fence for the tomatoes has blown over. Beau is sniffing at something down near the base of the ladder leaning against the house.

"What is it, boy?" My shoes squelch as I walk over to see.

At the tip of Beau's snout a soaked fantail lies with its feet curled, its feathers matted and head back like a drowned infant. It must have hit the window last night. I take the spade and dig into the wet soil. When I have opened a square of earth, I flip the fantail's limp body into it, then turn the dirt back over.

I'm conscious of the camera in the yard, so I walk slowly, with Beau at my side, toward the back of the block. The door of the shed won't open; I shake it, but it won't budge. I slam the head of the spade against it, turning back and looking up at the camera as if it might remonstrate me. The door still does not give. *What is he keeping in there?*

He said that if I was good, he would return my phone. In my desperation, I wanted to trust him. With my phone, I may be able to access the Internet and I could finally learn the truth. Of course, the online world is not without its dangers. Do you know what it is like to have a sex tape out there in the world? For a while, anyone could see every part of me; they could see how far up my legs those scars reached, and there was nothing I could do about it. Despite what Jim says, I know that once something has been on the Internet, it will always exist somewhere. The Internet is everywhere. I never thought I would be without it, but that was before he dragged me here.

Everything was different back home. I had Thom, Willow, and my dad. The thought of everything I have lost drains me.

I gnaw at my thumbnail, trying to decide what to do. I will never have a better opportunity to escape. I run back inside to my room. I quickly jam more clothes into my escape bag, remembering how cold I was when I tried to hitchhike. Is it possible he is watching the cameras right now? I leave the bag in my room.

I open the front door to check that the coast is clear. Up beside the mouth of the driveway a white sedan sits. From inside, the barrel shape of a camera lens is aimed toward me. I slam the door and lock it. It's the man in black; it has to be. He's still here.

Of course Jim has a plan B for if I don't stay inside. He would never leave me here alone unless he knew someone would be watching me. The man is not a reporter at all, he's a guard, a co-conspirator Jim has paid to make sure I don't go anywhere. How can Jim trust him? This man knows that I am alone in the house. . . .

I am startled by a knock at the door.

Beau leaps up from his bed, barking. He rushes to the door and hurls himself up against it, scratching with his paws. My heart pounding, I listen as whoever is out there tries the door handle and finds it locked. I hear footsteps receding up the driveway.

It must be the man, but then again, he knows I am here, why would he knock? I go to peer out the kitchen window. No one is there. Whoever it was has gone.

I eat lunch quickly and feed Beau, then I place the pills in my mouth in front of the camera for Jim to see. Immediately after I go to the bathroom, where I spit them into the toilet. The rain may hold off and if the man wasn't out there I could run, I could try the highway again. I open the door to check for his car at the road, finding something on the doormat. A note is scribbled on the back of a petrol receipt.

> *Hey, Evie, sorry I missed you! Heading out for a ride and wondered if you wanted to meet the horses. Otherwise, we're having a barbecue later if you're free. I've got good news and Mum would love to see you again, so I hope you can come by.*
> *Iso*

Iso has "good news." My pulse quickens; could it be a letter from home? I need to get down there. There is no sign of the man in black up at the road. I print a message in large letters and position it in front of the camera in the kitchen.

Beau is desperate for a walk. Won't be long. Will be careful.

I put the leash on an excited Beau, step out the front door, and head up the driveway.

Beau pulls me along, sniffing at the grass. I reach the road and begin down the hill. Somewhere a car door opens and thunks closed. "Kate," a voice says. *Kate.* I turn back. The man in black is rushing down toward me with his phone held out, a camera strung about his neck. *Where did he come from?*

"Kate," he is saying. "Kate, slow down." *Kate . . . not Evie.* His accent is Australian.

I begin to run, Beau streaking.

A car engine starts up behind me and the car accelerates past, then swings in against the curb, blocking my path. The man climbs out.

"Kate, please stop," he says. "I just want to talk to you for a minute."

Beau is growling, his body rigid.

"Kate, did you kill him?"

I look him in the eye before I can stop myself. There's a sudden movement at the side of the road and from my periphery I see someone leap over the fence. Another follows. It's the boys who threw stones.

"I can get your story out, give everyone the truth. The public wants to know."

"Leave her alone, cunt." The tallest boy shoves the man hard against his car.

The man looks at me. "What is this?"

I dip my head to avoid his gaze and walk around them, continuing down the hill, dragging Beau behind me.

"That's assault," I hear. "You can't touch me."

I hear something hit the ground—maybe the man's phone.

"I'm calling the police."

"Call the pigs, see if we give a shit. Fuck off and do it some-where else, though."

"Where are your parents?"

I just keep walking quickly with my heart thrumming. The car starts again. It zips past me. I hear the boys running down the hill and I brace myself. They pass me and hurl stones but the car is already rounding the bend.

"Hey, lady," they're calling.

I don't stop.

"Hey, lady—you all good?"

Someone touches my shoulder. I shrink away. My hair has grown a little but I wonder if they remember the harsh words they spat at me when my head was bare. Beau turns back and jumps up on one of the boys, who strokes his head. "Here, you dropped these."

I take the keys from his hands. When I meet his eyes, I see warmth, but I can't forget all the nasty words.

"Just tell him to fuck off next time. Fucking *palangi* bastard." He screws up his face like he's bitten into a lemon.

"Thanks," I say. "I will."

Beau is reluctant to leave, nuzzling the boys. *Traitor.*

At last I'm able to drag him away and continue toward Iso's place. *Kate, did you kill him?* Jim could have paid him to scare me, to make me believe that I'm guilty. Jim's book said scientists asked questions rather than making statements to manipulate memory.

When I'm near Iso's house I stop and stand on the road, trying to balance my thoughts and calm my body. *Did you kill him?*

Passing through the gate at Iso's, I walk down the long, muddy track that is the driveway. As I approach the house there's no sign that anyone is home.

"Hey." Iso's voice comes from the vegetable garden behind the retaining wall. "Is that you, Evie?"

"Hi," I say. "I got your note."

Beau pulls at the leash. I reach down to unclip him and the dog rushes forward, sniffing at the earth. Iso squats down and scratches behind Beau's ears, letting the dog lick his face.

"So," I say, too impatient to wait. "You said you had good news. Did you get a letter for me?"

His face goes blank. "No," he says, frowning. "No mail on the weekend, and didn't you only just send your letter?" Of course it would take more than a day—why did I let myself become hopeful? He plunges his trowel into the dark soil and changes the subject. "I'm just waiting for Mum to get back and then I'm going to take the horses for a walk."

"Well, what was the good news?" I demand.

"You said you wanted to go up to Auckland, right? I'm going to be heading that way on Monday if you want a ride."

That was only two days away. That's all. If I waited two days I could get a ride with someone I knew, someone who might pull over and help me if I had a panic attack. I smile. "Thanks, Iso. That would be really great."

"Well, I'll pick you up after lunchtime on Monday, if that suits."

"No," I say. "No, don't pick me up. I'll meet you down here."

He shrugs. "Well, that works too. So are you coming for a ride today?"

"A ride?"

"Yeah, on the horses. You could use Mum's saddle." He scratches his head, indecisive suddenly. "I suppose it would be all right for you?"

All right for me? His mum must have told him about the panic attack in her car. "Well, I've never really ridden a horse before. I mean, I rode like two times when I was a kid."

"You'll have to wear a helmet and be careful." He seems reluctant now. "I'm sure it'll be safe. Mum's old hack is perfect for beginners."

"Sounds good," I say.

"Great." He brushes the dirt from his hands, takes a mobile phone out of his pocket, and fires off a text message. I could ask now to use his phone, but Jim made it clear it is all traceable. "Just checking in with Mum," he says, "to see how far off she is."

We chat as he continues working in the garden.

"Your mum respond yet?" I ask.

I note the guilty shift of his eyes as he looks up at me. "Nah, not yet."

Soon Iso's mum pulls into the driveway. As she climbs out of the car, Iso gestures for me to get in.

"Hello again, Evie," she says.

"Hi."

"We're just heading over to the horses, Mum. We'll be back later."

"All right, see you then."

"Is it okay if Beau stays in the yard?" I ask.

"He'll be fine," Iso says, then to his mum, "Can you keep an eye on him?"

He wheels the car around and we set out.

We're not far from Maketu when the asphalt becomes gravel, which doesn't slow Iso down. The wheels flick up stones and the car bumps along. Soon we arrive at a farm, turning down a muddy track that runs between two empty paddocks, and at the end of it there's a long wooden shed. Nearby a chimney stands, like a solitary finger pointed at the sky. There's not much left of the house to which it once must have belonged.

Near the shed I can see three horses, two gray and one the color of a coffee bean. I recognize the smaller of the grays from a photo I saw at Iso's house.

Iso moves in and out of the shed fetching what we'll need for the ride. When the saddles are ready on the fence, one with a helmet for me balanced on top, he produces two halters and hands me one of them. "Like this," he says, concealing the halter behind his back. I do as he says and then we set off across the lush paddock.

"Are they friendly?" I ask.

"Yeah, really friendly," he says, reaching down to tug at a thatch of grass. He extends his palm with the grass on it and walks toward the horses. They watch him approach, curious. The brown horse comes forward first.

In the midday sun, I can see the veins in Iso's arms, the cords of muscle. He is wearing a singlet and his hair is knotted, falling in thick ringlets about his head. He worries the steel bit of the halter with his fingers.

"How old are you?" I ask.

"Twenty," he says. "Why?"

"I don't know—I thought maybe you were older."

He turns back with a grin. "Gee, thanks."

I could almost feel happy but there is something grinding within me, knowing I am going to have questions to answer when Jim returns. Watching through the cameras, is he wondering where I am? Where is he? Will he be angry that I went out when it wasn't an emergency?

The brown horse sniffs Iso's hand. It curls its lips back from its teeth and nibbles the grass. Iso works the halter up over the horse's head, running his fingers to the flat of its nose between the eyes. "Good boy." He strokes the docile beast's neck lovingly, then leads the horse away and ties it up to the rail running along beside the shed. I stand still as the other two horses approach and crowd around me. My breathing must be loud, or maybe Iso senses my rising panic, because when I look over he is striding toward me. He takes my halter and quickly guides his hand up the larger gray horse's neck. He passes the lead rope to me.

When I walk, the horse follows close behind. I keep looking back, anxious that it might decide to run over the top of me, but it just stares straight ahead passively. I begin to breathe more easily.

Iso saddles the horses. Mine is called Cracker, he tells me. I'm relieved to note that Cracker is as still and compliant as a tree stump. Iso doesn't even tie him up once the saddle is cinched on. I put on the helmet. Even after I've tightened the chin strap it feels loose. The extra space would normally be filled by hair, I suppose.

"All right," Iso says. "It's like riding a bike but easier." He points to the reins. "Pull this side and he'll turn left; pull the other side and he'll go right. Pull back to slow him down, dig your heels into his sides to make him go faster. Easy enough?"

"Okay," I say. "Just don't let him run or anything."

"You'll be fine." He crouches down and makes a cradle out of his hands for me to step on. "Hold my shoulder if you want." I do. I feel the tense ball of muscle. I put my foot on his hands and he stands, lifting me up. "Get your leg over."

When I do the horse walks a few steps. My pulse is uneven. It's not like when I rode a pony as a child; I feel much higher up now.

"It's okay," Iso says, taking the bridle. The saddle squelches beneath me. "Pull on the reins." I do and the horse stops moving.

Iso puts one foot in his stirrup and swings his other leg over his horse's broad back, and soon enough he is leading us along the muddy track out toward the road. Cracker's spine rolls beneath my hips. As we ride along, the track at the gate becomes gravel beneath us, then farther still the road becomes asphalt. Iso points out landmarks, things he remembers from his childhood, like the spot where a passing car beeped at them and his horse, spooked, threw him off onto the shoulder of the road. He broke his collarbone, he recalls—a fact that does little to abate the panic that's growing in me. When cars pass, most with blacked-out windows, their mufflers emitting a sonorous thrum, Iso raises his hand and nods to each one.

We pass a burned-out house. Licks of black creep up the rotting weatherboards. One wall has collapsed, leaving the interior exposed. Roof tiles have detonated on the concrete. Inside, the walls are covered in red graffiti.

"Tiri's old spot," he says. I watch it as we pass.

"What happened? Was there a fire?" I ask.

"Yep. It changed a lot of lives, that fire." Iso continues as if he can anticipate my next question. "My old man died there when I was young."

You never truly understand about death until you meet it head-on for the first time. It's a foreign thing, like a war in some place you've never been. When you are introduced, suddenly you think about life, you think about a body rotting in the ground, and all you want to know is: what comes next? I met death earlier than most. On occasion, I can't help but think about how different my life might be now if Mum didn't die. I understand then that Iso is the same as me. Perhaps that's why I thought he was older. When you only have one parent you grow up twice as fast.

"He was a paramedic and was driving home when he saw the fire. Mum raised me alone from the time I was eleven."

"I'm really sorry, Iso."

"Not your fault. It's probably the reason Tiri and I are so close." I recall the scars climbing up over her collarbone and neck.

"Did he save her?"

"Yeah. He couldn't save her sister, though. He ran back in and neither of them came out."

We ride on in silence but for the clip-clop of hooves and the distant boom of the surf. A shed comes up on our left, bare wood with patches of flaking white paint. The windows and doors are open like the eyes and mouth of a screaming face.

"We found a hanged sheep in there once. Someone must have dragged it in from the paddock and strung it up. I know people wrangle and pinch them for meat, but some of these kids just do shit for the fun of it."

I see Thom's face again in a passing car. When I go to speak, the words are trapped in my throat. I'm trembling, so I focus on my breathing.

We start to wind downhill. The helmet scratches the stubble on my scalp. The road is lined with native ferns in thousands of shades of green. There is no longer a shoulder next to the road as the scene opens up to a view of a sweeping river mouth and flat peninsula, so we ride single file on the edge of the asphalt. Fortunately, only a couple of cars pass us as we descend. When the road levels out we leave the asphalt and ride through a campsite to the beach. Seagulls swirl above.

We're on the sand now. I don't bother using the reins; Cracker moves of his own accord, as if he knows where he's going.

"Iso," I say, once again feeling rather than thinking I can trust him. Perhaps he's the only person left who I can trust. I need him to side with me, to not tell Jim my plans to leave. "Can you keep a secret?"

"What secret?" he asks warily.

"Promise me you won't tell anyone?"

He turns his head to me, raises his hand to block out the sun. "I don't know if I want to get involved in this."

"Involved in what?"

He grimaces slightly. "Look, your uncle asked us to watch over you, to make sure you don't do anything to put yourself in harm's way."

"What?"

"I figure you're going to do what you want anyway, so I don't mind telling you."

"I'm not hurting myself—he's hurting me!" Now I'm regretting the urge to confide in him.

Iso frowns. "How old are you, Evie?"

"Seventeen."

"Right," he says. "Well, I don't know the full story, but I have the impression that he cares about you and just wants to look after you. If that's not the case, then you should say so."

Jim is playing his games; he has gotten into Iso's head.

"What exactly did he tell you when you came to the house?"

"I've said my bit, Evie. I don't think I should say any more." He's clearly uncomfortable now. His frown deepens. "Come on, up here," he says.

We turn up a steep set of steps. Iso leans forward, and his

horse blows out its breath, then quickly mounts the rise to the beaten dirt of the car park.

"Lean over his head and dig in your heels," Iso calls.

I feel the horse lurch forward when my feet touch his ribs.

We cross the car park, then start up the steep road. I realize we are heading back through Maketu. A pair of old women sit at the top of the track and farther along a few kids wait, leaning up against an old shed with their BMX bikes. The iron roof is rusted and peels up like the cover of a well-thumbed paperback.

"Please tell me what my uncle said, Iso. I won't let him know you told me."

"It's not about telling. The way he put it, it'd be dangerous for me to involve myself."

"Dangerous?" I say, anger coming on hot and quick. "Dangerous how?"

"I don't know. Look, if you want to come to Auckland with me, I'll take you, but only if your uncle says it's okay."

"I need to get back to Australia, Iso," I say desperately. "I need to get home to the people who love and care for me. That's why I need you to take me to Auckland with you. I can get money, I can pay you."

"It's not about money, Evie." Iso stares in silence at his hands crossed over the saddle horn. Then, as if remembering something, he abruptly pats his pockets. "Shit," he says.

"What?"

"Oh, it's nothing. I left my phone in the car."

"Are you expecting a call?"

"Nothing like that," he says. "Look, why don't you just ask your uncle to take you home?"

I nod, focusing to keep the tears from coming. "He said we

were going on a holiday, then he brought me here." I hesitate; I only need to tell him enough to keep him from going to Jim, but not so much that he involves the police. "He doesn't let me out at night. He lies to me about what is happening back home, saying people are trying to find me to lock me up...." I stop. I'm in dangerous territory, edging too close to the truth. "He didn't want to bring us any attention. All I'm asking is if you are going to Auckland, you have to let me come with you. I promise you I'm telling the truth. He's been taking away my freedom bit by bit. I'm almost an adult now."

"Jesus, Evie. That's full-on. Why don't you go to the police? I can take you down there."

"No," I say, realizing how quickly my plans could backfire.

"Why not?"

"I can't—" Deep breath in, slow exhale. "I can't tell you that. We can't involve the police."

"Well," he says, clearing his throat. "What do you want me to say, Evie?"

I don't speak again. If I tell him the truth, or what I know to be true, he could do his own research; he might side with Jim, or worse, go directly to the police. If I can just get him to trust me, he will take me to Auckland. I don't need to tell him everything, just enough.

We continue along the road in silence. Back at the stable, Iso dismounts, then helps me off Cracker. I slide from the saddle and he holds my hips as I land on the soft grass. We are so close. I'm gripping his forearms. But Iso is already looking away. He scrubs his palms on the front of his thighs, then quickly takes Cracker by the reins and leads both the horses away toward the paddock. I twist my bottom lip between my teeth to feel the pain. How long have we been riding for? A couple of hours at least?

When Iso has put all the gear away we get back in the car. Before turning the key, Iso opens the glove box, lifts out a charger and a book, and finally locates his phone. It's so tempting to ask if I can use it for a moment, but according to Jim, one Google search could undo everything.

At the gate, he leaves the car idling as he steps out to open it. I notice a wallet sitting in the center console. He comes back, drives through, then climbs out to close it again. The second he gets out I snatch the wallet. Opening it, I see colorful cards. A coffee loyalty card littered with stamps. His driver's license. He is reaching for the door. I find a credit card. *Don't hesitate.* I shove it into my pocket, tossing the wallet back as he slides into the driver's seat.

"It's not my business, Evie. But you *can* do something if he is hurting you. There are options other than the police. There are youth and family centers." He doesn't say it but I read between the lines: *who will end up going to the police if you are telling the truth.* He holds the steering wheel in one hand and eases the car down the gravel track. "I don't understand what's stopping you."

I ask myself the same question all the time. Part of it is Jim. I don't want to be wrong. If Jim is telling me the truth, then I can't go back to my old life and I definitely can't go to the police.

"No. It's fine."

"Well, are you going to stick around for the barbecue?"

"Yeah," I say. "Okay, I'll come."

Beau races up and down the yard yapping at Iso's car as we bump along the driveway. When I get out and go to him, he leaps up in a frenzy, licking my fingers.

I leave him out in the yard and head inside. I'm once again

drawn to the photos lining the hall. There's the photo of Iso with the fish, and the one where he's holding hands with his dad. . . . And I see another photo that my eyes passed over last time. Iso is a child and beside him there is a younger boy. My heart almost stops. I have seen this photo somewhere before—but not here. The boy, I'm certain, is Thom.

"Evie," Iso calls from the end of the hall. "What are you doing?"

I look again at Thom's face, the sprinkle of freckles, the wide grin. It's him. I know it. And yet at the same time, I know it isn't. It can't be.

"Iso," I say, trying to keep my voice steady, "who is this?"

He walks back down the hall and leans in close, peering at the photo. "That's Stan, my cousin from Waihi." Then he glides past me back toward the kitchen. I pull myself away and head up the hall.

At the kitchen counter, Iso is dragging a knife through sausage links. He looks up with an inquisitive gleam in his blue eyes.

"So how did you like horse riding? Easy as pie, eh?"

"Yeah, it was fun. Thanks for taking me along."

He checks his mobile phone, sitting on the counter in front of him. "Mum's just at the shop getting stuff for a salad. If you want anything special let me know and I'll buzz her."

When I look up at him in his ripped singlet and board shorts, his arms lean and muscular, I feel I am intruding on something. That strange day comes back to me when I attempted to hitch-hike. When his mother stopped to pick me up, she already knew that I was Evie. *What else does she know?*

"Are you sure it's okay if I hang around?"

"Of course. There'll be a couple of others coming by later." Iso is rooting around for aluminum foil in a cupboard.

"Others?"

"Yeah, just a couple of mates."

"Um, okay." I could leave but then the man in black is still out there somewhere.

"You're in for a real treat, Evie. It's not every day I bust out my famous grilled snapper. Caught it early this morning."

I'm making an effort with Iso; he's the closest thing to a friend I've got. "I'm looking forward to it."

"So why's your, ah"—he pauses, scratches the back of his head—"your uncle out of town anyway?"

I hold my house keys in my hand, a habit I have when I'm nervous. I stare at him. "How did you know that?"

"What?" His gaze is fixed on the aluminum foil.

"I said how did you know that? How did you know he was out of town? I didn't tell you that."

He looks up at me. "Tiriana. She said she thought she saw him leaving town." He's a terrible liar, his eyes shifty, his teeth chewing at his bottom lip.

"Did she?" Jim left late last night. How could she have seen him?

Iso swallows, rubs the hollow behind his left ear. "Yeah, she said something."

The front door creaks open. "Hello." The gravelly voice of Donna. "Are you home?"

"In the kitchen."

Donna comes down the hall toward us, smiling. She holds up a bag of salad mix and says to Iso, "I got this. Hope it's enough. I can add a few tomatoes from the garden."

She turns her attention to me. "How was the ride, Evie?" Her smile is a nose wrinkle.

I force myself to smile back. "It was fun."

"Good," she says. "Good."

I follow Iso outside under the veranda beside the backyard,

where he sparks the barbecue. Sitting close by on a plastic chair, I watch him scrape the grill. Beau approaches and rests his head on my lap.

Over my shoulder, the view from the lawn makes me forget where we are; from here you could believe it really is paradise. Although it's not as high up as our place, the view extends further along the bay, deep blue with white veins where the waves break. There's a tree at the corner of the yard with low, spreading branches. It looks like a good sitting tree.

Iso drops a whole snapper on the barbecue and a platoon of sausages. He opens a package of lamb chops he had taken from the fridge and, using tongs, sets them on the grill one at a time.

When I walk down to the tree Beau follows me. I grip the lowest branch to heave myself up, then clamber through the limbs to a higher branch. There I sit and look out over the bay.

"Evie," I hear Iso call hesitantly. I turn back to him. Still holding the tongs, he has stepped away from the barbecue. "Are you ... you're okay up there?"

"I'll be down in a sec."

Monday. I can leave with Iso on Monday. It occurs to me that this might be another trick, that under Jim's instruction Iso will take me somewhere else, but what choice do I have?

Iso's friends start to arrive—two guys and a girl who seem about Iso's age—and I climb down from the tree and walk back up the lawn to join them.

They introduce themselves, Steve, Anaru, and Leah. Steve drags over three more white plastic chairs.

"Want a drink, Evie?" It's Anaru. He has a wetsuit draped over his shoulder; the arms and torso drip down his sweater.

"I'm okay."

He opens a beer for himself and one for Leah, before walking to the clothesline and folding his wetsuit over it.

"So how long you in town for, Evie?" Leah asks.

"Oh, I live here now."

"Cool. We're over near Pukehina, about twenty minutes away," Anaru says.

For the first time since we arrived almost a month ago, I feel close to normal.

Iso is still turning the sausages on the barbecue and Donna carries a bowl of salad over, setting it down on the wooden table. I hear the gate open and close, then Tiriana comes around the corner of the house. Beau rushes over to greet her. I can see the scars on her throat, pink and gnarled, yet with her green eyes and black hair, there is something beautiful about her. I squeeze the cuffs of my hoodie in my fists.

Beau sniffs at her heels, at the extra sausages she carries in her hands. "Sorry I'm late. Couldn't find anyone to cover at the shop."

"No worries. Help yourself to a drink."

Tiriana pours a few fingers of Jim Beam into a glass and tops it up with Coke. She takes a seat beside me. "Hey, Evie, I heard you went riding today. Iso texted me and said you were a natural."

I blush. "I don't know about that. It was quite scary actually."

Holding her cigarette in one hand, Tiriana reaches down to stroke Beau's head with the other. Beau ignores her and everyone else, focusing only on Anaru, who has taken a sausage from the grill and wrapped it in a piece of bread and is eating it.

"Dig in," Iso says, putting all the meat out on the table now. We each grab a plate and load them up. I only take a little of the salad, one of the lamb chops. I'm not feeling all that hungry.

Iso piles his plate up last, sits down, and pops another beer bottle before taking a long drink, his eyes on the sun descending behind the moss-colored hills. Heads turn. For a few seconds, we watch in silence.

"Not a bad view, eh?" Anaru says.

"It's really pretty," I say.

Iso pulls his phone out. "Speaking of which, take a peek at this." He passes his phone around and each of them looks down at it. "Oh, wow," one of them says, eyes cutting toward me. When Tiriana hands me the phone, I see myself silhouetted by the descending sun flaming through the clouds. I'm sitting way up in the tree and the bay sweeps out beneath me. I could be a boy with my strong legs, my hair short, the hoodie hanging loose from my body. I delete the photo and hand the phone back to Iso.

"Don't take photos of me," I say quietly, looking him in the eye.

No one speaks for a moment.

The glow of the sun is waning beyond the hills like an ember knocked from a fire, as dusk softens the edges of the day. Iso lights the steel brazier and we all turn as the back door closes. A guy with clippered hair and gray unfriendly eyes saunters toward us, carrying a couple of bottles of beer by their necks.

"Mick," Iso calls. "You made it. You know everyone, I think. Oh—this is Evie."

When the man shakes my hand, he narrows his eyes and leans in closer. "Did you go to Ohope?" he asks.

What is Ohope? "Me?"

"Yeah, where did you go to school?"

"Oh, no. I'm from Melbourne," I say.

"Far out, the big smoke, eh?" He shakes his head, taking a plate. "I know you from somewhere, though. I'm sure I've seen you before."

I shift in my seat, staring down at the grass. *They'll find you.*

The bag in the bottom of my wardrobe seems so far away now. I will never outrun what Thom and I did. Jim took all the sharp objects, anything I could defend myself with, but not the ax. Despite the heat emanating from the brazier, I am suddenly cold. I wrap my arms around myself.

"Uh, I don't know, I haven't been here long." I can feel my cheeks burning.

"You used to have long hair, right?"

A pulse of fear runs down my back. "No." Within hours of arriving in Maketu I was bald. That was—what?—four weeks ago, I realize. "It's always been short."

Whiskers poke through beneath his long pink-tipped nose. "Maybe it was someone else. She looked exactly like you, though." He dips his head but I catch his sly grin.

"You're a tripper, man," one of the other guys says.

"So why'd you leave Melbourne?" It's Mick again.

Everyone falls silent. I find myself scowling at him. He takes a lamb chop and pulls the meat away with his teeth.

"We wanted a change."

He doesn't wait to swallow before speaking again. "A change, huh?"

Can they hear my heart, see the pulse in my neck? I count my breaths slowly in and slowly out.

Mick is looking down at his phone.

I still have food on my plate, but I can't eat for the foaming anxiety in my gut.

The others begin chatting and laughing, teasing each other. Iso rocks back with his empty plate in his lap and the legs of his white plastic chair bow beneath him.

Donna is busy with her hands and I realize she is rolling a joint. I put my plate down, thinking about running away, but I stay still, with Beau at my feet. Iso tosses him half a sausage and Beau snaps it out of the air. Mick is still staring at his phone, his lips curving in a nasty smile.

"I've been wanting to get one of those," Iso says, reaching over and touching the key ring I'm fiddling with. "Expensive for what they are, though."

"What?"

He takes the keys from my hands and holds the key ring between his thumb and forefinger. I notice it is slightly thicker at one point. "This thing, here?"

"What is it?" Mick asks, slipping his phone back into his pocket.

Iso tosses my keys to him. "That has a chip in it that tracks movement. You pair it with a phone and it has all sorts of settings. I was looking at getting a couple and embedding one in the tail of my surfboard to see how far I paddle and how fast I move along the wave. But some people put them in their car so if it gets stolen they can track it. That sort of thing. Pretty handy really."

My stomach sinks. Jim is one step ahead again. "Just going to the bathroom," I manage to gasp. It comes on quickly, that fizzing rush. I just make it to the toilet in time. Lurching forward, I aim the spray of vomit into the bowl. It rocks me, leaching my energy and throwing my stomach into jolting spasms.

When the nausea passes, I splash water on my face. I can't go back out there. I think about running but I can't leave Beau behind.

He has my keys.

When I return to the table, Mick has Beau on his lap. He watches me take my seat again.

"Can I have my keys?" My words slur. I blink.

"What?"

"My keys?"

"Where did I put them?" Mick pats his pockets. "I must have dropped them."

"Please," I say, willing my voice to stay steady.

"Oh," he says, pulling them from his pocket. "Here they are." He tosses them to me and continues stroking Beau.

"Jesus," Donna says, rising. The herby tang of pot floats on the air. "Evie, you don't look so good." She touches my back and my skin crawls, my shoulder blades rise. Her eyes are half closed.

Someone presses a glass of water into my hands. I take it and sip. Jim was right, as usual. I should have stayed home. I should never have come here. The joint comes around to me and I take a small puff, hoping it will quell the panic.

I rise on unsteady feet. Everyone is watching me but there is something loaded in their looks. I find Beau's lead on the grass and clip it to his collar. "I think I might go. I need to get home and lie down."

"I'll give you a lift, if you like." It's Mick again. *He knows.*

I shake my head.

"Are you sure you don't need a ride?" Donna asks. "I'll run you back home myself."

"No, it's fine. Come on, Beau."

"We'll see you again soon, doll."

"Let me know about Monday, Evie," Iso calls.

I look back at him, trying to decipher the expression in his eyes. Eyebrows angled upward; kind, open face.

"Sure," I say.

As soon as I'm out of sight around the side of the house I quicken my stride, almost stumbling in my haste, up the driveway to the road. I have only moonlight to see by until I reach the bottom of Iso's road near the beach, where the streetlights glow. The keys I hold firm in my hand. He has always known where I've been. I wonder if Jim is watching me now, if I'm a dot on a map that he can follow.

I start up the hill toward the house. The incline is easier now than when I first arrived. I'm fitter and stronger, but still the anxiety burns in my gut and the cold crawls over my hands and face. I try to keep the pace up, reminded of the park, *the spot* near Thom's house. Those nights I walked home and my dad told me to take the long way unless I was with Thom. Dad would know what to do, he would know exactly how to escape. *Don't cut through the park; it's not safe for a girl to walk alone.* His warning drew to mind images of grown men waiting in the shadows. There had been *incidents* there. A team of football players drinking at night and a teenage girl. There were no CCTV cameras and no security. Her word against theirs. I had cut through the park a lot, but always walking quickly, my pulse fluttering. Never looking back. I think of this as I climb the hill in the darkness. A car approaches from behind but I don't look over my shoulder. I sense eyes staring out the window as it draws alongside and slows a little. Eventually it creeps past and disappears around the bend.

I imagine Mick, with his sly grin, showing everyone his phone. I'm sure he has found the video of me and Thom. Soon enough the whole town will know.

I can hear the harsh strain of air rushing into my lungs, the thrumming pulse in my chest. Inside, I sink down on my heels and Beau leaps up against me as if to hug me, as if to say, *It will all be okay.*

Twenty-eight

scratching sound in the night. It's coming from up on the roof. Down below, twigs snap. The sounds are amplified by the stillness within the house. Then comes a knock at the door. My heart leaps up into my throat. Beau barks.

I wait in the stillness, holding my breath. Two more firm taps echo through the house.

"Hello?" someone calls. Beau's barking grows louder. "Hello? Evie, are you in there?" It is a woman's voice.

I climb out of bed silently, my thighs aching from the horse ride. I inch toward the front door, leaving the lights off. My body quakes with the cold.

When I get to the kitchen, I scissor open the blinds and peer outside.

The shape by the front door is stooped, with dark hair, hooded eyes, and a pale stare. The eyes turn on me; I am frozen to the spot. My hands tremble and blood thrums at my temples. The figure smiles. "Evie," she says, her voice thick with booze.

"What do you want?" My own voice is high.

She lifts something up. "It's me," the figure says, too loud. "Tiriana?"

"Open up, girl, it's chilly out here. I brought you leftovers."

With Beau pressed against my leg, I open the front door.

Tiriana is on the doorstep. "What took you so long?"

"I didn't know who it was."

"It's all good," she says with a sniff. The stink of alcohol fills the room; she must have just finished up drinking at Iso's. She holds up the plastic bag. "I brought some sausages and snapper— you hardly ate anything tonight."

"Thank you," I say. "But I'm not really hungry."

Her face seems to fall with disappointment. "Well, you can heat it up for breakfast then." She hands it to me.

"How did you know where I live?" I demand.

Her head tilts to the side. "You told me, when you arrived. The lodge. Remember?" She looks about the interior of the house from the doorstep with a grin. "Looks a bit different in here these days."

I glance back toward the oven. "It's almost midnight."

If Jim were here, with his rifle, what would have happened?

"Oh, not so late for a Saturday night. Can I come in?"

"I was in bed."

She nods, puffs out her cheeks. "I see. Well, I'll get out of your hair then. Just thought I'd say hi. Iso said your uncle was out of town and I thought you might want some company."

"Iso told you that Jim was out of town?" My stomach heaves. Either Iso is lying or Tiri is.

She takes a step forward and my fingers itch for the safety of the ax behind the door. Almost unconsciously I find myself stepping toward it.

"I think I want you to go now." Beau is tense beside me. "Please."

Tiriana's eyes move from my face to Beau, then back to me. She stands for a few heartbeats longer. "Yeah," she says, her demeanor becoming dark. "If that's what you want." She turns and walks away on unsteady legs.

I close and lock the door behind her, then watch from the kitchen as she walks up the driveway. She turns back once to look down at the house, pausing before continuing on.

I wake early the next morning. Last night, lying there in the darkness and hugging Beau against me, I was so scared it's a wonder I managed to get to sleep at all.

I feed Beau, then go to the front door, opening it a fraction to peer up toward the road. The coast looks clear. I walk up the driveway and check the mail. There is nothing but a square of paper with no message, only an image. My face. My dark brown hair, still long, pulled over my shoulder. My hazelnut eyes glazed with a drunk detachment. My skinny body nude. It's a still from the sex tape. I know at once who must have put it there: Iso's friend Mick. He was so certain he recognized me. And if he was able to find this image, it means he must have known what to search for. He must know my real name. Jim will fix this, but I can't trust him, I can't trust anything he says.

I look up and down the street. At first I think it's deserted, then I spy a small head poking out from the bus shelter. *Awhina.*

Her head withdraws as I start to walk toward her.

"Hello," I say when I reach her. "How are you, Awhina?" I squat on my haunches so that I am at her eye level. Her brown eyes settle on mine.

"Good," she says.

It's Sunday. No school today. "What are you doing in here so early?"

She shrugs, twisting her slim body like a ribbon.

"Hey, Awhina, did you see someone put something in my letterbox?"

"When?"

"I don't know—since you've been here."

She shakes her head. "I've got to go home."

"No," I say. "You don't have to. Your dad hurt you, right?"

The child looks uncertain.

"What if I told you that I could make sure he never hurt you again?"

Children are perceptive, I know that, but Awhina's face changes. It is filled with such skepticism that my heart sinks.

"It's true," I insist. "I could help you so he never hurts you." I remember the man holding her up on his shoulders at the park. Was it delight or terror on her face?

"Do you want to see my house?"

The girl looks past me to the street. "I'm going to go home now."

"Don't be shy, Awhina."

"I'm not. I just want to go home."

"I have a dog," I say. "Did you see him? He's cute."

"No."

"Do you want to meet my dog? His name's Beau. I could make you a hot chocolate and you could pet him."

She bites her bottom lip.

"Or maybe," I say with an encouraging smile, "you want me to piggyback you?"

Again the child doesn't speak.

"Come on, Awhina," I say, turning to present my back to her. "On you get."

Obediently, the girl stands up on the seat and puts her arms around my shoulders. I take her legs in my hands and rise with straining calves. Her head rests against the base of my neck.

"Where are you taking me?" she asks.

"Just to meet my dog, Beau, that's all."

She tightens her grip.

I carry her down the driveway. On the doorstep, I free one leg to open the door and she squirms. "Hold tight." I step through the door into the house. I place her onto a stool and she releases her grip. Beau rubs up against my leg, then rests his head in the child's lap, and she squeals with delight.

I remember the photo in my pocket. I take the box of matches from beside the fireplace and in the bathroom I light the corner of the image, holding it angled away from my hand. The flame creeps up, consuming the picture, flaring the shadows in the mirror. I can hear Awhina's laughter. I drop the photo, almost entirely consumed by flames, in the sink and run water to chase away the ashes. The cameras would see us, me and Awhina. What will Jim say?

I stared up at Thom's camera. As drunk as I was, I knew what was happening—but I trusted him. I was so naive, so stupid, just like everyone said. I wanted it so badly, the gaze of the lens on me. The gaze of Thom. I had felt such a surge of power and excitement. His eyes caught something the mirror never did: a side of me that was beautiful. In the end he took something that had liberated me and twisted it into something that caused me immense pain. I feel a flash of anger.

"Okay," I say, emerging into the lounge. "Hot chocolate time."

Beau goes over to his bed and flops down. I set the kettle on the stovetop and spoon the powdered chocolate into two mugs. The girl watches me from the stool.

"What happened to your hair?" she asks.

"My hair?"

"Yeah. Why's it so short?"

"I cut it."

"Why?"

"Because I needed a change."

"My mum and dad told me not to talk to you."

I clear my throat, hurt but trying not to show it. I turn back to her, hands on hips. "Why?"

She shrugs, looking down, her bottom lip jutting out.

"Why?" I say, a frayed edge to my voice.

"Because . . ."

"Because why?"

"You're the crazy lady. They said you might hurt me."

I lean forward over the island so my face is close to hers. The kettle begins to whistle behind me. "Awhina, they are lying. I would never hurt you," I say, before giving a little laugh over the scream of the kettle. "And I'm not crazy, okay? Tell them that."

I kill the stovetop and pull the kettle off the burner. Steam rises from the mugs as the hot water splashes in. It is easy to imagine the boiling water pouring over skin.

I add milk, then carry the hot chocolates over to the island. I climb onto the stool beside Awhina's. The girl blows into her mug, then lifts it to her lips tentatively.

"Would you like to move away from here, Awhina? Do you want to come away with me, somewhere where you will be safe and happy?" What could I do with her? I could get a job and maybe she could go to school wherever we end up living. Could I really look after a child? I think about my dad. He raised me alone. A twist in my heart; I miss him. I miss home.

She grimaces. "I want to go now." She puts the mug back on the counter. I see tears forming in her eyes.

"Careful, Awhina. It's hot."

"Let me go home!"

"Go home?"

She slips down from the stool and runs to the front door. I rise and, as she reaches for the handle, put a hand to the door, holding it closed. Has she noticed that I keep an ax near the entranceway? Maybe that's why she is afraid.

"Just wait for one second," I say. "Why are you leaving?"

She glances up fearfully. "Please let me go."

"You haven't finished your drink."

"I don't want it."

I step back, holding my hands up in surrender.

"Okay, there you go." I begin opening the door. "No need to panic, Awhina." The child darts out, fleeing up the driveway.

I tip our hot chocolates down the drain. I do all the dishes in the sink. Jim will be annoyed when he gets back, annoyed that I left.

I tidy up. I wipe down the counters and take the trash out to the bin. In the laundry, I put the washing into the machine, turning out the pockets for any change. Then I feel something flat and rigid. In the pocket of the jeans I wore yesterday, I find Iso's credit card. I take it and press it deep into my escape bag at the bottom of my wardrobe.

I've just finished eating when I hear a car pull up outside the house. I take up a position behind the door. It could be the man in black, or Awhina's parents. It could even be Iso's friend from last night. A key in the lock. The door opens. I brace.

"Hello?" It's Jim. "Kate, where are you?"

"Hi," I say. He jumps.

"Shit, Kate." His eyes venture from my face to the ax clutched against my shoulder. He reaches out and takes it from me, resting it against the wall. "What are you doing lurking with an ax? What's going on?"

"Nothing," I say. "I was scared."

He opens up his arms and pulls me into a hug. I can smell his oaky aftershave. Two nights he was away, that's all, but it feels like weeks.

"How was your trip?" I ask.

"It was okay."

"What was it for?"

I feel his body tighten and he steps away from me. He just looks into my eyes and says, "I'm home now, that's all that matters."

Home? Is that what this is?

"Tell me where you were," I demand.

Ignoring me, he takes up the ax.

"This should be outside, Kate." He exits through the back door, taking the ax down beside the wood. He comes back inside.

"Tell me where you were," I say, forcing my voice to stay loud and steady. "Did it have something to do with Thom?"

His expression changes, a little color seeping into his cheeks. He brings his hands together and then drops his face into them.

"What did you do?" I ask.

"Don't, Kate. Please don't talk to me in that tone. And what I was doing doesn't matter; what were *you* doing? I saw your note to say you were taking Beau for a walk. You were gone all day...." He pauses. "And today you brought the little girl inside. What were you thinking?" What else does he know? Is it possible that he knows Iso is going to Auckland tomorrow and that he's going to take me?

"She's my friend. She needs help."

"Jesus, Kate. Don't be so naive. You locked a child in this house. I saw it all."

"You lock me in this house." My voice is low. My neck tight with anger.

"Did you take the pills I left out for you? Did you swallow them?"

"Shut up!" I say, blocking my ears. "I don't need those pills. Stop trying to make me take them. I don't need them."

"Come on, Kate—you can't just stop taking them."

Frustration is quickly becoming anger. "Tell me why you went away. What did you do? Tell me."

He looks at me. Eyes serious. Hands closing into fists. "This is not the time to talk about it."

"I hate you!" I run to my bedroom and he is on me like a shot. He seizes my wrist, whipping me back. He looks down at my forearms, then up into my eyes.

"I hate you!" I scream. "I hate you, I hate you, I hate you! You made me leave everything behind—my whole life."

He steps back. "Kate," he says. "Stop."

"I hate you." I hit myself once, hard, on the side of the head. I tighten my fist and do it again.

He grabs my arms. "Stop it, Kate. Please, stop it."

I struggle to free myself but he's holding me too tight. I bite his shoulder.

"Fuck!" he yells, pushing me away. His face is red with fury. "Everything I've done has been for you. Everything! And we were happy, until you had to go fuck it up with this business with Thom."

I can barely look him in the eye. My hands are still balled into fists at my sides, but the urge to strike myself, to punish him, has gone.

"You're a child still. You think you're not, but you are. You need to grow up because we are running out of time. It'll all be over soon and you're still sick." I can tell he is willing himself to speak calmly. "You invent things. You make things up because the truth is too difficult. You think I know what the fuck I am doing? I don't." He shakes his head. "I don't." He looks me in the eye. "He's dead, Kate. Accept it and we can move on."

"You're lying."

He narrows his eyes. "Why would I lie?" His tone is incredulous. "You were remembering things. Come on, Kate, think about it. The night he was hurt, what was I holding in my hand?"

"He's alive," I insist. "He's alive, that's why you won't let me go; that's why you keep me here. You want me to believe I am a murderer." Suddenly I find that I'm laughing.

He just shakes his head slowly, looking at me with something like horror. "You're getting worse. Jesus Christ, you haven't gotten better at all." Then, quietly, to himself: "What have I done?"

You're getting worse. Despite his reasonable tone, I know what he's doing: he's trying to convince me it's all in my head.

We eat a late breakfast, then he makes me take my pills in front of him where he can watch. There is one extra pill: a little blue diamond. He runs his forefinger around in my mouth to check that the pills are gone. Does he know how tempted I am to bite down?

"Now go have a lie-down and read, okay? I need you to relax and get some rest."

I know what the blue pill does: it puts me to sleep. So in my room I make myself stand up and move around to keep awake. It's still the morning and he wants to put me to sleep but I'm not going to let him.

Soon enough I can hear him on the phone. He speaks in a low, melancholy tone at first, and then his voice rises, as if he is arguing with someone. It's when he is loud that I catch snatches of the conversation. *It doesn't matter what it costs, I'll organize enough money that you won't need to worry about it. Soon she'll be alone.* A tremor rips through his voice. *I'm not going to be able to meet you, it'll be too late. You'll just have to pick her up.* . . . His voice lowers to a murmur again, then the call ends. I hear him coming up the hall. I slip in beneath the covers and lie there, holding my breath and keeping everything perfectly still.

Twenty-nine

want to talk to you about something," he says when I emerge
from my room into the warm lounge early in the afternoon.
His eyes are sunken, sleepless, and red rimmed. The fire is
blazing. He pats the couch beside him. "Something we should
really have talked about but I didn't think you were ready. I have
been going over everything in my mind. I thought you were getting better. I thought maybe you were nearly ready to confront
everything, but now I realize it's best for me to be honest with
you." He is gazing into my eyes. "I just want us to be happy in the
long term, and if that means you have to go through hell in the
short term, well, I guess it will be worth it in the end. But I can't
risk you doing something rash, Kate."

I don't respond. I think about when I felt like I really loved
this man and I'm sick with it. The silence thickens the air between us. I think about times from before when I really could
have done "something rash." When Willow said those nasty
words, when I discovered that Thom's video of us was on the
Internet. Then I think of Thom's words. *I'll kill him.* I thought of it

as a throwaway line, something a boy might say to sound tough. *I'll kill him.*

"I've organized for you to get help. But before you can leave this country, I need to know exactly what you remember." He drops his head forward. Then he looks up again and grips my hands. "It was an accident, Kate. However you remember it, just know that it was an accident. The plan was just to scare him."

I feel sick. Tears sting my eyes.

"What do you remember, Kate?"

"I remember seeing him. And you."

"Me?"

"Yes."

"What was I doing?"

"You had something in your hand." I swallow. "You were holding something."

His nod is almost imperceptible.

"What else?"

"That's it."

"You don't remember anything else, Kate? Do you promise me you can't remember anything else?" He's pleading now, a sort of desperation in his eyes.

Blunt-force trauma to the skull is defined as nonpenetrating damage—more of a crushing, twisting, knocking force. Gunshots, for example, are penetrating. A blow with a golf club or a spade is not.

Jim is still speaking but I just watch him, trying to block out the words.

"They know you were there when it happened."

"They're going to lock me away?"

"No, Kate. You just need to tell them you were with me. Always tell them we were together and that's all you remember. Okay?"

"Okay." My voice is barely audible.

"It might raise questions of what you were doing with me when you should have been in bed, but leave me to face those questions."

"Sure."

"We can't risk you breaking down. You need to be strong and ready."

Don't trust him. "What about the people here, who knows?"

"No one. Did someone say something?"

I recall the image in the post. The barbecue. What Awhina said. *Crazy.* "No, it's just"—I draw a long breath—"that man, he was back here yesterday."

"I see," he says. He grits his teeth and sucks in a breath. "Don't worry, you won't have to worry about any of that soon enough."

He gets up and walks away.

Whatever he is planning to do to me, it will happen soon. He wants me to be a reliable witness, to be his alibi, but he could easily decide that it's too risky to keep me around. He's just trying to protect himself. But what happens if I refuse to play along? What then?

I am lying on my bed staring at those words in the book, finding each of the underlined letters to spell *Don't trust him*, when he goes out to the shed. I can't stay cooped up in here all day. I need to find my passport, and I need to see Iso to organize my getaway. I need the Internet to book flights and to know the truth about what happened. The Internet is traceable, but Jim made it very clear our time is almost up; by the time someone could trace us and turn up here, he'll have done whatever it is he is going to do to me anyway. Outside a light rain has begun to fall.

To escape I need to take down the cameras—the one in my room and the one in the yard, at least. Jim's still out in the shed, working on what? I have no idea, but I can only assume he wants to keep it from me.

I walk outside and climb up the ladder near my window to the camera that surveys the yard. It needs to look as if something natural has happened to obscure its vision, like a bird or a possum could have done it. Glancing around, I notice a branch reaching out near the corner of the house. I lean across. The ladder seems to yaw. I look down; the ground is a long way below. If I fell, I could break my neck. I lift my gaze back to the branch and extend my fingertips a little farther. This time I manage to grasp it between my fingers. I listen for the sound of the shed door but all I can hear is my pulse thumping in my ears. I pull the branch. The ladder wobbles underneath me and my breath catches. I wait till it's steady, then try again. The tree resists, so I bend the branch back and forth until it snaps and is hanging by the skin of the bark; I twist it in a way so that it partially covers the camera's lens.

I quickly descend the ladder, cross the lawn, and knock on the door.

"One minute," he says.

He opens the door but blocks the gap with his body. I can make out a faint light glowing in the shed behind him. "What's up?"

"I just wanted to know what you're doing down here."

His mouth quirks to one side in irritation. "I'm working."

I stand on my toes to look past, but he steps out of the shed, closing the door behind him.

"What's in there?"

"Nothing, Kate. It's just a private space for me to do some work. I'm just assessing our options." *Could he have been watching the cameras?* He glances down at his watch. "I'll come inside soon. I'm thinking we should have a special dinner tonight and try to enjoy each other's company. I just want to make one nice memory of this place. How are you feeling anyway?"

There is something about his forced smile and the unnatural cadence to his voice that chills me. Something is going to happen tonight. "I feel okay."

"Good girl."

"I guess I'll go read," I say. "Hey, you said I could have my phone."

"That's probably not the best idea at the moment, Kate." He turns and goes back into the shed. "Everything has changed."

"What do you mean? Can you show me?"

"I can't, Kate. Just go make a start on dinner and I'll be up soon enough." He slips back into the shed and closes the door.

I go back inside. I'm feeling anxious, edgy. I need to do something. I can't leave anything up to chance.

Beau jumps up and runs over to me, pressing against my legs. In the kitchen, I open the cupboard beneath the sink and scoop out some biscuits for him. He guzzles them hungrily.

Anger sears my veins. If Jim refuses to show me the truth, I'll find it out for myself. I rush to my room and fetch Iso's credit card before setting off.

I feel different, still a little drowsy but something is thawing inside. I still need to follow the plan. I need to book flights. Then I'll find proof that I'm not in trouble: I need evidence that Jim has been lying, that he has dragged me here to punish me, or to keep me to himself. Or worse, because I'm the only one who witnessed him at the scene of a crime and he won't risk my going to the police. I can find all of this on the Internet at Iso's.

Next I need my passport. I've rummaged through his bedroom more than once and the passport's not there; it must be in the shed. This will be the hard part. Finally, I need to lock in transport to the airport. That's where Iso comes in, if Jim hasn't turned him against me completely. Assuming part one goes to plan, I can show Iso the evidence that Jim has been manipulating me. That he is dangerous. If there is enough evidence to go to the police, then perhaps we can involve them. If there's not, I will need to get back to Melbourne to clear my name.

I keep running, against the fire in my throat, the ache in my chest. Against the burn in my legs. I run as fast as I can down the hill to the beach, then up the hill all the way to Iso's gate. I twist through, closing it behind me, then rush down the driveway. I knock; the door opens.

"Evie," Iso says, standing in the door frame. No greeting, just my name. He seems cold.

"Hi," I say. I haven't thought this through; how do I get to the computer? I'm angry at myself suddenly, but then my anger vanishes. I am here, I just need to do this. "I was out for a walk and, well, I was wondering if I could use your phone."

"My phone?"

"Yeah, my uncle's been away and I need to call him. I locked myself out of the house."

"Oh, right," he says. "Well, why don't you come in and use the landline?"

"No," I say. When I smile it feels like it's held in place by tacks. "I'd like to use your mobile."

"My mobile?" He frowns. "Ah, okay . . . sure. I think it's out of battery, though. But if you're happy to wait for it to charge . . ."

"Have you got a computer? Maybe I could e-mail him."

"Evie," he says, leaning against the door frame, "what's going on?"

"Nothing." A little laugh. *Don't act crazy, Kate.* "I'm fine. Look,

I just need to use the Internet, okay? Not your phone but the Internet. Is that all right?"

His blue eyes bore into mine. "Why didn't you just say so?"

"I need five minutes. That's all."

"Look, I heard what happened with Awhina."

I swallow. How could he know about that? It was only this morning. The entire town is against me. Jim has turned them all.

"What do you mean?" I ask, trying to sound surprised.

"You scared her, Evie. Her parents were pretty shaken up. I mean, you locked a little girl in your house. . . ."

"That's not what happened, Iso. You've got to believe me. I just wanted to help her. I wanted to look after her."

He's exasperated, but I can sense he is softening. "Look, I can understand it's hard moving somewhere new, and you might have things going on at home. But you've got to be careful what you say, who you scare."

"Scare?" He is making it sound as though I'm like Jim—taking her captive in that old house. I suppose I *did* lock her inside and try to keep her there but only for a few minutes. I never wanted to scare her, I just wanted to help.

"Her parents are not happy, Evie. Look, it's fine. I shouldn't have said anything. So, you want to use the computer?"

"Yes, please." I've already been gone ten minutes. Will Jim still be in the shed? I don't have my keys, so he won't know where I am.

He turns. "Come in."

He leads me into a stuffy little room containing a desk littered with bills and books. A moth-eaten curtain covers the window.

The computer slowly whirs to life. I turn to Iso, who has been standing behind me. "Can you give me a minute?"

"Sure," he says, raising his eyebrows. "Do you want a cuppa?"

"Yes, please. That would be nice. Milk and no sugar."

He pulls the door closed and makes his way up the hall. I can hear him out there, the murmuring of a phone call. Who is he calling?

Once the computer has finished booting up, I click on the browser. I begin by logging in to my e-mail. One hundred seventy-four new messages. It has almost been a month. A quick scan. There's nothing worth opening.

I go to Facebook, but my password doesn't work. Jim must have changed it or deactivated my account. The same goes for Instagram.

Next I search flights for Wednesday morning. There is one departing at 9:15 a.m. If Iso takes me tomorrow, that will give me a full day and two nights in Auckland to organize a passport if I can't find mine. I choose a seat at the back of the plane and fill in the passenger details with my real name, my real address. When it's time to pay, I pull Iso's credit card from my pocket. I'm punching in the numbers when I hear the front door open again. I jam the card back in my pocket and click confirm. The flight costs $439. One day, I promise myself, I will pay Iso back.

Finally, I go to Google. This is the part I have been dreading. The part that fills my guts with concrete. I tap the keys.

Kate Bennet   Thom Moreau

I press enter and results fill the page. Hot bile rises in my stomach, moves up toward the base of my throat. I swallow hard. The photos of me are not the old ones; in these I have no hair. There are photos of me piggybacking Awhina from this morning. Photos of me on Cracker with Iso beside me. It looks like I'm on holiday. Sweat starts in patches on my back. They know where I am. There are other images, of course. . . . Police hunched over something beyond a ribbon of yellow police tape. The headline reads SEX TAPE AND VIOLENT ATTACK. I know that spot. It's *the* spot, *our* spot.

It's true, I realize with dawning horror. Jim was telling the truth about one thing. I read the article again. In the early hours of Tuesday morning, a local man was struck in the head and is in a critical condition. . . . I close the page and open another one. The stories are days old.

> . . . with no realistic chance of recovery, the family
> made the decision to turn life support off late last night.

Something else Jim was not lying about. I find a more recent article. This one is from two days ago. The day Jim left.

> Police are reviewing new CCTV footage that appears
> to show a black Mercedes-Benz heading to the scene.
> They have allegedly identified the driver.

I know exactly what they found when they reviewed the footage. They found an image of me and only me in the car. Jim was already there when it happened. In every memory, I was alone in the car. I realize it then: he has framed me. He has been leaking the photos to the media, making me out to be someone unstable, just crazy enough to commit murder. What if this was his plan all along?

> It's believed an arrest is imminent.

I click another link, open an earlier news story. There is a photo of Jim and a photo of Willow. There is a photo of me and a photo of Thom. Four faces. I scroll down and there is another photo; this one is grainy, as if taken from afar by a mobile phone. The caption credits the photo to a Facebook account. It's clearly me; there is blood on my face and on my hands. It's not from that night but from daytime. I look exactly like a psycho killer from a movie. It must have been a photo from someone on Thom's street.

I hear Iso coming down the hall. The credit card is burning white hot in my pocket. I open the history and delete all activity from the last hour.

"Are you all right?" Iso says as he pushes the door open and places the cup of tea on the desk beside me. "I hope Mum didn't leave any of her holistic healing shit open."

There's no conviction in his voice; he's a desperate salesman selling something he doesn't believe in.

Breathe, Kate, for fuck's sake. You need to be calm and ready. I try to empty my mind and focus my breath. *In. One, two, three, four* . . .

Iso is watching me, alarm spreading across his face. My body is quaking, my breathing is growing faster and faster. *Out. One, two.* "Evie, are you all right? Evie?"

I try to pick up the tea, but it spills, scalding my fingers. "Give me. A couple more. Minutes," I say. It's clear that the police believe I killed him, they have enough evidence to arrest me, Jim is going to hand me over to them.

"Evie, I can't . . . I can't let you do this to yourself. You're crying."

I touch my cheek, find it's damp. "I need to get away."

"From who?" he says. "From what?"

"I think . . ." I can't tell him. He already thinks I'm unhinged. The day I hitchhiked and ran from his house. Not letting Awhina leave. If he finds out I'm the lead suspect in a deadly attack, what will he do? He needs to know Jim is controlling it all.

Iso's eyes are wide. "Jesus, Evie. You're scaring me. What is it?"

"They—"

He squats down beside my chair and touches my back, his face close to mine. "What, Evie?"

"They think—"

There's a knock at the door. Three urgent taps, followed quickly by three more.

"They think I killed someone."

"Who?"

"They think it was me."

The knocks sound again, this time louder.

"Hold on a sec," Iso says, but I'm still speaking over him.

"He set me up."

He leaves the room and hurries down the hall to open the front door. I hear a male voice, hurried and loud. It's Jim. I hear Iso saying, *Sure, sure, come through.* He says, *She's right through here.*

I'm in some distant place where I can barely move, where I can only sit and listen.

"Evie," Jim says.

I turn. Jim's lips are tight, his face pale. I can't read his expression.

"It's the dog," he says. "We've got to go, right now. It's Beau." He looks at me the way a man might look at a river in which his best friend was swept away. "Something has happened."

BEFORE

Thirty

A maelstrom of glass and fists. Screaming. More bottles hurled. My memories of the party come through the warped lens of alcohol and concussion. It's possible, of course, that I don't remember anything, that what I remember are not memories at all but newly imagined wisps of a night I will never truly understand. An amalgamation of all the stories I heard.

It was Willow who found me stumbling around dazed with blood running from my head, and she pulled me away from the melee. I wasn't in any state to resist, I was just grateful to be away from the violence. She called her dad, who pulled up in his car shortly after. He got out to help me as I tottered away from the party, then he lifted me up and deposited me on the front seat, wrapping my bleeding head in a sweater he had in the car. I imagine people were torn between the spectacle of my bloody skull and the spot fires of fighting that continued to flare along the street and near the house.

"Don't let her fall asleep. If she's concussed she shouldn't sleep," Willow's dad said.

"She can't go home," Willow said, slurring but insistent. "Her dad will kill her."

"I was thinking of heading to emergency, Willow."

I remembered the way my dress flew up, Willow's nasty smile.

At the hospital we sat in the fluorescent white glare of the waiting room. It was busy. Most people seemed to be in a state of inebriation. When Willow's dad rose to go to the bathroom, Willow slid closer to me on the bench seat.

"Kate," she said, grabbing one of my hands in hers. "Are you feeling okay?"

I simply shrugged.

"You know I'm sorry, Kate. You have to know that. I felt so angry that you chose Thom over me. I know it's no excuse, but it's hard to lose your best friend and I guess I was . . . jealous."

Her father was striding back toward us.

"We're not talking about this now," I said with more anger in my voice than I intended.

"Tomorrow? Can we talk tomorrow?"

"I don't know, Willow."

Surprisingly quickly a nurse ushered me into a room.

She slicked the cut above my right ear down with medical wipes; I winced at the sting. The wipes continued to come away blood soaked. Then I felt the nurse cutting a patch of hair. When the cut was clean and the hair cleared away, a doctor came over with a needle—a couple of pricks in the back of my head, then numbness. After that I felt a slight tug of skin as my wound was stitched closed.

Finally, at around two in the morning, with my head bandaged and my legs unsteady, Willow's dad helped me back to the car.

Willow was already asleep in the front seat. "We'd better take you back to our place," he said. "Probably not a good idea to drop you off home at this time."

When we got there, Willow went to bed while her father carried me in his lean arms over to the couch and propped me upright with pillows behind my head. He fetched an ice pack from the kitchen and held it to the throbbing spot where the bottle had hit.

"They cut my hair," I said sadly.

"Only a little, almost nothing—you can't even notice it," he said, his voice tender. "But you should let me take a couple of photos in case you decide you want to go to the police in the morning."

My head was pounding, my vision shifting in and out of focus. My eyes fluttered against sleep.

Willow's dad gave me a gentle shake, his hand on my shoulder. "The nurse said that you may have a mild concussion, so you can't go to sleep just yet. You're going to have to stay awake for a while, okay?"

I nodded slowly, trying not to move my head too much.

"I forgot what the nurse said. Let me check online for other symptoms," he said, patting his pockets. "Have you seen my phone?"

"No," I said. I pulled my phone from the pocket of my jeans. "Do you want to call it?"

He took my phone and dialed his own number. Seconds later there was a vibration down the side of the couch. He rummaged for it, pulling it out. He opened the Internet browser and conducted a search.

"It says here that you shouldn't sleep if your eyes are dilated." He turned to cup my chin and peer into my eyes. His palm felt surprisingly soft and warm.

"You're lucky, you know," he said softly.

"It could have been a lot worse," I agreed.

"I meant your eyes. They're so . . . dark. Just lovely, Kate."

I leaned against him. "I'm sleepy." My voice was thick and syrupy with alcohol and tiredness.

"I don't want you to feel any worse. Are you still dizzy?"

"I don't know."

He placed his hands on my hips and pulled me upright, tight against his shoulder. The ice pack slipped and he grabbed it from down my back before pressing it against my head. We talked for a while. He asked me about Thom.

"Thom?"

"Sorry. I couldn't help but notice that you had ten messages and a few missed calls from him on your phone. Is he your boy-friend?"

"Yeah," I said, then added, "Kind of."

"He didn't make it to the party?"

"He was there," I said.

His body tensed against mine. "So where was he when all this happened with the bottle?"

Where did he go? Why was it Willow's dad and not Thom who picked me up and took me home? Did he run? Did he fight?

"I don't know. He was walking away from me when it started."

"Really? He left you?"

"Thom would have been there but he was jealous. We had a fight."

"A fight?" he said. "You're too young to be fighting."

I felt heavy with fatigue, and the room spun in a slow, sickly twirl, but I knew I wanted to stay awake, I wanted to talk to him. "He doesn't like it when I talk to other guys. He got mad and said the other guys there could have me."

"Sounds like a prick—if you don't mind me saying. You're not his property to give away."

"He was just drunk," I said.

"Kate," he said in a soft voice.

I pulled his hand away from my head down over my shoulders and shifted to nestle into his side. He dropped the ice pack and rested his palm on my hip. My dress slid up my legs, slowly revealing more of the shining swirls of my scars. Thom had left me. Jealous Thom.

"Take care. It's easy to break a man's heart."

"Mmm."

His hand crept from my hip onto my thigh. I smelled cotton and oak; it smelled like home.

PART FOUR

Thinking about
Ending Things

In the past month, how often have you been fixated on the
possible recurrence of your traumatic experience?

0. never;   1. rarely;   2. sometimes;   3. often;   4. all the time

Thirty-one

Transcript from 3RA newstalk morning radio show:

HOST: You're listening to 3RA newstalk, I'm Des Holder and today we are talking crime. We've got Joe from Melton on the line.

CALLER: Morning, Des.

HOST: Now, you believe you've got some information regarding the Hawkesburn Park case. If you've been living under a rock for the past month, you might have missed the story. But the girl involved, Kate Bennet, vanished under what some have described as dubious circumstances days after an attack in the inner east, which she may very well be linked to.

CALLER: That's right.

HOST: A lot of it is speculation, of course, but what have you got for us, Joe?

CALLER: Well, I'm at the pub last night with a couple of others, and one of the boys just got back from New Zealand.

HOST: Very nice. Business or pleasure?

CALLER: He did a four-week tour—lots of skiing and booze, by the sounds of it.

HOST: All right, so what's this got to do with Kate Bennet?

CALLER: Well, on the flight over he gets a free upgrade—and guess who's sitting there in business class?

HOST: It wasn't Elton John, was it, Joe?

CALLER: Des, it wasn't Elton John, no. All bundled up in a hoodie and jeans facing the window was Bomber Bennet's daughter.

HOST: Your friend, is he normally one to spin a yarn, so to speak?

CALLER: He swears black and blue it was her.

HOST: Did your friend say who she was with?

CALLER: He didn't, no. But they've got the car that was involved on CCTV, did you see that?

HOST: I certainly did.

CALLER: It's a black Mercedes-Benz, right? Now, guess who else has a black Mercedes-Benz?

HOST: Tell us who, Joe.

CALLER: I read online that Bomber Bennet drives the exact model in the CCTV footage. I'll bet my bottom dollar that when this CCTV image does get out, Kate Bennet will be behind the wheel.

HOST: More rumors, quite frankly, Joe.

CALLER: Well, the girl is in New Zealand, and my friend saw her on the plane one or two days after it happened. So if she's been there for a month now, she's either having a bloody good holiday or she's fled the country.

HOST: The *Sydney Morning Herald* broke the story last week, releasing a set of images that appears to be shot in New

Zealand. Although the source of the images won't reveal exactly where in New Zealand. It's also possible she was over there at first and has since moved on. She's not currently wanted by police and is not listed as a missing person, so it's all academic at this stage.

CALLER: Well, she was absolutely loopy. No one can deny that.

HOST: We can't really speculate as to her state of mind, though, can we? She's definitely involved in this mess with the boy, you think?

CALLER: Things are going to blow up, mark my words. This thing isn't done.

HOST: I agree. It's been good to speak with you, Joe. I'm looking for more information on the case. I say this with a caveat: we do not encourage any form of vigilante justice at all. On the other hand, you can be cleared of involvement in a crime and still be a person of interest, and out of respect for Bomber Bennet, I sincerely hope this is all a misunderstanding and his daughter fronts up to clear up this mess. Weather and news up after the break, then we will be talking protesters: when is it okay to use force to disband a public nuisance? Have something to say? Taking your calls shortly.

AFTER

Thirty-two

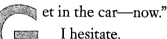et in the car—now."

I hesitate.

"I'm not playing games, *Evie*. You want the dog to die?"

Leaving Jim with Iso, I go out through the front door to the car. Beau is lying on his side across the back seat. He doesn't move when I approach.

I pull the passenger-side door open and get in. Beau's tail thumps the seat twice. He lifts his head a fraction, eyes on me. He's alive. Thank God, he's alive. I reach back and stroke his head and his tail thumps once more. He doesn't get up, though; he seems weak, lethargic.

The door to the house opens again and Jim comes storming out. He drops into the driver's seat, slams the door, and starts the car. He does a U-turn, the wheels skidding on the dirt, then shoots along the driveway onto the road, not even stopping to close the gate behind us. He barely slows as we turn onto the road. Beau slides along the back seat.

"Careful!" I say.

"Careful?" he echoes, taking his eyes from the road for a second. "*Careful?* Did *you* just tell *me* to be careful?" He slams the car into another turn; we slip again, edging across the center line. For a split second I imagine someone standing in front of us on the road.

"Slow down," I beg. "You're scaring me."

"You've probably killed him, Kate. Do you realize that?"

For a second I'm confused as to who he's talking about. Then I turn to look at the back seat. Beau's eyes are half closed. "What did I do?"

"How many times have I told you to close the damn cupboard? How many?"

"What happened?"

"I came up from the shed, looking for you, but I couldn't find you anywhere. I thought you might have done something crazy." He screwed the heel of his hand into one eye. "I noticed the door to the cupboard beneath the sink was ajar, where Beau's biscuits are kept. Then I found the yellow wrapper of the rat poison."

I closed the cupboard. I'm certain I closed it. Is this another one of his tricks?

"How did you know where I was?"

"What?"

"How did you know I was down there?"

"I didn't. I just drove around everywhere I thought you might be."

I reach back and stroke Beau's side. He doesn't move.

"It can't have been more than an hour since he ate it. It says online if he shows symptoms within the first couple of hours— well, it doesn't look good. You can't even look after a bloody dog. The poor thing."

"Where are we going?" I ask as we start up the hill toward our place.

"You're going home. I just can't trust you enough to take you anywhere."

"Home? We don't have time."

"You haven't left me any choice. I found a vet not far out of town. She said to bring Beau immediately. This could be our last night together and you just have to go fuck it up."

Another sharp turn into our driveway. I'm thrown against the seat belt when he yanks on the hand brake.

"Our last night? What do you mean?"

He ignores me. "Come on, quick."

I reach back and pet Beau once more, stroking his head before I get out of the car and head to the house. Jim follows.

"Move, Kate. In your room." He stalks behind me down the hall.

"Go—you don't have time," I say.

He slams the door behind me and walks away. A drawer opens, slams closed, then I hear him coming back up the hall. Beau is dying in the car—what is he doing?

I hear the drill. The lock is going back on. Over the sound he calls, "We're leaving here tomorrow."

"What did you do? You killed him, didn't you?"

"What do you remember, Kate? What was I holding?"

A brick. He was holding a red brick. I'm sobbing. "I just wanted to see the news. I just wanted to read about what happened."

"I could have shown you," he says. "If you really wanted to see it. Just stay in there and think about what you've done to the dog." ·

"No," I say. "No, I—I closed the cupboard, I know I did."

It's happening again; I'm weak with it. Grief makes us feeble. The longing to have the warm dog there in my arms. It comes on like waves in the sea, rocking me. The front door closes. The car revs and he is gone.

I do not feel Beau's hot breath against my leg, I do not see his wet pleading eyes staring up at me. I do not hear his paws scratching on the wooden floor. The bedcovers waft stale air as I collapse on them, drained of energy, the familiar anxiety foaming inside.

Why is he always in the shed? Why was *he* not inside? Is this another game of his? The stories were there: the *Sydney Morning Herald*, the *Herald Sun*, the *Huffington Post.* There is nothing for me in Melbourne but the opportunity to clear my name. What will I tell the police? Will they investigate Jim if I tell them what I remember: Jim holding the brick? *He* was *holding the brick.*

I have my flight to Melbourne booked. Maybe when I get to the airport I can choose to fly somewhere else. If Jim has convinced all of Australia that I'm a killer, and if I am going to be locked away, maybe I really can go to Europe, or South America. I just need my passport. For that, I have to get into the shed.

I rise, go to the window, and look down into the yard. The sun is setting, making long shadows up the back lawn. I press the window open, feeling the crisp cool on my skin.

The ladder is still there.

After glancing up to check that the branch is still obscuring the camera's view of the yard, I climb down to the ground. I find the ax beneath the stairs near the woodpile and stride across the lawn to the shed. Without aiming, or considering what I'm doing, I swing the ax as hard as I can. The blade crashes into the steel door. The birds in a nearby tree take flight. I swing again, this time striking above the door handle. A snapping sound. One more strike and it swings open. I step through into the darkness. Something touches my face. I swat at it. It swings back. It's a cord. I snatch it, pull down, and a single bulb lights up the shed.

A filing cabinet, an old cupboard, a desk with sheets of paper, pens. Then I see something else. Long, sleek barrel and wooden stock. The door swings on the breeze, whining like something dying. The rifle stands at the rear of the cupboard. I creep toward it and reach out, touching the cool steel of the barrel. Above me the light swings, oscillating all the shadows. For one term at school we had lessons at the rifle club every Tuesday afternoon. At first we were only allowed to handle fake plastic guns, practicing safety procedures and how to aim before they let us touch the real thing. This gun looks different. I lift it and pull the bolt back. It's empty. *At least he doesn't keep it loaded.* I find a box of ammo and take it outside with the gun beneath my arm; I must hide it from him, there's only one reason he has this gun. I hold it over the neighbor's fence. Dropping it, I hear the crack of twigs snapping. It doesn't hit the ground; it must be caught in the bush. Next I drop the ammo.

My heart thuds as I return to the shed. I try the filing cabinet but it doesn't open. There's an empty key slot at the top. I pick up the ax again; I can't stop now. The blade crashes into the lock. The corner folds about the wedge of steel, but the drawer won't open. I hit it again, harder, the sound making me flinch. The top drawer rolls open.

Inside, there's a broken wine bottle and the tannic whiff of wine hits me. I find other bottles of alcohol. The drawer below won't budge; I twist the ax head into it and jerk it back until it comes unstuck. Papers, lots of them. I pull them out and hold them beneath the light. Sheets and sheets of articles are blood-stained with red wine. I scan them quickly. *Fractured skull ... found on the road* ... There are photographs. I recall that night, taking the car keys, setting out. Some photos show yellow tabs like morbid Post-it notes all over the road and the footpath. More photos of me ... more stills from the video, the same as the one I found in the letterbox. It wasn't Iso's friend Mick who put it there; it was

Jim. He left one in the letterbox and kept these others for future use. He did it to frighten me. Or is it possible these are others left by the same person and Jim was collecting them, hiding them from me? Is it possible someone else has known all along?

Then I find the envelopes. My letters. The letters he handed to Tiriana. She was in on it too. This entire town has conspired against me.

Blood pulses in my chest and everything—my breathing, the sliding clatter of the drawer, the whine as the shed door moves in the wind—is too loud.

I open the doors of the cupboard and feel around on the top shelf. My hand touches something small and hard: a wallet. I pull it out. Not a wallet—a passport. I open the first page. My face looks out. *My passport.* It's happening. It's coming together. I jam the passport into the pocket of my jeans and keep looking.

On the next shelf down I find a pile of magazines, a dozen of the same issue. And pages, the missing pages from my magazine, are here: the pages he cut out. I see my face; I see Thom's face. I look happier, my face rounded and my hair long. It barely looks like me at all. He must have bought every copy so I wouldn't see it. It's a story about the sex tape. Maybe Jim bought them all so no one else in this town would find the article.

On the bottom shelf I find all the sharp objects he took from the house: the scissors, the knives, his razor blades.

The door creaks. The light in the room changes.

"What are you doing?"

My heart stops. I don't turn around. I can't move at all. The ax is beside the door. I cringe, bracing for the blow. I can feel myself fading; the scene before me blurs. I close my eyes and breathe. No flee, no fight, just resignation.

BEFORE

Thirty-three

Y ou're a tough old boot, aren't you?" Thom asked me. In his sly, laughing way he had spoken of this meeting at our local café as if it were a date. He reached across the table, the one I had chosen in the far corner near the window, and clasped my hand. I resisted the urge to pull it away. He had had a week to apologize but he still hadn't, even though my concussion and these stitches in my head were caused by his jealousy. I had been obsessively combing my hair down over the bald patch to hide it from Dad. I lived with the consequences while he was the one who had started the argument that led to the fight. He had abandoned me, yet here he was joking about it.

"My head's still very sore, Thom," I said. I chewed my thumbnail and watched the people passing by the window.

"So what happened afterward? I was really worried when you didn't answer your phone."

I turned my gaze to him. "Willow looked after me. I slept on her couch." Willow's dad had sat close to me, his long, lean arms around me, his breath on my collarbone. I knew he wanted me. I craved the feeling it gave me. The sense of power.

"Willow? So you're friends again." He sounded annoyed.

I pulled my hand away from his. Anger came over me quick. "She looked after me. And it doesn't matter if we're friends. The fact is, she was there and you weren't." My voice was rising. "And where were you, Thom? Where did you go when I was bleeding and concussed?" I tried to calm myself but something had changed between us. This wasn't the Thom I had dreamed about, the Thom I thought I knew.

His face dropped. "I didn't see. It all happened so quickly."

"But you started it. It was your fault. Can you not see that? You got so jealous and if you had kept your head we could have just walked away."

"You were the one flirting with them."

I bit down, clenching my teeth to keep from screaming. Only my lips moved when I spoke again. "So what if I was? Would that justify what you did? Would this inch-long cut to my head be justified then?" The café was almost empty but the only other diners, a family at another table, had fallen completely silent now.

"I wasn't the one that hurt you, Kate. We can still get them. We should go to the police."

"No," I said. "Definitely not. I can't risk Dad finding out. I wasn't supposed to be there." I glanced over my shoulder as more people entered the café. "So you've got nothing to say? You're not going to apologize?"

"Okay. I'm sorry that you got hurt, but you've got to accept some responsibility too."

What would he say if the tables were turned and I'd left him bloody and barely conscious?

"That's a bullshit apology, Thom. You can't even say sorry."

"Those guys are the ones who should be apologizing," he said. "People like that get away with too much."

"Just fucking say you're sorry. Not you're sorry I got hurt, but you're sorry for being such an arsehole."

I could feel tears coming.

"Hey," he said, reaching for my hand again, but I pulled it back into my sleeve. The barista was watching us over the coffee machine. "Don't cry, please, Kate. I fucked up, okay. I'm sorry for being an arsehole that night. Just please, we're making a scene."

I glanced at the barista and mouthed, "Sorry." *But for what? Sorry for crying? Sorry for being angry?* It was Thom's fault. Boys are so skilled at drawing apologies when they're the ones who owe them.

"It's okay. We're going to be okay," he said.

But I didn't feel okay. Something had shifted between us and I wasn't sure it would right itself again. I didn't kiss him when he walked me home.

Up in my room, I took out my phone and went to the recently dialed list. I knew which number was his; he had called his own phone from mine to find it at 2:39 a.m. on the night of the party, the night I had fallen asleep in his arms and woken in Willow's bed.

I was out in the yard lying beneath the eucalyptus. A magpie cawed from up on the eaves of the house. I pointed at it, making a gun with my fingers. "Pow." The bird continued undeterred. The sun warmed my ankles where the shade didn't quite reach. I peered past my phone up at the branches cutting pieces from the sky.

There was something about communicating in the digital

realm that didn't feel real, I thought as I scrolled through my messages. It was like there was another world where my messages existed but they were sent by someone else. In that space, I was someone who was always happy and uninhibited.

> Kate, do you think it's a good idea that you message me?
>
> I don't think there is anything wrong with two people sending text messages.
>
> It could reflect badly on us both.
>
> I think it's okay. No one has to know. I like it. I like you.

I took a photo of my face, angled in such a way that you could see my collarbone and the skin on my chest. I looked pretty in the photo, lips slightly pursed, dark hair fanned out on the grass, eyes narrowed a little against the light. I held my breath and hit send.

I hadn't seen Willow since the night a week ago when she had tried to reconcile our friendship, but I said yes when she invited me over. And if it was someone else in her house I really wanted to see, well, she didn't need to know. I deliberately wore my sheer black top that Thom hated—he said it was "attention seeking"— and my tightest black jeans. I knew I was overdressed for the casual shopping trip we had planned, but I wanted to look nice for *him.*

Willow was up in her room getting dressed, so it was her mum who let me in. I went into the lounge to wait. Sitting on the couch, I was conscious of my heartbeat, the fluttering in my stomach. There was no sign of Willow's dad, though I had seen his car parked in the driveway. After a while, I walked through his study as if on my way to the bathroom. *Does he know I'm in his house?*

Footsteps. I turned to see him coming into the room. "Hello, Kate." His voice rolled over me, honeyed and warm.

"Hello," I said, my voice barely audible. I dragged a finger over his desk. He stood close by. I turned to him, my heart thumping in my chest. I wet my lips.

He glanced back toward the hall once. When he spoke it was so soft, I found myself stepping closer to hear him. "I've been thinking about you." So frank, so direct. None of the irony I had come to expect from Thom. A blush scorched my cheeks.

"I know the feeling."

I stepped so close that he would have to touch me to get past.

"You have the most beautiful hair," he said. "Did you ever think about cutting it?"

"I like it long."

"I think you could pull off a bob."

I could hear the footsteps on the stairs.

"That's probably Willow," he said without urgency. "It would be best if she didn't find you in my study." Did he realize I could barely breathe? Would it be the end of the world if Willow found us? I walked away, deliberately pausing at the door and looking back. His eyes traveled my body. *Good.*

That night I got a message. You looked stunning today, Kate.

Thirty-four

We arranged to meet for coffee. If we were caught, it could be explained away. We might have both been at the same café, coincidentally, and bumped into each other.

He was there before me, one ankle on the opposite knee, looking down at an open newspaper. I scrunched my hair with my fingers, caught a look at myself in the reflection of the window, then entered. The café was busy.

"Kate, hello," he said, rising. He kissed my cheek, and suddenly I realized this was real. No one's parents had greeted me like that before, like a peer. "Grab a seat."

I ordered a latte. He already had a black coffee half drunk in front of him; how long had he been waiting? I reached for the sunglasses sitting beside his keys.

"Are these yours?" I said, pushing them on. I had to hold them to my face to keep them from falling off. "How do I look?"

He smiled. "Sophisticated." He closed the paper and folded it on the table. "Are we eating?"

I shrugged. "I'm not so hungry."

"Let's get something small," he said.

When my coffee came, I loaded it up with sugar and quickly stirred it through while he spoke to the waiter. He ordered a slice of carrot cake.

"So how's school going?"

"School? It's okay. It's just . . . school—kind of boring."

"And what about next year, what are you planning to do?"

"I want to study architecture at uni."

His dark eyebrows rose. "Architecture. My brother is an architect. I could put you in contact if you wanted. You know, to find out what it's like. Hard work, but I'm sure it's a rewarding career." Dad had never really spoken to me about my dreams and ambitions, and the offer, to meet his brother, a real architect, was not one Willow would ever have made.

"That would be great. Thank you."

"Don't mention it. And if you're looking for work while you're at uni, I'm sure I could talk him into taking you on, even if it's just answering phones. It would be good experience and you'd see how an architect's practice worked." The carrot cake came out with two small forks. He took one, trimmed off the tip of the cake, and ate it.

"That would be cool, if you could introduce me." I sipped my coffee. It still wasn't sweet enough but if I added any more sugar I would look like a child.

He leaned forward, and a curl of dark hair fell down his forehead. "So what's happening with the Thom situation, Kate?"

I took his fork and sliced off a small piece of the cake, bringing it to my mouth. "Thom?"

He smiled. "You were having some issues."

"Right. Well, we still are, I suppose."

He took another slice of cake from the same fork. "So where are you going to go with it?"

"I'm thinking about ending things." As I said it, I knew it was true. I was still angry with Thom. That night at his house had been so special but something had changed. I needed a break at the very least, although I couldn't imagine things ever going back to how they were.

He lowered his head a little closer to mine. "Well, you need to make sure you're doing what's best for you. It sounds like you've got a great future ahead. If that future doesn't include Thom, it might be worth acting on it sooner rather than later."

"It's been a year now. It feels like a long time, you know? It's hard to walk away."

He rested one hand on the table. I didn't care who saw us there. I reached out and ran my forefinger up and down his.

"What would you do," I said, "if you were me?"

"That's a loaded question."

I waited, letting the silence urge him to continue speaking.

"You seem earnest about this, so I'll answer in kind. Say you meet someone when you're young and you believe you're in love," he began. "You seem perfect for each other. Perhaps you are, but as you grow older you find yourself making concessions. You give up on dreams and plans you always wanted, you lose friends and start to realize you weren't as happy as you once were. You begin to have some doubts that the person you fell in love with is the same person you're married to but you're too afraid of change, or afraid of"—he waved his hand—"let's call it the unknown." I thought of how I used to feel about Thom, those words in my journal. I compared that feeling to now.

He glanced once to the door as someone entered, then back to me. "You start a family and even as the doubts grow, even as you begin to feel something a lot like regret, it's not just about the two of you anymore. Every decision you make affects more than just the two of you. Years go by and you grow more and more distant but you think soon you'll have the courage to make a tough decision and all the while you are getting older and older and you begin to resent each other. You get no joy or love out of the relationship but you are obliged to stick it out.

"Then you promise yourself when your daughter turns eighteen, when she is an adult, you will do what you should have done years ago, because regret doesn't fade away, it only gets bigger and bigger. Do you understand what I'm saying?"

"I do," I said. Willow would be turning eighteen in the next few months. And just like that I knew what I needed to do. I smiled and pressed my fingers between his.

Thom's mum let me in. I had turned up unannounced, and Thom was in the shower. I had come straight from the café, energized after the conversation with Willow's dad. I went to his room to wait. His laptop was open on his desk. I thought it would be nice to have some of the photos he took of our trips to the beach and days in the park. Would he send them to me if I ended things? Or would I have to take them? Maybe I could choose a few of my favorites and put them on my phone.

I sat down in front of his laptop. There were a couple of movies on his home screen. I found a folder titled *Photography*. I clicked it and began to scan through hundreds of photos. I recognized the settings. Some were from the tennis courts, others from the beach. In a few I wore a pair of sunglasses I had since lost, buried in sand at Brighton beach, two black dinner plates that covered half my face. I kept scrolling all the way through. Toward the end of the list, I found another file. *School stuff.* Curious, I clicked it. The photos were of me.

In one image my dark brown ponytail hung over one shoulder and I wore a sedated sort of smile, all gums and closed eyes. I loved that feeling, his words spurring me on as he took photos. The thrill of knowing someone desired me. Above my own narcissism I felt liberated; Thom's lens was the antidote to those venomous words Willow had spat. For just the fraction of time it took for the shutter to click, that lens salved the pain of the bullying, the torment of being different, all the lingering stares. The feeling inside now was the inverse of that excitement.

I continued to scroll. There was a series of shots taken at a dam, the place where a man had once deliberately swerved his car off the road and into the water. He'd had his three sons in the back. The man swam to safety while the car sank. What constituted *good* photography was a mystery to me, but it was clear Thom had an eye for it. I scrolled further until I heard the hum of the shower stop.

Then I saw a photo of myself. One I had never seen. I was asleep on Thom's bed, one arm thrown across my face as if to keep the light out. My small breasts were bare, peach-colored nipples floating atop pale skin. I ran my gaze down my own body, then clicked on the next image. The camera zoomed in between my legs. I felt my face flush. I clicked again. Then I found the video file. My finger hovered over the icon but I could hear him coming up the hall; I didn't have time to watch it. I sat with a hot new feeling bubbling inside me. *Why did he keep it?* I remembered the video, but it was never supposed to be permanent. It was an experience, a memory, something that should have disappeared in the cold morning light. *Can you delete it?* I had asked when we woke. *I already have.* So why was it still there?

I closed the lid of the laptop and moved away from the desk to sit on his bed.

He entered the room, a towel around his waist.

"Kate," he said. "This is a surprise."

"A surprise. Yes." The anger was bubbling inside.

"What?" he said, watching my face. "What's wrong?"

"Nothing." I clenched my jaw.

"Oh, wow, are you still that pissed at me about the party? I said sorry. What more do you want?"

He glanced over at his laptop, then sat at the desk and opened the lid. "Were you snooping?" He turned to look at me.

"Why did you take those?"

"I'm a photographer. I don't know. I thought it would be nice."

"You never asked my permission."

He made a horrible little sound with his nose, not quite a laugh, rather a sharp exhale. "What's wrong with keeping a reminder of how beautiful you are? Most girls would be flattered. I just want to be able to look at you when you're not with me."

"That's not the point, Thom." I was trying so hard to keep my voice even, to keep the feelings inside. I needed him to delete them all before I broke it off. "The video, that was a private, intimate moment. You said you deleted it." I needed to keep breathing. It wasn't the time to let my simmering anger boil over. "Why would you say that if it wasn't true?"

"Well, I deleted it off the camera but I had already downloaded everything from the memory stick."

"So it was a lie.",

"You said, 'Can you delete it off the camera.'"

"That's because I didn't realize you had uploaded it onto your computer already. You never had my consent—"

"Consent? Shall we watch the video? Do you want to check that you were consen—"

"Let me finish. You never had my consent to *keep it.* I trusted you. It doesn't matter how you spin it, you can't deny that you knew I wanted it deleted, that I didn't want you to keep it, and still you saved it."

"Grow up, Kate. It was a special time and I wanted a way to remember it, okay? I'll delete it, don't worry."

"What about the photos? I was asleep, Thom. Do you know how creepy that is?"

"Creepy?" Again he made that ugly sniffing sound. "You wanted me to take them."

"I was asleep, Thom!"

"I asked you and you said yes."

"You're lying. You're full of shit. You took nude photos of me when I was drunk and asleep. You kept a sex tape of us after you'd told me you had deleted it." The words made me angrier and angrier, as if by speaking about it I was reminded of how disgusting he really was. How little respect he had for me.

"You were drunk, you can't remember. This never would have happened if you hadn't snooped through my stuff."

The anger was cresting into rage. My voice did not rise but fell, cold and fierce. The words came from deep inside me. "Don't you dare blame me."

"What if I went through your shit?" he said, snatching my phone from where I'd left it on the desk. "Huh? How would you feel?"

I leaped off the bed and tried to snatch it from him. He held me off him with his forearm and opened my messages. Then his face changed abruptly and he shoved me back onto the bed.

"What is this?" he demanded.

I tried to sit up but he pushed me again, hard. I fell back. I wanted to cry. Then I did and he began to cry as well.

"Who is it?" His face contorted.

"No one."

"Tell me," he said. Every tremor in his voice went through me as sharp as shrapnel. "Who is it? Who is this old bastard messaging you, sending you photos?" His voice dropped. "Did you fuck him?"

"Don't make this about him. You ruined this relationship."

"I'll kill him. I'll fucking kill him."

"Delete the video, Thom. Delete it right now."

He shook his head. "Get out." His voice rose, high-pitched with pain. "Get the fuck out!" He stood up and his towel began to slip. Absurdly he clutched at it, as if shy of being naked in front of me. "Get the fuck out now, Kate." His eyes, his nose ran. A vein stood out in his shoulder. "I fucking hate you!"

I climbed up again and strode toward the laptop. Thom's sadness was a distraction. He'd betrayed my trust first. He'd kept the video.

Thom shoved me hard again. He was so much stronger than me and this only made the rage grow.

"Don't you touch me," I said, straining, baring my teeth. "Don't you dare touch me."

"You're disgusting, Kate. I always knew you were a slut."

My scars, my naked body, were on his computer. "Delete it!" The rage took over. I rushed forward and shoved him, scratched at his face. He pushed me back. I could hear footsteps up the hall. *Thom's mum.*

I got to my feet, my vision blurring. I rushed at him again.

. . .

I don't know if I hit my head or what happened, but the next thing I knew I was outside, hammering on the front door of Thom's house with my fists, blood on my fingertips, blood streaming from my nose. Suddenly aware of my surroundings, I stopped, stepped back from the door, and tried to collect myself, to steady my breathing. I looked around. My phone was on the lawn, as if it had been tossed outside. A neighbor was peering out the window of the house across the road and the builders working next door were watching me. I had blacked out. Was this an aftereffect of the concussion? Had that bottle broken something inside my brain?

I sobbed all the way home, tears streaming down my face. It felt as if nothing would be okay ever again.

I didn't hear from him for several days after that. I had called and messaged him on Facebook. It was clear our relationship was over, but it was important to me that he knew why I was angry. I needed him to understand that what he had done was also a betrayal and he needed to delete everything.

Dad knew something was going on but he didn't ask any questions. He let me mourn the death of my first proper relationship in my own way. In silence and darkness in my room, binge-watching TV shows. I typed a message to Willow's dad.

I broke it off.

Oh, Kate. It's not easy, it never is.

I just wish I could jump forward in time to when I feel better.

> Sounds like you need an escape.

But I had no energy for lust. I was too preoccupied with the guilt, the fear and anger.

> I don't think we should be sending each other
> messages for a while.

Around the same time Willow messaged me.

> I just saw Thom's Instagram post. Are you okay? Who is
> this older man?

It was accompanied by a love heart and a winking emoji. I began to notice something happening online. Thom had posted a plain black image to Instagram captioned with a simple sad face. Beneath it I read the string of replies:

> Some things happen that should surprise you but they
> don't.
> What happened?

Thom had responded.

> Turns out she's into old men.
> What a slut.
> Forget her man.

I received one or two direct messages from his friends.

> What the fuck is wrong with you?

How could you do this to Thom? Scum.

Did they understand what Thom did to me?

After a few days I deleted my Facebook, my Snapchat, and my Instagram apps. I would stay away from it all and go e-incognito until things blew over. Another message came through from Willow's dad.

Kate, we need to talk. It's urgent. Can we meet?

I didn't respond.

I often wondered how much Dad knew. Those first few days when I told him I was too sick to go to school, did he know that there was nothing physically wrong with me? Did he know more than he let on? Did he know about the text messages to Willow's dad? He would touch my shoulder and give me a sad look. He would heat chicken soup and bring me books to read, although I never opened any of them.

Later that week, I heard a knock on the front door. I was up in my room and when Dad opened up I could hear Willow's voice.

"Hi, Willow. Haven't seen you in a while."

"Is Kate here?" No greeting.

"She's sleeping right now. She hasn't been well."

"She hasn't been well. I bet." She sounded mad; did she know?

"Right," Dad said. "Would you like me to have her call you?"

"No. Just tell her I'll be seeing her soon."

Later that night, the text message came through.

We all know what you did. Everyone knows. How could you? One of Thom's friends figured it out. And he is spreading the word. Mum is leaving. This is my family.

> He's my fucking dad! This isn't a game, Kate. You've
> ruined my fucking life.

For an hour I drafted replies, but in the end nothing I wrote seemed appropriate. Anyway, we hadn't had sex, and Willow's dad had made me believe their marriage had run its course. I had one missed call from him, but he didn't leave a message.

No one approached me when I walked through the school gate, but I could feel their eyes tracking me. So it was true what Willow had said, word really had spread. The inner east of Melbourne was far too small to escape a scandal like this. Thom and Willow both had friends at Windsor Girls' Grammar; they were all connected online.

At first I mistook the other girls' expressions for sympathy, but in fact it was closer to mortification, or perhaps awe. Awe at my stupidity. Everything was too still, too calm. Hands trapped secrets between mouths and ears. Eyebrows rose as I passed. The breeze of a whisper swept by, chilling my skin. Tara and Anika, girls I had once been friends with, walked quickly away when they saw me heading toward them. I didn't need them, I told myself. I'd be going to uni next year. I'd make new friends, start a new life. I'd just have to ride it out.

Each step across the quad was harder than the last. *Slut*, someone hissed. I turned to look at the cluster of girls I'd just passed, but no one would meet my gaze. Slut-shaming and bullying were taken seriously. Girls could be suspended for it, but what would happen if I went to a teacher? In the end it would only get worse.

My first lesson that morning was biology. As I entered the classroom, Mr. Dornish raised one eyebrow in the way he did when delivering a sardonic line. He didn't say anything, though; he simply nodded to a vacant seat near the back of the room. Someone muttered *skank* loud enough for me to hear, and this was greeted with a few sniggers. I wondered if Mr. Dornish had heard. If he had, he didn't react.

Skank. It rattled around like something loose in the engine of my mind. It made me mad that other girls couldn't empathize with me; would it help if they knew what Thom did to me? My thoughts grew so loud I couldn't hear anyone else, I couldn't read. I sat frowning at the page. Eventually, when I had mustered the courage, I raised my hand.

"Yes, Kate, you may be excused."

I sat in the bathroom and cried. It might have been five minutes, it might have been half an hour; I was still there when the bell rang. When I got back to class I found my bag open. On top was a note scrawled on the corner of a torn page. *We know what you did. Do everyone a favor and kill yourself.* I packed up my things and left.

I crossed the quad alone. Tara came up beside me. Tara, the barnacle that stuck to sinking ships. Tara, who would be the first to stand on your face in her effort to climb another rung of the social ladder. She linked her arm through mine and leaned in close.

"Seriously, Kate," she said. "I'm hearing some weird things from lots of people. What actually happened?"

I pulled my arm free and strode away. "I've seen it anyway," she called after me. "We've all seen it."

Seen it?

Seen what?

PART FIVE

The Man in the Dark

In the past month, how often have you experienced flashbacks or other dissociative reactions in which the traumatic event is recurring?

0. never;   1. rarely;   2. sometimes;   3. often;   4. all the time

Thirty-five

MYSTERY SURROUNDS 17-YEAR-OLD
FOUND UNCONSCIOUS IN HAWKESBURN

Victoria police are attempting to piece together how a
teen was rendered unconscious on a sleepy suburban
avenue in the inner east early on Tuesday morning.

Thom Moreau, 17, is currently in a critical condition at St. Vincent's Hospital Melbourne after sustain-
ing blunt-force trauma causing extensive bleeding in
the brain.

Police are trying to determine the cause of the
trauma and as yet have not ruled out assault, investiga-
tors said.

Moreau, a promising young photographer who
planned to travel the world next year, was described as
"outgoing and fiercely intelligent" by his teachers at
Melbourne Boys' Collegiate, where he is in his final
year.

Text messages recovered from Moreau's phone suggest he was on his way to meet his ex-girlfriend when the incident occurred.

Moreau was found outside of his family home in Hawkesburn and police have appealed for any witnesses to come forward.

"We are asking members of the public to come forward with any information about suspicious vehicles or individuals around Lachlan Avenue, Bellpark Drive, and Dorcus Road, or Hawkesburn Park between Lachlan Avenue and Dorcus Road," Detective Inspector Peter Collins said.

Police believe the incident occurred between one and three a.m.

CCTV images from the surrounding area are being reviewed. If you have any information regarding this or any other open case, please call Crime Stoppers.

AFTER

Thirty-six

can't face him. I tense everything, ready for what is coming.

"Evie?"

Evie. I expel all the air from my lungs at once and hang my head for a few breaths before turning around.

"Iso."

The lightbulb still swings gently in the draft coming in through the door. I suddenly feel claustrophobic in the small space with him blocking the doorway.

"What are you doing? Your uncle said that you poisoned the dog."

"I've got to go."

"Jesus," he says, his eyes traveling about the damage to the door and within the shed. "Hope you weren't trying to kill a mouse." He laughs nervously.

"No," I say. "No."

I step past him out the door. He follows me up the back lawn toward the driveway.

"Where's your uncle now, Evie?"

"He's at the vet, and I'm running out of time. I have to leave right now. I think he deliberately poisoned Beau in order to blame me. I think he killed someone back in Melbourne and has set me up."

"At my place you said that people think you killed someone, now you're saying it was your uncle. It sounds like a fantasy."

"A fantasy? You think I'm making it up?"

"I know he's had a couple of run-ins with the locals—he chased some kids on their bikes and one of them flipped into a ditch and hurt himself—but that doesn't make him a killer."

"He's not my uncle, Iso."

"What?"

"I said he's not my uncle. Don't call him my uncle." I turn to look him in the eye. "If you care about me, you will take me from this town right now."

"Let's go to the police."

"I have someone waiting for me in Melbourne. That's where I'm going. I just need to get to Auckland."

He scratches at his patchy stubble. "Who is it?"

The question takes me by surprise. "Why does that matter?"

"What?"

"Why does that matter?"

He looks offended for a second. "I was just wondering. Is it, like, a boyfriend or something?"

"We don't have time for this, Iso. We can talk in the car."

"You said you killed someone, Evie. You said—"

"No, they think I did but I didn't. It's him—Jim. He's controlling everything."

"Let me take you to the police."

"No police."

Iso's jaw clenches, and he squints up toward the road before turning back to me. I know the look he's giving me, somewhere between concern and skepticism. He doesn't believe me; he sees a crazy girl.

"No," I say. I reach forward and grip his wrists. "No. You need to believe me, Iso. You've got to take me to Auckland. We need to go *now.*"

A car is coming up the road. The sound startles both of us; the red light of urgency fills the air.

"Please, Iso, get me out of here."

"Let me talk to him." The car turns down the driveway.

"Iso, no," I say. I can hear the desperation in my voice. "We have to run—now!"

It is all happening so quickly. The car jerks to a stop and Jim climbs out.

"What the fuck?" The door slams.

He's on Iso in a heartbeat. Shirtfront knotted in his fist, dragging him right up close to his face. He pulls his arm back, ready to strike. Iso raises his palms, turns his face away, bracing for the blow.

I can see it takes all his self-control to refrain from hitting Iso. His face is red with anger. "Stay the fuck away from her," he snarls. He drags Iso toward the road, then throws him to the hard gravel at the road's edge.

"Hey, relax, I didn't mean to—"

"She's sick, okay? She's not right in the head. She makes up stories, her entire life is a fucking fiction. She has a condition and you're taking advantage of it."

"Okay," Iso says, his hands out in front of him, placating. "Okay, I just wanted to help. I didn't realize."

He will come for me next. I reach into my jeans and surreptitiously throw my passport under a shrub.

"I asked you to keep an eye on her, but you just sneak over here when I'm out to do . . . what? What exactly do you want from her?"

His gaze swings back to me, but I can't for the life of me look up and meet it. I could run, but I wouldn't get far. What will he do when he sees the shed?

Iso gets to his feet and brushes the gravel from his hands. "I'm sorry, man. I didn't mean to get involved."

A snatch of memory. Jim scrubbing his hands at the sink. It's just a beat, a flash of recollection, but I know it was from *that* night. *He was scrubbing his hands.*

His dark-ringed eyes run over my face. His drawn cheeks shape a sad smile. He has aged a decade in the past month. The late nights, it is all making sense now. He has the nightmares too.

"Where is Beau? Is he okay?"

"We'll have to wait and see. He's not coming back to us anyway."

"Why not?"

"Well, you're getting your way, Kate. We are going home."

"You're lying."

"I wish I was, but it's true." He nods toward the door. "Come on, let's go inside. This is our last night."

We go to the kitchen and I sit on a stool at the island with that cold, tight twist in the pit of my stomach. How can I defend myself when the ax is still in the shed?

He smears his hand down his face. "I'm going to miss you," he says. "It's going to be tough."

"Miss me?"

"It's going to be so bloody hard," he says. He rests his hand on my forehead. He has lied to me so many times; he's doing it again now. "They're going to put you away. I can't protect you from it any longer."

"You won't let them take me," I say. "You're just trying to trick me again."

The room is still. "Enough," he says.

My anger boils over. "You didn't send my letters. You knew that if you did he would come for me. You didn't want me to leave you behind. It's another trick."

"It's time to face reality, Kate. This can't go on. You've got to grow up. I'm not going to beat around the bush anymore." He grabs my shoulder and leans in close, his voice just a whisper. "Your boyfriend died. You remember that, don't you? Remember what happened to Thom?"

An uppercut of memory hits. My eyes turn to liquid. I breathe in and out. It's so clear. Thom is lying facedown, his skull dashed on the curb.

"I fucking killed him, Kate, and you just stood there and watched."

BEFORE

Thirty-seven

wasn't able to watch more than a few seconds before rushing to the bathroom to retch over the toilet bowl. Nothing came up but a throat full of scorching bile.

You could tell it was me in the video without even looking at my face; you only had to see those swirling pink clouds on my thighs. The sting of betrayal and anger filled in my veins like venom. How could he? How could he do that to me? And I had let him film it—I had been so stupid to trust him. All those times we were warned at school about what we put online, about who we had contact with, where our photos and videos ended up. They never warned us about people we loved and trusted, about what they could put out there. A video was being watched around the world of me and Thom tangled in a breathless tryst. He was holding the camera so it didn't show his face, only mine. I would never have a good life, start a family, get a job with this hanging over me.

Dad had spoken to his lawyer, Paul, who had been a family

friend for years—someone Dad could trust. I'm sure even Paul watched the video. Dad also contacted the police. Dad didn't watch the video but he knew what it was and that I was in it and that was enough. He knew my life had changed. Was he disappointed that I was no longer his little girl?

I had loved Thom for a time. But love, I learned quickly, is fickle. The anger didn't abate, and the fantasies began. I wanted to hurt him. I wanted *him* to feel the pain and embarrassment that I was feeling.

On Monday evening, when Dad and Paul had gone out to meet with Thom's parents and *their* lawyer, I texted Willow's dad. I told him I needed to see him. I couldn't talk to my own dad about what was happening, but I could talk to Willow's. He had filled two needs, the comfort I missed from Thom and the lack of communication with Dad.

I waited and waited, but I didn't hear from him. I went to the cabinet in the hall with the dusty old bottles of whiskey, unopened gifts from years gone by. I opened one and tipped it back until my throat caught fire and my eyes watered. The coughing came on so strong and fast it bent me double.

I took another long draft, the warmth, the buzzing energy, diffusing within me, into my limbs, the tips of my fingers. Another swallow, then another. The more I drank, the easier it became.

I took the bottle to the couch and turned on the late news. Talking heads on TV. The screen split in three for the three commentators. I lay on the couch listening. A man's voice explained that I should have had enough self-respect not to let someone film me having sex. That I had been asking for trouble.

"... *obviously we can't name anyone, but rumors have circulated on social media and let me just say, there is a well-known member of the Australian sporting community at the center of the story."*

Another voice added, *"I've heard the same rumors and, given the profile of the father, I would have thought that this girl would have had more sense—"*

"That's victim blaming," a third voice objected. *"And quite frankly, Rob, you are feeding the trolls with this speculation. Consenting to have sex and consenting to film a sex act is not the same as consenting to share the footage. You need to underst—"*

I lifted the remote and muted the sound.

I continued to drink. Normally Dad and I would both have been in bed by now. I'd have been thinking about school, fretting over assignments, messaging friends. Dad would have been setting out his clothes near the foot of his bed ready for the morning, his watch and underwear sitting on top. Pumping out his evening set of press-ups.

I checked to see if any new messages had come through from Willow's dad. Nothing yet. I sent another one, just a series of question marks, then took another long drink from the bottle. I sent a message to Thom.

> I hate you, Thom. I wish I never met you. I wish you would disappear.

Tears stung my eyes. I had nothing to look forward to ever again. My life was over. A reply came through from Thom but I didn't open it.

I went to the kitchen and pulled a small paring knife from the drawer. I pressed the tip against my wrist, gently at first, then a little harder until a pearl of blood appeared. My breath came on fast. I couldn't press any harder; I didn't have it in me.

I dropped the knife, slamming my palm down on the island. Eyes clamped shut, chest trembling. Eventually I grabbed my phone and texted Willow's dad once more.

> I don't know if I will get through this. I just want to end it. I just want him to feel the pain I feel. Please help me.

I pictured all sorts of tortures befalling Thom. The rage was swelling and swelling. I imagined all the pain in the world, but in the end it just made me weaker in the limbs. It began crowding my brain, overpowering my thoughts.

I put the bottle to my lips and drank as long and hard as I could. The blood had smeared a little on my wrist and between drinks I put my tongue to it, the metallic taste mixing with the whiskey. I couldn't just sit there while Thom went unpunished. I couldn't just be alone.

I was still drinking when Dad got home. His eyes went first to the bottle, then to my face.

"What are you doing, Kate?"

I looked down at the trail of red at my wrist. Dad's face went slack. He took my wrist in his hand and stared at it. He looked like he was going to cry.

"No," he said. "Please, Kate, no. This can't happen, not again."

Not again.

"This is Thom's fault," he was saying, more to himself than to me. "That fucking boy's ruined your life."

He picked up the bottle and took it away. I could hear him opening cupboards in the bathroom—searching for disinfectant and a bandage no doubt.

I opened Thom's message.

Let's talk. Can you meet me at the spot? I'll head down
now.

I'll head down now. The message had been sent half an hour ago.
He would already be there.

I picked up the keys Dad had left on the kitchen counter and
went to the garage, my stride unsteady. I clambered into the driver's seat and lifted the lever to drag it forward. It wasn't far; I'd be
there in no time. This was my chance to make him pay for what
he had done.

The car seemed less responsive than when I had driven before. As I backed out I heard a scraping sound and saw too late
that the side of the car was sliding against the brick wall. On the
street, I shifted the gears into drive and saw Dad rush out from
the house and sprint toward me. I swerved to avoid him and ac-
celerated up the street. In the rearview mirror I saw Dad running. He would never catch me. When I looked up again he
wasn't there. I swerved to avoid a car parked by the side of the
road. It was becoming harder and harder to concentrate. Thom
had ruined my life. All my visions of the future, all my ambition
and dreams, he took it all. My anger was growing. I sped up.

AFTER

Thirty-eight

The scene is so clear, I can see it all. The blow to Thom's skull, him collapsing. Jim standing there with a brick in his hand. I'm lying on my bed with it all playing in my mind when his broad frame fills the doorway.

"What exactly were you planning anyway?"

Does he know about the flight I booked? The passport?

"I wasn't planning—"

"Don't lie to me. I'm sick of the lies."

"I'm sorry."

"That doesn't answer my question."

"I wanted to go back to how it was. That's all. I thought if I got back to Melbourne, Thom would be alive. It's impossible, I know. But I thought I could clear my name and my life would go back to being normal." Even as I say the words, I know it doesn't make sense.

"This all ends tomorrow, Kate. Okay? I'm sorry, but I can't do this anymore."

What ends? My captivity? My life?

"You've put on seven kilos in a month. I thought if we healed your body your mind would catch up, but it didn't." He looks grim. "So tomorrow you're going somewhere new and we will just hope that it'll all work out."

"Where am I going?"

"Let's not think about it now; we'll cross that bridge tomorrow."

I swallow and try to smile. "Did you want me to light the fire?"

"That's not a good idea," he says. "You stay in here and try to get some sleep." He fishes in his pocket and produces another of those blue diamond pills. "Take this for now." He watches closely as my hand comes close to my mouth, but I drop the pill, feel it catch in the front of my pajama top. I mime swallowing. "Open up."

I do.

"Good girl, rest up." He closes my door and slides the bolt in place. "Just knock if you need to use the bathroom," he says from outside, his voice muffled.

I hear him pad up the hall to the bathroom and then, a few minutes later, the thrumming of the shower. I glance at the book on my bedside table. *Don't trust him.* There's something I'm missing. He is telling me one thing, but what if he is telling the police another? What if he's framed me for his crime and now he wants to hand me over to the police? And it has become suddenly urgent for him. Is it because of new CCTV evidence or is it because he knows how close I am to the truth?

I reach for the book, taking out the photo of me as a baby, staring at it. Then I read the words once more. *Don't trust him.* The ax would do the trick. One firm blow and it would all be over. Or maybe I could use the rifle? Whatever I decide, it has to happen tonight. I lie in bed, waiting, plotting how I will do it. Down the ladder once more and into the night.

I think of Mum. Where would I be if she had survived? I could never live with that sort of torture, with her sickness.

I hear the back door slide open and stand to look out the window. He's crossing the lawn, holding his mobile phone to his ear, but there's a tea towel folded between his mouth and the microphone.

He stops at the open door of the shed. He can see what I have done. He lowers the phone and turns to look up at my window.

I brace myself and wait for the pain to begin.

Thirty-nine

The door explodes inward. He crosses the room in two strides and is on me. His hands grip me viselike.

"Where the fuck is it, Kate?"

I don't resist. He twists my arms behind my back, up my spine. I feel a crack in my shoulder. Something binds my wrists, then he shoves me up against the headboard. Tears are rolling down my cheeks but I can't move my hands to wipe them away.

"No more games, Kate. This is fucking serious." He grabs my head in both hands, shouts into my face: "Tell me where it is!"

I avoid his gaze. He shakes my skull. "Look at me." He shakes again until I look into his eyes. He's not wearing his glasses now.

"Why are you doing this?" I sob. "Are you going to kill me?"

"What are you planning on doing with the gun, Kate?"

"With what?"

A spark of anger in his eyes; his nostrils flare. "Don't play dumb." When he swallows, his entire neck seems to expand and contract. He springs a single tear in each eye. "What the hell am I going to do? I just wanted you to be different from her." *From who?*

Crocodile tears. He will do anything to fool me.

"I'm sorry, okay? I'm sorry. Please just leave me alone," I beg.

"No. I'm not leaving you. I'm staying right here until you tell me where the gun is."

I can feel the muscles in my face betray me. A tightening of the jaw. "What gun?"

"I know you were out there in the shed. I know you've taken it. I'm not letting you leave this room until you tell me where you've put it."

"What are you talking about?"

"We both know I can't let you have that gun."

"You bought it for me—to kill me."

He laughs, sounding almost delirious. "I'm just so exhausted. I can't do it anymore. Sitting up all night, waiting for the day I discover you're gone."

The restraints around my wrists are too tight; my fingers are growing numb. "It's hurting me."

"I'm not letting you go. I can't risk it."

"Please, I can't feel my hands."

He leaves the room; I can hear him out in the yard, climbing the ladder. The drill screams into the wood outside my window.

When he comes back he's carrying a pair of pliers. Jerking me by my elbow, he flips me onto my stomach. There's a snap and then the tension around my wrists eases.

"Put your hands in front of you."

I do.

He binds them once more with cable ties, this time a little looser.

"Last chance, Kate: where is the gun?"

"No," I say. "No."

His hand comes across my face. My jaw snaps to the side and

suddenly I am dizzy. "Where the fuck is it?" He has a trickle of my blood on the palm of his hand.

"Go on, kill me. Kill me like you killed Thom."

He lifts me by the collar of my pajama top and pins me against the wall. A button pops. "Where is the gun?"

I spit in his face. Blood and saliva drip from his nose. He releases me and I slide down the wall.

He begins with the dresser. Ripping the drawers out one at a time, tipping them upside down. Then he flips the mattress, the bed base, and I tumble hard to the floor. He strides to the wardrobe and kicks at the door, his foot passing through it. A crack like thunder and flying splinters. He kicks again. The door folds forward. My clothes, my escape bag, my shoes all fly across the room. He tears the curtains from the rail. One end of the rail comes away from the wall and hangs down.

"Where the fuck did you put it?"

"It wasn't me. I didn't take it."

He storms from the room and I notice then that his limp is back; his knee is bad again. The door slams and I am left sitting amid the wreckage. My head is still singing from the blow. The lock closes.

The man who was once my father . . . once a husband . . . always a killer.

PART SIX

Both Sides

Is there a history of mental health issues in your family?

__ Yes __ No __ Unsure

BEFORE

Forty

My coach has given me *personal time* away from rugby. It was that or quit altogether because someone has to look after Kate, and God knows it's not going to be Bella. So while my career should be peaking, and all of my plans and goals slip through my fingers, Bella is nestled up in bed reading that book of hers and using Kate's photo as her bookmark.

She seems to have it pretty good to me. Other than her trips to the psychologist, she hasn't left the house in a week. I have lost my parents; I have felt the weight of sadness. Hopelessness shares a fence line with fatigue but the problem is Bella isn't even trying. Would it kill her to show the child a little attention? How the hell can she expect us to keep raising Kate properly when she can't even get out of bed?

I remind myself of what she was like five years ago in the weeks after Kate was born. The way she squeezed the baby against her body and gently stroked her cheek with the back of her finger. Bella often cried when she touched Kate. They weren't tears of joy or gratitude, they were caused by something else entirely.

Immediately after the birth, I asked her to resume taking her medication but she didn't want to breastfeed with the chemicals in her system. Formula wasn't an option because she had read somewhere how important breast milk was for an infant. Bella's sister, Lizzie, was visiting from London at the time and she liked to throw the word *postpartum* around as though it was worse than usual, as though the sadness hadn't been with Bella since she and I had met in our teen years. Lizzie also pushed her view of what she called "Big Pharma." As far as Lizzie was concerned, organic food and "natural living" were far more restorative than Western medicine. When Lizzie disappeared back to London, she left behind her half-baked ideas. The *fair-weather sister* hasn't been back to Melbourne since.

That first year was tough for both of us. Then when I finally convinced her to start taking her medication again—Kate was on solids and we had found an organic milk formula—she only lasted one month before stopping again. She said it was like living under dense fog.

Since then everything in this family has been about Bella. Whenever it seems like she might be feeling better, I find another mark on her body, or more of those horrible words she writes in her journal: *Physical pain is a footnote in the ledger of my suffering* and *How long can I last with this ache?* Despite what Bella wanted, I made a plan then that I would fill her prescription myself, I would take it into my own hands to get her medication into her body.

Maybe I left it in the wrong place, or open at the wrong page, but somehow Bella knew that I had been reading her journal. Her anger flared like a struck match, then very quickly fizzled out.

"How dare you? Those are my private thoughts. How could you breach my trust like that?" When the tears began I closed my arms around her and stroked her back. While I held her, she spoke. "You know, James," she began, "Bill at the pharmacy called today. He just wanted to let me know my repeat was almost up; they said I would need a new prescription. But I haven't been filling my prescription for a while." I drew a breath. I knew what was coming. "You've been feeding me them, haven't you?"

"Bella, you have to take them. Think about Kate."

"How can you say that? I think about her every second of every day. Kate's the only thing keeping me here."

"What do you mean?"

"I mean we've tried your way and it doesn't work. We've tried everything."

The burns on Kate's legs are just as much Bella's fault as they are mine. Eloise, the nanny, was supposed to come down to the Portsea house but she had called in sick and Bella was staying up at the hospital in the throes of a particularly dark period. The hot-water cylinder was scheduled for repair later in the week and Kate was sitting in tepid water, yelling my name. It was too cold, she said.

I thought I'd take a look myself. Kneeling in the garage, staring at the thermometer, hopelessly I tried to divine what could be wrong. When I rose to my feet again, I noticed a plastic bag I hadn't seen before tucked in behind my golf clubs. I reached and pulled it out. Kate was shrieking again but I couldn't look away from what I'd found. Within the bag there were a few meters of hose and a new roll of masking tape. You add a car to that equation and you have everything you need to drive somewhere with a view and comfortably put yourself to sleep.

There could only be one reason it was in the garage: Bella had left it there. She must have had it all prepared and faltered at the last minute. Or possibly an even worse scenario: she had it all set up and was planning on doing it soon. My stomach clenched. A sudden rage swept over me. She didn't trust me, she would never talk to me about it. How could she even think about abandoning our daughter? She wanted to leave me to raise Kate alone, to explain to Kate that her mother didn't care enough to stick it out.

"*Dad*," Kate called in one long, drawn-out syllable; I could hear the angry tears in her voice. I tried to calm myself but I couldn't. Rushing back into the house, I dumped the bag and its contents in the bin. I put a large soup pot of water on the stovetop. I ran my hands through my hair. *Will Bella deny what she was planning?* My mind still wheeled and my hands were shaking. Kate called again.

"Just wait one damn minute, I'm fixing it!"

The water seemed to be hot enough; it was steaming in the pot. I took it from the burner, marched to the bath, and tipped the pot up so the water splashed in. Kate screamed. *What is it? What is it, Kate, use your words.* When I saw the skin, flayed from her thighs in long strips of blisters, I realized what I had done. I reached for the drain, but the water was too hot for me to grab it. I ripped her out of the bath, running to the shower downstairs with her in my arms. Cold water sprayed over us both while she howled.

"It's okay, darling. It's going to be fine."

Her screams didn't stop, not even at the hospital. They went on and on.

That was two weeks ago. I can see Bella is better after her time in the hospital because she is making attempts to interact with Kate, who now shows her burns off with pride. Children don't mind being different at that age, but it's only a matter of time before that pride she feels morphs into shame.

That evening, for the first time in months, Bella and I have sex. She drags me down onto her, pressing her lips hard against mine, pulling my shirt up over my head. I feel like a teenager. It almost seems like she really is happy, but when I look down into her face, I can see the detachment, I can see her wince with each thrust. Afterward as we lie there holding each other and when she thinks I'm asleep, I hear her sniffles, I feel warm tears running from her cheek to burn my chest like battery acid.

The following afternoon I drop Bella at her psychologist. There is no kiss or farewell; she simply wanders, dead-eyed, into the building. I wait a moment, watching the door to ensure she's inside before heading back home. Soon I head to pick Kate up from daycare.

With her dark pigtails bouncing, she runs from the gate into my arms.

"Kiss for Daddy." She lays one on my cheek. "Ready to go pick up Mama?"

We drive to the clinic, parking at the rear. Bella's appointment started forty-five minutes ago at one fifteen, which means any second now she will walk out the door. I turn to Kate in the back seat. She's staring out the window. Five minutes pass. Then ten and there is still no sign of her.

Something is wrong. I can feel it in the base of my neck, in my bones and chest.

"Can you wait here for one minute while I go get Mama?"

I lock the car and briskly walk to the entrance. The receptionist is on the phone. She glances up.

"Where's Dr. Lewis's office?"

"Hold for one second please," the receptionist says into the phone. Then she presses her palm over the microphone and looks up.

"Where's Dr. Lewis's office?" I repeat.

"Dr. Lewis is with a patient."

Relief washes over me. She's still here.

"Okay, thanks. Will she be much longer?"

"I'm sorry, who are you?"

"I'm here for my wife. She should be finishing up at any minute."

The woman glances down at her watch, then back up. "Dr. Lewis will be in her current appointment for another forty minutes."

It all comes crashing down. I dropped Bella off and watched her walk inside. Today is Tuesday. She has an appointment every Tuesday. *It's just a mix-up.*

"Did Bella Bennet stay for her appointment?"

"I'm sorry?"

"My wife had a one fifteen appointment with Dr. Lewis. I need to know if she went into it."

"I'm afraid that's confiden—"

I don't let her finish. I storm past reception and begin opening doors.

"Bella," I call. "Bella?"

First I find a doctor with a patient. I can hear the receptionist's heels clapping on the tiles behind me. *Excuse me, excuse me.* But I don't stop. Behind the next door I open, I find Dr. Lewis with a man sitting across from her. They're both startled to see me burst through the door.

"When did she leave?"

"Sorry, what is this about?"

"Bella is my wife, I'm here to pick her up."

"Bella," she says, removing her glasses. "She left"—glancing up at the clock on the wall—"almost half an hour ago. She said you were here early and you were going to pick up your daughter together."

"She's gone?" I say. I don't wait for a response.

I sprint from the building to the car, ripping the door open. As I drive out of the car park onto the road, the wheels skid. Traffic is light. I know exactly where Bella is going but I have to get there first. She must have taken a taxi. I race down the highway, with Kate sitting in the back, her seat belt across her lap. Her eyes are stretched wide with panic.

"Where's Mama, Daddy? Where is she?"

"We're going to see her now, darling. Don't worry."

The car flies into the bends, the engine growling as I press the accelerator harder to the floor. There's a near miss as I pass a truck. I hear the bassy drone of the horn receding behind us. I clench my jaw, urging a green light ahead to stay green. Mixed in with the fear and sadness is a rage that makes me squeeze the wheel like I'm choking it. How could she make us live like this? Why wouldn't she talk to me about it?

It takes an hour before I reach Portsea. I slide in beside the house and sprint to the door. I reach out and find it's unlocked. *She's here.*

The first thing that I notice is a strange dark stain on the pale rug in the lounge. Then I see the tiled floor shining as if wet. I look up. Water is flooding down the stairs, dripping between the banisters. Taking off at a sprint, I slip, my knee twists, and I collapse with pain, but I can't stop. Back on my feet, I hobble up the steps toward the bathroom. Water flows out from beneath the door. When I turn the handle it doesn't open.

"Bella," I call with a tremor of desperation. "Bella, open up!"

I kick the door. It doesn't budge. I kick again as hard as I can.

My knee explodes with pain. The handle snaps and the door swings in. Water flows over the edge of the bath. My heart stops. I rush to her. Floating, eyes closed, arms out. The water has a rose tint. On my knees I drag her body from the bath, howling, screaming. *No, no, no, please. No, no, Bella.* I'm pressing my ear to her cold lips when I hear her voice. Not Bella's but Kate's.

"Mama?"

AFTER

Forty-one

The fog drifts off the sea, swallowing the village. Sleep drifts too, but before it can overwhelm me, I rise and walk around the room, determined to stay alert, not to drop my guard. Jim—it's surprising how quickly it's become second nature to think of him that way, as Jim rather than Dad—left me hours ago. He may be searching for the gun—maybe he thinks Iso took it—or perhaps he is sleeping.

Out there, in the empty night, floating up from the sea, comes a single word carried on the back of the waves to the shore: *Run, run, run.* He killed Thom, and he may kill me next.

As I pass the dresser, now missing its drawers, I see a glint in the empty cavity. It's the spare car key I hid there all those weeks ago. I reach for it, still hampered by the cable ties binding my wrists. I try to yank my hands, but they're bound too tight. After piercing the tie with one of my canine teeth, I begin to saw at it with the car key. Finally one tie snaps and relief floods my body. My hands are free.

Many would-be murderers fail to appreciate the durability of the skull. Extreme force exerted will crack bones, but there have been countless incidents of brains and skulls surviving extreme trauma. Nothing is guaranteed to collapse a skull but repeated and focused pressure.

No sound comes from the house. It could be two in the morning, three, four. I change out of my pajamas into track pants and a hoodie and retrieve my escape bag from the mess of the room. I reassemble my bed, then use clothes to create the shape of a human body beneath the covers. It's the small details that might save my life. The red dot of the camera watches me from the corner of the room. I never figured out how to obscure it but perhaps it won't be necessary. He could be watching the feed on his phone. But if he were, he'd be coming up the hall by now.

In the morning when he finds me gone, he will watch the recording from the camera. He will see me. In the darkness, I look up at that red light. *You made me do this.* I will be a pale green shape in the night, my eyes shining white and ghostly.

The window is fixed closed from the outside with two screws.

I take the pillow and press it against the wood of the window frame. Holding my breath, I draw myself back, then, with as much force as I can muster, I rock my shoulder into it. I pause a few seconds to catch my breath, then slam into the window frame once more. It hurts but this time there's a pop. One corner of the window has come unstuck.

Breathing heavily, I turn toward the door, anticipating a shout, footsteps. But all is quiet.

One more blow and the second screw snaps loose and I hurriedly push the window open.

The fog outside is so thick I can barely see the ground. I drop my escape bag down onto the frosted grass, where it lands with a thump. Then I ease myself through the window, feeling with my toes for the ladder. I reach further, and further still, until—too late—I realize it's no longer there. I try to pull myself back up onto the sill, clawing for purchase, but my fingers slip and I fall.

A second of flight. My body twisting through the air. Then a splintering pain. It takes all my willpower to contain the shriek as a sharp throbbing starts in my shoulder. The pain is so intense I feel like throwing up. I lift my head and am almost overwhelmed by dizziness. I can feel one of my headaches coming on as I try to stand. A shock runs up my leg when I put weight on it and each small movement is agony. I lower myself to a crawl. It's all I can do to keep from howling.

Gritting my teeth, I pull myself across the icy grass with the escape bag on my back. When I reach the side of the house I stand on my good leg, then hop toward the shrub into which I tossed the passport. I scrabble around, grasping with my fingers. Leaves, cold hard earth, twigs . . . Finally, my hand lands on the passport. *Move, Kate, move.*

I shove the passport into the bag. Pushing through the pain, I stagger toward the car. The door unlocks with a *thunk* and I wrench it open and fall into the driver's seat, slinging the bag onto my lap.

The car will be easy enough to drive, I assure myself. I have done it before. *But with one arm?* I slide the key into the ignition and start the engine. As it roars to life, I recall the last time I drove a car; I see Thom running, see his head rock back and his body become still by the roadside. *But it wasn't me. I didn't do it.* It was Jim; he admitted it. He has been manipulating me all along, making me believe I did it.

The headlights come on automatically. The cab steams up, misting the window, and outside the fog is so dense I can barely see the house at all. I push the gearstick into reverse and step on the accelerator. The car won't move. It just revs and revs. *Go, go, go.*

A light comes on inside the house. *Fucking move.* I press harder but still the car is stationary and he's coming. I see his silhouette flying through the kitchen toward the front door.

The car shoots back as if of its own volition. I can't turn the wheel fast enough with my one hand. A crunching thud and I'm thrown back hard against the seat. I press the accelerator and the wheels just spin and spin. The car is grinding against the tree. He's coming.

I open the door and dive out. I hit the driveway and roll with my bag held against my chest. I crawl into the bushes running up beside the house as the front door is thrown open.

Peering through the foliage, I see Jim. He switches on a flashlight and stands still, scanning the driveway with the beam. I hold my breath.

"Where are you?"

He is circling the car, shining the flashlight through its windows.

Next thing I know, he has a phone to his ear. "Police . . . Hello, I'd like to report a—" He stops, starts again. "Someone—er, my daughter—has just attempted to steal my car. She's slammed it into a tree and now she's run off. I believe she may be armed. . . ." He's bluffing. He said "daughter," not "niece." He's not really talking to the police. He just wants me to think he is. "Maketu," he says.

He starts walking up the driveway and I shuffle closer to the house.

"Yes, a rifle . . . Well, how long will they be? . . . No, she's not going to hurt me—it's her I'm worried about."

She may be armed. The gun—I need the gun.

"All right, all right. Just please come quickly." He goes back inside.

So, are the police coming or not? The call sounded convincing, but he might be bluffing. He hasn't involved the New Zealand police all this time; why would he involve them now? It will only incriminate me further. I'm a killer who tried to steal her father's car.

The cold needles into my clothes; it creeps into my flesh as I squat in the bushes, trying to decide what to do. I could run to Iso's. I sense he was starting to believe me about Jim. He's my only chance.

I crawl out from my hiding place, pulling myself along the grass toward the fence I threw the gun over. I reach the fence and pull myself up. *Keep going, Kate. Don't stop now.*

Gripping the top and hopping with my good leg, I get up onto it. I fold myself over and balance for a second with the edge of the wooden fence digging into my waist. I let go and tip over. The hard earth rises suddenly and thumps the wind from me. I'm flat on my back, my lungs burning with each breath. I crawl to the bush, see the glint of the gun barrel. I grasp the rifle and find the small box of ammunition.

Now, with everything I need, I move in a hunched limp up the neighbor's driveway. Each step sets off an electrical storm of pain in my body. As I reach the road I hear something behind me and below: a car starting. *Is it his car?* There's the sound of metal scraping as it moves off the tree.

I stumble on as quickly as I can. When I look back, headlights blind me. I dive into the cover of the bushes lining the road. Lying there, I fumble in my pocket for the box of ammunition. Finding a bullet, I pull back the bolt on the rifle's barrel, press it into the cavity, then slide the bolt closed. Now it's loaded.

The car slides to a halt at the road's edge a little way behind me. A door opens and closes. A flashlight beam plays over the foliage on either side of the asphalt. I grip the rifle with my left hand, aim it back up the road. *Could I pull the trigger?*

He is back in the car now, moving along the road slowly. I hold myself still, hardly daring to breathe. Adrenaline courses through me.

The car stops again, nearer now. I can hear the engine ticking as it cools. A flashlight beam leaps out into the night. I can barely contain myself; the bush seems to rattle with my body. The beam skims just above my head. A fire burns in my right shoulder as I use both hands to aim the rifle. My breath stops. I can feel warmth pooling between my thighs, down my front. If he finds me he will kill me. The stranger inside is taking control of my arms and legs. My body is running on pure instinct now, my mind merely a spectator.

The light returns, slowly moving toward me. The bush seems so thin and flimsy, the latticework of twigs too fine to conceal me. Only the fog covers me now. A calmness comes over me. The stranger is in control. My breathing steadies and the rifle becomes still, aiming up toward the light. Then I squeeze the trigger. I'm almost surprised by the explosion. The gun slams itself against my body. The barrel jerks up. No thoughts. No emotions.

The echo comes back from down across the bay. Dogs start up. One or two at first, then more and more. An animal's hoarse breath whistles close by; I realize it is my own.

I open the bolt and thumb another bullet in. I point the gun and pull the trigger. This time the explosion is more violent, and my hands and arms are so fatigued I can barely keep hold of the gun at all.

The flashlight beam drops to the grass, where it remains. Seconds, minutes, hours, there's no telling how long I stay there, how long I am still before I thumb one more bullet into the gun.

I shot him.

Eventually I leave the cover of the bush and move off down the road. At one stage I look up and there ahead of me is the white dog, its three-legged gait strangely graceful, lighting my path. The next time I look, it is gone.

I reach the bottom of the hill. The dawn chorus is beginning in the trees and people will soon be waking. The long night is nearly over.

By the time Iso's house comes into view, I am nearly rigid with pain and fatigue. One arm is little more than a weight attached to my shoulder and I am dragging my bad leg. But I'm so close now. As I open the gate and stagger through, my tears flow freely. Tears of liberation? Of joy? The relief comes now like warm water on the coldest, darkest nights. Will they understand why I had to shoot him? I had no choice: it was me or him.

The security light comes on at the front door as I approach. I let the rifle rest against me, raise my good arm, and, with the last of my strength, I knock.

Forty-two

so is not wearing pajamas; that should have been a warning. If I had turned and looked back, I might have noticed a second car parked in the shadow of the house. He barely reacts when he sees me; there's just a subtle shift of his eyes, and his lips part. His gaze slowly travels down my body, taking in my injuries as if following the path of a falling feather.

"Iso," I croak.

"Jesus," he says, stepping forward. He reaches out and prizes my fingers from the rifle. He opens the bolt, tips out the bullet, flicks the safety on, then leans it by the door.

My body quakes with fatigue and chill.

Before I can move, his hands are on me, helping me inside. "Let's get you in beside the fire."

"He wouldn't let me leave," I say. "He was going to kill me."

"Shh," he says. "We will get you help."

It's early for a fire. "He was hurting me and he kept me locked away. I had to do it, Iso." How quickly I have slipped into the past tense, as though he is long dead.

"Hey," he says, guiding me along the hall. "It's okay." Then, a little louder, he calls, "It's her."

It's her. . . .

I can hear his mother murmuring in the lounge. *Who is she talking to?*

"We were expecting you," Iso says.

The heat presses against me as he opens the door to the lounge. The fire is roaring. I remember the first time I was here, how they tried to make me take a bath. A hot bath. It was a bath that took so much. . . .

My mother hadn't turned off the tap; the water just kept flowing and flowing, up her slender throat. Scarlet-tinted water. I remember how her body was suspended. Her face still damp, her eyes closed. I am my mother's daughter and my father's. The melancholy is hers, the rage is his. Choose either or both.

"I'm sorry, Kate," Iso says. *Kate . . . he knows my real name.* Something is wrong. It punches me right in the gut. "I'm so sorry."

Then I see why.

BEFORE

Forty-three

Fragments swam through my mind like strangers passing by in fog: turning my head and feeling the cool bite of the car window; the phone in my hand; intermittent flashes in the dark as the car sped past streetlights. Was it a dream or a memory?

Another sliver of light, a gasp of cold air as the car door opened and I stepped out into the night. Dad was there. Then I was back in the car. Dad opened the door, placed a brick on the back seat.

I fell asleep and woke again. We were back in the garage.

Where's my phone?

Here.

The headache drilled the base of my brain, and my vision was blurred. An echo of pain in my throat, a sort of mild burn. I was still in Dad's car. The Mercedes, not the Range Rover. My hands were trembling. No, not trembling, they were vibrating. Looking down, I saw *Suzie* on the screen of my phone. Thom's mum was ringing. Why? She hated me. I didn't answer the call.

Something wasn't right and I needed to figure it out but my mind felt sluggish.

The call rang out, then, almost at once, began to ring again.

I heard the door to the house open; Dad was coming back into the garage. I closed my eyes, feigning sleep. I cracked them open enough to watch him. The car door opened, then closed. I saw him again as he passed across the windscreen. He was holding something in his hand: it was the red brick. Then the lights went out in the garage and the door closed. He left me sitting there.

AFTER

Forty-four

K ate." That voice. The man who now hurries toward me is Jim.

"No, no, no, no—"

"Shhh."

I shrink away but he grabs me, pulls me into a hug, squeezing the air out of my lungs. It feels like a white-hot blade sliding into my shoulder.

"I'm so glad you're okay. Jesus, you had me worried." He releases me and I stumble back until I hit something firm. I collapse against the wall and slide to the floor.

Jim squats down beside me, touches my face gently. "I explained it all, Kate. They know who you are and what has happened to you. They know about Thom." He looks deep into my eyes. "You're not a killer."

I know—you *are the killer.*

"No," I say, so quietly that I wonder if anyone hears it at all. "No, please don't, please."

"Every day I think about what I could have done differently.

It's only now that I realize it's out of my hands. You pretend it never happened. You stopped taking your medication. You disappear into the night. You almost *kidnapped* a girl."

"He's lying," I say. "He's lying!"

"You refused to acknowledge what happened. The media, that city where everyone wanted to know your secrets, it was too confronting for you. I thought I could take you away to a place where I could control everything. I wanted to help by slowly reminding you, slowly drawing out your memories of that night . . . but I failed. You fired a gun at me. You tried to kill me, your own father." He exhales. Eyes weary behind his glasses. He is still disguising himself, even now. I watch his tongue run over his cracked lips. He's playing to the audience.

"Lies!" I yell. "You killed him, you admitted it."

He turns to Iso's mother and shrugs as if to say, *I told you so.* She stands with her arms crossed, those dull eyes sad.

"Kate, you shot at me. Can you imagine what that is like—after all I've done to protect you, that you should turn on *me?*"

"He's lying to you," I say. "He's lying, he's lying, he's lying." I realize I'm screaming but I can't stop. The look on Iso's face is one of deep sorrow, but I realize the sorrow is not for me—it's for him. Jim has won.

I scramble to my feet and try to run, but my leg collapses beneath me. I scream even louder. Iso and Jim both rush forward to restrain me.

"I should call an ambulance," Iso says.

"No," Jim says. "It'll take too long. I'll drive her straight to the hospital now."

"Should I come along?"

"I'll be okay," Jim says. "Thank you both for your help. I'll let you know how she goes."

Iso's gaze lingers on Jim's face. "All right, let me help you get her to the car, at least."

Donna steps forward, her eyes on me. "God gives us what we can handle, doll." With her warm, forgiving smile I think she could be anyone's mum. She could very well be my own.

Jim and Iso help me up. I am limp, delirious with pain and fatigue.

"Iso," I say, my voice ugly and desperate. "Iso, please. You don't understand. Are you in on it? Did you know Thom, is that it? You knew him, didn't you?"

Iso adjusts his grip, taking me by the elbow of my right arm, and the pain cuts through my mind. As I open my mouth to scream, darkness swallows me.

Rocking. Explosions of pain. The sound of the engine.

I blink, try to raise my hand but I can't.

Straps run across my body; I'm in the back seat of the car and my hands are cable-tied.

"You're awake," he says, eyeing me in the rearview mirror. "If only you had listened to me, none of this would have been necessary. Our last weeks together as a family could have been a happy time." His expression has changed; no longer earnest and open, but himself again, controlling and manipulative.

"It's my own fault, I suppose." He clears his throat. "I thought we'd got away with it, but the noose kept tightening and tightening, and at the end of the day it was either me or you."

The pain is back, fireworks exploding all over my body. My shoulder is numb and I only notice the ice strapped to it when it crackles against the seat belt. I don't recognize the places passing by outside the window.

"Where are we?"

"We're on our way to your new home, Kate. A place where you won't be able to do any more damage, not to anyone else's life and not to your own." He continues, "The smallest lie can protect you from the harshest truths. We own our memories, Kate. We can change them and move on."

"You killed him."

"I had to."

"Why? Why drag us here?"

"When you became unstable, you could have said anything to anyone. You didn't remember how it happened. You're not right in the head. You began to get closer and closer to the truth, but the truth can be white-hot, and when you touched it, you retracted into yourself again." He takes a breath. "I thought that you were the only one who could give me away. All it would have taken was a slip of the tongue."

"Are you going to kill me?"

"Kate, everything I have done has been to protect you. *Everything.* I couldn't sleep with worry. I couldn't look away from the cameras and the GPS. We were so close to escape. But then someone who'd been away on a cruise when it happened returned to the shit storm and offered up their CCTV footage, which looked out from their front door to the street. There are images of the Mercedes. It contradicted the statements we gave to the police, that we were both at home together. All of a sudden, the police began to piece it together. They saw you driving toward Thom's house."

The anxiety is coming back along with the fatigue. I throw myself against my constraints. I twist and howl.

He sighs and swerves through a roundabout. "You could have killed me with the gun, but that's not the worst part. It was the car. What did you plan to do? Drive off the cliff, into the sea?" He shakes his head slowly.

"No," I say. "I just wanted to go back to how it was. . . . I just wanted to go home."

"Do you know what it's like to expect to see your daughter hanging every time you walk into a room? Or with her wrists opened? Can you even imagine the toll that would take?"

"I wouldn't do it. Never."

"Promise me, Kate. Promise me that. Promise me that no matter how bad it gets you won't do it." His voice cracks.

"Never, I would never. I promise. Please, just let me go."

"Tell me exactly how you remember it. You remember me taking the brick and hitting him, right? Just once. Not so hard. If anyone asks you, that's how it happened, okay? Tell me you remember."

I don't, but I lie. "Yes," I say. "Yes, I remember it all. He provoked you. He started the fight." I will tell him anything now, anything to escape. "He tried to grab the brick to hit you but you ripped it from his hand."

He clenches his jaw and winces, blinking slowly, as though he is coming to some realization. Then I see that he is crying. "I did it, Kate," he says. "I left you in the car, I set it up so you would think you were involved. You wanted to stop me but it was too late." He sniffs hard.

I can't find the words. A drip of ice races down my spine.

"Do me a favor, one last favor for your old man. Just please try your hardest to be calm, to behave yourself today. Just do what the people ask of you, okay? Can you do that for me? And when it comes time for us to part, one last hug and a kiss. No screaming, no hysterics, just me and the old Kate. Like that little tot that used to walk around on my feet, holding my hands and giggling as though it was the best thing in the world." He sniffs again and smiles through the tears. The pitch of his voice rises a little. "You are everything to me—everything. I would do anything for you. When your mum died it was just us against the world. Wasn't it? Wasn't it, darling?"

The truth, I realize, doesn't matter.

Forty-five

As I step from the plane, I am greeted on the other side of the Tasman by plainclothes police officers waiting for me. They cuff me right there before all of the other passengers. It's over. They have me. It was inevitable. I suppose it didn't help that we fled the country, but of course the police, and in the end the media, knew exactly where we had gone—the end of the earth, I suppose, wasn't so far away after all.

I have been e-mailing someone from the hospital for the past week, organizing an assessment to determine an appropriate inpatient program for Kate. I have no doubt that if they see what I saw, she will be committed. I just couldn't take her with me to Australia; I couldn't risk it. Memory loss can have any number of causes: *PTSD, anger blackouts, drugs and alcohol.* I know exactly what caused Kate to forget.

By the time I touched down in Melbourne, Kate's aunt, Lizzie, was on her way to Auckland. I hadn't seen her in a decade, and if we had any other options, I wouldn't have bothered contacting her at all. She wasn't there when her sister needed her most, but at least now she is making an effort for her niece. She'll stay in Auckland for as long as it takes, waiting for Kate to get better before returning with her to England. I wish I could say she is doing it out of the goodness of her own heart—who knows, maybe she is—but I offered up a lot of money to be paid out yearly for the next three years to make certain Lizzie will do the right thing. Kate will always have the family trust to fall back on when she turns twenty-one.

It was clear back when we first left Australia, as we sat in the departure lounge, that I was in deep; sweat on my spine, barely able to keep my hands still. Thom had hand-delivered a letter to Kate. The morning the cops turned up, I found it in the letterbox and shoved it into my laptop bag. It's as though someone knew what had transpired the night before and wanted to mess with me, but of course in all likelihood Thom had simply placed it there a day or two earlier and we hadn't checked the mail.

Waiting for that plane to New Zealand, I expected the police to turn up at any moment. But if we made it all the way to Maketu, I knew we would be in the clear for some time. If only I could control everything, gather my thoughts and ideas, find a routine to get Kate healthy again. I just wanted to help her understand what happened and why. I had to protect her from the media, the vitriol, the scrutiny. There was always a sliver of a chance that we had gotten away scot-free but people would always speculate and form conspiracy theories about what transpired. All the crap in social media, in the papers and the news, would screw with her head.

Most important, I needed her memories to conform to the narrative of that night. The *true* singular narrative. I couldn't afford deviations or cracks in the veneer. Kate's mind was much more broken than I'd anticipated and yet she still showed signs of *knowing.* Then I found out Thom's life support had been turned off. Grievous bodily harm became manslaughter—or worse— and all of a sudden the investigation heated up.

Now the plainclothes police are marching me past all the queues of people at customs. A kid holds a phone up as I walk by. They escort me outside and sit me in the back seat of an un- marked car. We wind along the motorway into the city; eventu- ally we turn in at the St. Kilda Police Station. There I am escorted along a corridor to a gray interview room with four chairs and a table. I call my lawyer, Paul. The cops are cordial, removing my handcuffs, offering coffee, and asking about my rugby career. Paul must have been ready in his suit and tie because before five minutes have passed the door swings open and he comes striding in, his hand stretched out for mine. And now the formal inter- view begins. It's the preliminary stuff first, names, ranks, time, location.

I answer yes when asked if I understand that I am under ar- rest. Then the fun begins.

"Can you tell us what you did with the brick?"

"How . . . how do you know about the brick?"

They have me and they know it. Someone has tipped them off; it's written all over their faces.

When I called Paul from Maketu he said we had a case; he talked about insanity and plea bargains, he talked about reason- able doubt. But when I said I was going to confess, his tone changed. *They'll skewer you, don't do it.* I figured if the truth was going to come out, they might look on me more favorably if I owned up to it. In the end it would spare Kate the misery of tes- tifying against her dad.

Now, beneath the stark lights in that featureless gray room, a cop sits before me with another man, a detective in a shirt and tie. As the tape runs, prompted by their questions, I continue talking.

I explain how Kate had been in those dark days before the attack. Desolate, suicidal. The night it happened, I saw a puncture mark on her wrist. It was an echo of that awful night I'd found her mother.

"I can show you photos of the cut, and also photos of how skinny she was, what she did to her hair."

That was why I was so angry that night, I explain. I was terrified of losing Kate, the same way I lost my wife.

I describe the lead-up. The meeting with Thom's parents had not gone well. We had sat together, along with Paul, their lawyer, and a counselor, with the intention of working out what to do next. *Mediation*, they called it. In the business world I was known as the anvil, immovable when it came to negotiations, but that night I made a show of being reasonable. The Moreaus understood the precarious position their son was in; without consent he had distributed an explicit recording of a seventeen-year-old. If we pressed charges he was looking at time in prison. Yet still that woman made it out as if Kate and Thom were in as much trouble as each other.

"But I had a plan of my own; I wanted to meet with Thom and talk to him man to man, I didn't want the kid to go to prison over this," I explain. I look down at my palms, thinking about Kate. "When he texted Kate while she slept on the couch, I saw my opportunity."

The detective leans forward, turning his head a little to aim one ear at me. His tie hangs down away from his shirt. "What were you planning to say to him?"

"I just wanted to give the kid a scare," I reply. "I wanted to put the fear of God in him, truth be told. After what he did to my girl . . . Anyway, I found the message and decided it would be me turning up instead of Kate. I didn't know that Kate would wake up and see the messages on her phone. I didn't know she would jump in the car and follow me down there. She was . . . well, she wasn't in any state to drive."

"What do you mean?"

"She had been drinking."

"She was inebriated?"

"Correct, yes."

"Tell us what happened next."

I draw a deep breath. "I was diagnosed with something when I was younger. Intermittent explosive disorder. I've had counseling and I had been managing it for years, but sometimes I get overwhelmed by rage. It can be so bad that I black out. But this is what I've managed to piece together from that night." I take a few seconds to let this information sink in before continuing. "He was near his house when I arrived, I remember that. But when he saw me instead of Kate, I think that pissed him off. He kind of got cocky, you know?"

"What did you do then?"

"Well, he shoved me. I've got a dodgy knee, so when he pushed me again I kind of stumbled. Then when I stood up I realized he'd grabbed something. He was holding a brick."

"*He* was holding a brick."

"Correct."

"What happened then?"

"It put me on the back foot. He was a big boy, you know. Taller than me and strong as an ox. I was a little scared but then I got even angrier. I came to talk to him, that's all, and he had a weapon in his hand. He kept telling me to leave or he would hit me."

"He said he would hit you?"

"That's right. Then he did."

"He hit you?"

"He tried, yes. He swung the brick at me. And this is where things get hazy. That really pissed me off. I just remember prying it from his fist. Then I blacked out."

"You struck him with the brick?"

"I believe so. I kind of came to and I was breathing really heavily. The brick was still in my hand and Thom's head was on the curb. There was blood."

"Where was the blood?"

"Around his head, in the gutter, and on the sidewalk. There was blood on the brick, but I think that was from my hand."

"You were bleeding?"

"I guess I scratched my palm, maybe when I was trying to take it off him."

"Did you touch him after you hit him?"

"No," I say. "It was clear he was . . . Well, I thought he was already dead."

"Then what did you do?"

"Well, I heard a car coming and I went to run but then I saw it was *my* car. I stopped her, flagging her down before she could see Thom."

"By 'her' you mean your daughter, Kate?"

"That's right. I convinced her that I hadn't seen him, that I was just out on a walk."

"Could I please have a moment alone with my client?" Paul interrupts. His ruddy cheeks have been growing redder throughout the conversation.

"It's fine, Paul," I tell him. "This is what I'm here to do." I turn back to the detective.

"With the brick?"

"Yes, with the brick."

The officers share a look.

"You got in the car with it?"

"Yes. I'd never intended to do any serious damage to Thom. I never intended to kill him, but when he tried to hit me I had to protect myself. I didn't want her to know what I had done, so I was lucky she had been drinking. Well, not *drinking* but plastered drunk. She could barely keep her eyes open. So I put her in the passenger seat and she quickly dozed off."

I didn't want her to know what I had done. . . .

I will never forget the day I burned her. The blisters all over her tiny legs, tears streaming down her face, her screams. They had to sedate her at the hospital. The truth doesn't change but memories do. I told her it was Eloise who caused the scars. And everything we talked about, everything I asked and said, conformed to this version until subtly the story merged with Kate's memories, as stories so often do. I knew if the time came I could do it again.

It is like a defense mechanism of the mind. She will forget this whole ordeal. First you need to understand what the mind remembers, then you can break it down and rebuild it.

Soon after the police had left us that day, Kate asked me, "What happened to Thom?"

"What do you mean, Kate?"

"Did someone hurt Thom?"

I realized then that I wouldn't need to break down her memory of that night. She had no memory at all. I would simply need to excavate and find out where the memory faded and where it started again. "He hit his head last night. His skull is fractured," I said.

Later I found her at my laptop, a news story on one tab and a Wikipedia page about the human skull on another.

"Then you drove home?" the detective asks.

"I did."

"Which route did you take?"

"I doubled back along Dorcus and took the long way. I drove for half an hour as far away from the scene as possible. Then I had to stop for gas."

They share a look. The CCTV at the service station would show me get out to refuel the car while Kate sat asleep in the front seat.

"Mr. Bennet, when we met with you on Friday last week, when we showed you the CCTV image of your daughter driving your car on the night of the death of Thom Moreau, you agreed to bring her in for questioning. What changed between now and then?"

"I was scared for her. She knew what I did to Thom. It was coming back to her. She's already been through enough without being grilled by you lot and then living the rest of her life knowing she put me in prison."

The younger cop slumps back in his chair. The detective scratches his jaw, watching my face. "So," he says, "the weapon, the brick. Where is it now, Mr. Bennet?"

I swallow. "It's in the basement at home."

They both sit up straight at this. They know where the brick is already, but they're playing the part.

"If we take you there now, will you show us?" They are anticipating the solve, the successful prosecution. Like most people, police have bosses to please, and to please their bosses these men have to lock up a bad guy. I suppose I am the bad guy, even though all I ever wanted was to protect my daughter and make sure she was always happy.

I've read online that it's difficult to lift fingerprints from a brick. DNA, on the other hand, is much easier. On the brick they'll find both mine and Thom's.

Forty-six

Today, just like every other day, I take my pills and then I sit in the sun near the window, watching the trees move in the breeze outside and waiting for the food to come. The first thing I discovered when I arrived was that most people here were just like me. We talk and sit together like normal *sane* people. No one is strapped to any chairs and people are generally kind. It's a lot like school in some ways: we have a schedule; I must listen and speak when it is my turn. I'm not in control of my time but I really don't mind it at all.

After lunch I have a meeting with Jess, who asks me all the questions, the ones that help me move on with my life. She wants me to rate my feelings from zero to five. What do I feel? What do I think? What happens inside my body when I recall the past?

I saw Dad on television yesterday. He was being mobbed by photographers. His head was lowered and his hands were cuffed before him at his waist. A banner had scrolled across the bottom of the screen: *Australian rugby legend James "Bomber" Bennet charged with murder.*

I still feel rage, I still feel anger bubbling inside—but who am I angry at? Thom is dead, I am alive. Am I angry at all those men who watched the video and shared it? Angry that no one ever asked me *why* I am so angry? I remember how angry I was at Willow that time she pulled my dress up at the party: *Show everyone those scars.* But all the anger is distant now, as if it is someone else's anger. I can observe it and laugh at the impotence of it. Being angry is such a waste of time and energy. That's what we have been working on here: expunging bad feelings in a healthy way.

Jess asked me to write about my thoughts and feelings in a notebook and today I bring it along to our meeting. My handwriting is very messy because my arm is still in a sling. She says I can read it to her if I'm comfortable doing so, although I don't have to. The main thing we are focusing on, she says, is helping me to reconcile the traumatic events in a way that makes sense. It's impossible that I killed Thom because Dad killed Thom. But sometimes I have a feeling inside that I can't shake. Dad had been telling me all along I was there, he kept asking what I remember about the brick in his hand and what he did to Thom, but still that nagging feeling won't go away.

Jess says this is survivor guilt. She says these are thoughts that my mind has grabbed on to because it's hard for me or for anyone to accept that my father is a killer and that the person I once loved died. We are going to find a way for me to cope with these episodes in the real world. It's an entirely new language: *false memories, trauma-induced psychosis, manic episodes.* I trust her when she says I will be healthy again soon. Soon Aunty Lizzie will be able to take me with her back to England. Then I can put everything behind me.

L et's talk. Can you meet me at the spot? I'll head down now.

    I walk out into the chill of the night, gently pulling the front door closed behind me. I tie my Chuck Taylors and turn the collar of my coat up. There are a few stars and the cold has brought on a crisp mist that turns the streetlights into huge orange orbs.

I hear something in the fog. *Steps.* A figure forms in the darkness and mist.

"Kate?" I say, just loud enough.

They continue closer. Then as the figure passes beneath the streetlight I see who it is.

A current of nerves travels across my skin. I realize my pulse is racing. *It's her.*

She looks different. Her hair is teased and wild, her pupils all iris, her face still but for her lips, which part slightly with each exhale. The sour smell of alcohol emanates from her skin.

"Kate?" I say. "Are you okay?"

She stands so close. I glance down and see what she is holding. The brick looks huge in her hand.

"What are you doing?" I look past her again. Her father's Mercedes is parked on the street. *She drove.*

"Kate," I say, my voice trembling. "You're scaring me now. Can we just talk about everything?"

Then I see him: Kate's father. He's running toward us, drifting silent as a shadow. *Fuck.*

"Kate, what is this?"

No answer. A vein pulses in her throat.

My heart knocks. I've got to get inside. He's closing in. I step past her toward my house. He's still meters away when I hear his voice.

"Don't do it, Kate! Put it down."

Don't do what? A footstep behind me, her animal groan. A seismic knock. My legs become liquid. No time for thought; my arms and legs don't respond. I'm falling, falling. Black, red, then nothing at all.

EPILOGUE

AFTER

I feel much more lucid now that I have settled in at Aunty Lizzie's flat in England and I don't have to take all of those pills anymore. Sometimes I think about Willow's dad; I wonder where he is now that his marriage has broken up. That's how it all began—with my plan to have something over Willow for that horrible thing she did to me at the party. She thought she had gotten away with it. She thought she could embarrass me like that. I didn't seek him out first. But when he gave me his attention I buzzed. There was a connection; I mean, I really did like him, but as my desire fizzled and it became clear that he was still keen, I saw an opportunity. I never expected Thom to find the messages and then react the way he did.

The letters I addressed to Willow were as much for her father as her. *I miss spending afternoons lying in the study, listening to music ... what we would do if we ran away together and left everyone behind.*

Willow would regret her nasty words and in the end I took her advice: *Don't get mad, get even.*

I wonder if she knows why I did it, if she even remembers what she did and the fact that everyone saw my scars? I wonder how much she suffered as her family unraveled around her?

Of course, my own family unraveled too. I do miss my dear old dad at times. Sometimes I try to imagine what his life is like now. One day I will visit him and tell him I forgive him. I forgive him for everything.

It's a dream. My first in some time. *Memories would come through like grass pressing between cracks in the pavement,* Dad had said. Some memories I know will be false reconstructions.

The smell of the night, the suburban quiet, all the stars in the sky, and the grip of the cold air. This is more than a dream; it is so rich and vivid. This I know is a memory. And Thom is there. But I am angry. There's a rage burning in my arms and legs. Like I said, the skin remembers, the fingertips remember. The gritty bite of the brick. The crack of bone. The memory is like something physical, a scab I can worry, something I can make bleed again.

Acknowledgments

This book would never have been published without the tireless effort and insight of my agent, Pippa Masson. Dan Lazar and Gordon Wise both provided crucial feedback and helped to get this book out into the world. Many thanks also to my team of publishers, Robert Watkins, Lucy Dauman, and Margo Lip-schultz, along with Ali Lavau, Brigid Mullane, and all of the team at Hachette.

I am also grateful to the writers and friends who have supported me and helped with this project in various ways, including Sue Werry, Antoni Jach, The Tiffaneers, The Clifton Hill Writers Group, Ben Steele, my brothers Ben and Kent, and Marion Barton.

To my tribes, thank you to the Pomares, especially my father, Bill, who are storytellers to the last, and the Tracys for being my cheer squad.

Finally, thank you to my wife and first reader, Paige Pomare: without your balance, insight, support, love, and, most of all, encouragement, this book would still be a secret.